VALLEY OF THE SHAMAN

ALSO BY ARLAN ANDREWS SR

SILICON BLOOD
FUTURE FLASH
OTHER HEADS AND OTHER TALES

VALLEY OF THE SHAMAN

ARLAN ANDREWS, SR

Hydra
Publications

ISBN: 978-1-942212-57-7

Hydra Publications

Goshen, Kentucky 40026

www.HydraPublications.com

There is a longing that Truth cannot tell,
*   a yearning that Fact cannot satisfy,*
*   a thirst that only Myth may sate.*
*   There, is a Valley.*

– El Viejo

THE VALLEY

Located in the human soul in a place accessible only by those so invited, lying physically in a region of northwestern New Mexico, exists an unearthly dimension, tucked up close to majestic mountains, so unlikely located at the edge of a barren flatland. Unidentified except by those who visit there, it is unknown by

most who drive by the insignificant dirt road entrance that leads to a world Beyond.

A world of grace and living, a small world and lovely.

A world that waited all my life for me to find it.

A world that waited for me.

A world that waits for you.

A world that waits forever.

There, is a Valley.

❧ I ❧

Where was the mystery?

From where I was standing on the hotel verandah, nothing strange was visible, only the mystical beauty of an enchanted summer evening in high desert New Mexico – tall, blue-tinged mountains, billowing white clouds, and the light brown of low-lying Spanish-style adobe buildings blending into the landscape. I breathed deeply of the scented winds, felt the oncoming coolness of evening, and wondered what the night would bring. Something more substantial than breezes, I hoped. Maybe an explanation for why I was there?

Go to the Plaza in Santa Fe for the Summer Solstice celebration, the e-mail message had read. *There you will meet a man wearing white pants and a blue shirt. He will give you what you need to know.*

I hadn't been able to trace the sender of that terse command, and curiosity as usual had the better of me. So here I was in "The City Different," about to visit the site of that celebration, hopefully to meet an unknown man and obtain unknown but interesting information. Whatever any of that meant. I walked down the broad stairs and started toward the Plaza, the center of town, my old friend and sometime investigative partner, Ol' Zack, keeping up with my stride.

Invisible torrents of sweet-smelling wind continued to sweep through the shadowed streets, cascading down from the *Sangre de Cristo* mountains to the east, bringing with them a promise of impending rain. The English translation of that melodious name, *Sangre de Cristo*, is "Blood of Christ," an appellation incongruous for such a beautiful locale. The Spanish place names, in their resonant syllables, today mask the stark and brutal mindset with which the early Conquistadores viewed the magnificent landscape, assessing their reign only in the value of gold and blood and slaves. However, a few dedicated priests, more concerned with immortal souls than transient riches, had at least moderated the material with their spiritual designations. *Good old guys,* I thought. Their ethereal nomenclature had outlasted the rusted steel of the warriors' swords.

"The color comes from the evening light," Ol' Zack (he always insisted I call him that, which I inevitably shortened to just "O.Z." a strangely appropriate abbreviation at times), said, "Sunset turns these mountains a really pretty red." I nodded. Further to the south, in Albuquerque, where my plane had landed, they had named their mountains to the east for the same rosy phenomenon but with gentler names, "Watermelons" and "Apples," again, in the much more lyrical Spanish, "*Sandias*" and "*Manzanos.*" What a world of difference in cultures, in language; no Anglo settler would have called them anything like that. They would have been the "Lincoln Mountains" or "Teddy Roosevelt Mountains." I marveled at this history lesson; it was a wonder that with such diversity of backgrounds the human race co-existed as well as it did, wars and all. At least here in New Mexico's rugged rocky peaks there were no Spanish equivalents of the French *Gran Tetons*!

That morning I had picked up a rental vehicle at the airport in Albuquerque, an SUV big enough to warrant its nickname, "Suburban Assault Vehicle", driving it to Santa Fe, and leaving it at the hotel about six blocks from the center of town. Zack had met me there, giving me a brief report on his findings. "O.Z." was a tall, lanky old codger with sun-darkened skin, brown and wrinkled like the mountains, dressed in jeans and denim jacket like a working cowboy. He had emerged from one of the overstuffed brown leather chairs in the hotel lobby as I came in.

"Haven't been able to find out much, pard'ner," he said, a puzzled visage crackling the topography of that face. "Nobody's expecting you that I could find out, no special welcome for the famous New Age writer and all that, and nothin' unusual about a guy in a blue shirt and white pants. That's a few thousand folks out this way. And that valley you asked about? Hell, there's hundreds of them out here in all directions. Take your pick!" I had thanked O.Z., looking over the two typed sheets he handed me. All that was happening in Santa Fe today was the Summer Solstice celebration, probably just another excuse for real New Age believers and their wealthy Santa Fe groupies to throw a party and market or buy some esoteric items. I never had seen why people believed in drumming and dreamcatchers and crystals and such, but my own unusual experiences all over the world had taught me not to judge others' values. I learned to agree at a gut level with Shakespeare when he said *There are more things in Heaven and Earth than are dreamt of in your philosophy, Horatio.* And that festival was the reason I came, after all. That was all the mysterious email revealed.

"Be real busy downtown tonight, sir," the desk clerk had said. "A big party, no place to park. Might want to leave the vehicle in our parking lot."

O.Z. said he had mostly enjoyed the previous two days in Santa Fe, although he hadn't been able to uncover any data for me. I always enjoyed the old man's company. O.Z. and I had a history; more than once he had dug around (sometimes literally!) for me, investigating some bit of Southwest or Native American history, mystery or legend or other when I was doing books and articles and TV productions on various New Age nuances. He was used to my peculiar ways of doing business, and it suited him fine. He'd retired as a rancher in southern New Mexico a few years before we met, and always enjoyed (paid!) outdoor research, particularly liked coming to the "City Different" once in a while "to absorb some culture," he put it.

So because of our other "adventures" at the fringes of archaeology and history, O.Z. didn't think it crazy for me to travel halfway across the United States on the basis of one strange e-mail. Or at least he didn't act like he thought so. He was being paid, after all.

"I'll check out the celebration tonight," I told him over a cold beer in the hotel bar. "If anything happens, I'll look into it a bit further. Hopefully, an article or book can come out of it, with all the recent interest in Native American legends and tales. If not, then it won't be the first time I've been led on an unfulfilled quest for untamed fowl." Smiling, O.Z. seemed satisfied with that. Myself, I would have been full of questions. I was *already* full of questions for myself. Maybe he saw something about my look of resignation and decided that was enough. Or maybe that was just the Western way – few comments, no questions. I hadn't been out this way in several years; back East was a lot noisier and nosier. We set out from the hotel to find our destiny. Or at least, mine.

From the sidewalks, Santa Fe was a wonder of nicely-maintained brown adobe buildings and sparsely spaced trees. As we walked, O.Z. waved his hands this way and that, a long cigarette drooping from his bottom lip, telling me tales about the good ol' days in the state capital, "Back when Santa Fe was a nice little old Mexican village, afore the jet-setters prettified it, and afore the crystal-gazers oozed in from ever'where."

The Springtime afternoon was already becoming twilight, sliding rapidly into Summer with low shadows of the buildings and trees somber omens that, cloudy or not, sunset was less than an hour away. The sky grew ominously darker, a mottled blue dome animated by scudding gray clouds in the west and deeper darkness in the east. A few dark blue patches of western sky emanated golden rays of sun, but these soon closed shut. Far to the south, graceful dark curtains drooped from the cloud-line, signaling summer showers. The breezes were cooler now, and the long sleeves on my shirt felt good. The smell of imminent rain was a friendly reminder of the impending "monsoon season," when New Mexico would receive over half its annual rainfall within a three month period.

I answered O.Z.'s unspoken question, whether to satisfy myself or him, I couldn't have said. "You saw the e-mail. All I know is I'm supposed to meet a guy here in the Plaza this evening some time, somebody with a blue shirt and white pants," I told him as we arrived at the Plaza. "Let me know if you see any particular suspects." I couldn't figure whether he was as convinced as I was that the myste-rious message had any meaning.

"It's party time, pard'ner," he replied between puffs of his cigarette. I'd long since given up tobacco, but the pungent smell of it sometimes aroused a long-dormant sensory apparatus, and the addiction struggled to break loose. Sighing, I suppressed the urge to bum one from O.Z., if nothing else just to hide the nervousness I felt, an apprehensiveness about what was to come. O.Z. frowned slightly at my hesitancy, but smiled and patted me on the shoulder. "I'll be around here quite a bit, pickin' up on whatever makes sense. But I'll keep an eye out for ya. And for our friend with the blue-and-white." I smiled and he walked away into the gathering crowd, greeting this one and that. He was never without friends, even new ones made on the spot. I envied him that ease, something I'd never quite been able to accomplish.

Located in the center of town, the Plaza was one full block square, shaded by a few dozen trees, mostly mature ash. The plaza square, set off by red brick streets, was surrounded on three sides by brown, *faux*-adobe buildings of the style derisively called "Adobe Disneyland" by the locals, featuring touristy art shops, upscale restaurants and souvenir shops jammed side by side. On the north side, a fairly new bandstand or stage faced the ancient Palace of the Governors across the street, the latter a low-lying adobe structure featuring a series of brown wooden posts supporting a massive shaded porch – *portal*, in Spanish – that maintained a quiet dignity in contrast to the festivities now commencing in the Plaza.

Among the rows of canvas-sided, bazaar-like booths, diagonal side-walks of faded red brick converged onto a circular pavement at the center of the square, culminating in a fenced-off garden containing a concrete pedestal topped by a ten-foot stone obelisk on a rectangular base. Intrigued, I took a couple of digital pictures of it. An inscription on the north face of the pedestal read "This monument is dedicated to the Army troops that fought" – here a word was chipped out of the recessed inscription, probably "wild" I thought, shaking my head, or "savage"? – "Indians..." I smiled; here in Santa Fe, political correctness involved using a chisel. Similar testimonies commemorating other battles – both political and Civil War – marked the other three faces.

To my astonishment, a newer plaque on the south side apologized for the derogatory terms used by the early settlers for their Indian opponents and by the Union victors for the Confederate ("Rebel") troops they had fought nearby at Glorieta Pass. I wondered which of today's popular sentiments future generations would be apologizing for. On the other hand, the shape and size of the obelisk seemed totally appropriate for the New Age-y activities advertised in some of the Solstice booths. With some hieroglyphics here and there instead of English lettering, the monument would have fit right in with those I had visited at Luxor and other sites in Egypt.

THIS FESTIVAL TIME, THE PLAZA WAS DECKED OUT IN STRINGS OF tiny white lights scattered like curtains of stars, or perhaps flights of fairies. Ordinarily, the walking paths and dark-green iron benches would host a few dozen people out for a stroll or a smoke or lounging on the grassy areas. But today, in honor of the Native American and the New Age holiday, it was filled with a couple of dozen booths of colorful fabric stretched on aluminum frames, some selling beer and fast food, some displaying local Indian and other art work and handicrafts, some curtained with strings of crystals and other occult curios, some still in various states of assembly.

Amidst novel odors of cooking food, mixed with a rainbow of fragrances from smoking incense sticks and vases, I wandered around, admiring what art displays were visible among the crates and cartons and pickup trucks. The streets on the west and south sides of the block were blocked off for pedestrian traffic and more lines of booths. A steady stream of bumper-to-bumper traffic filled the streets to the east and north, the murmured deep engine noises punctuated by random bursts of rap music, Mexican mariachis and even a few twingy-twangy East Indian New Age instrumentals coming from the booths, each genre competing in volume for my ears. *Only in America,* I smiled to myself.

At the western end of the plaza, a very attractive, dark-skinned Indian or Hispanic woman, dressed in tight black jeans and a bright red sweater, was struggling with a large rectangular package as she attempted to unload it from the back door of a white minivan. "Can I help you?" I asked politely, approaching her. She turned and smiled, revealing a perfect brown face with rosy cheeks framed in black hair, and dark eyes full of infinity. I was instantly in love. "Sure," she said in unaccented English, not commenting on my sudden intake of breath, "This carving is a lot heavier than I thought it would be."

The package measured about three by four feet by about six inches thick, wrapped in brown paper. I gave her a hand, and we wrestled the – *heavy!* – carving onto the sparse grass. "This really is heavy, isn't it?" I said, panting. "Must be a couple of hundred pounds. Strange for a carving."

"Well, they said it would be unusual when they brought it over. And thanks, *amigo*, for the help." In her mid-twenties and only about five feet tall, her upturned face was all smiles. "Maybe you want to come see it when we get it all set up over there at my aunt's booth?" *Over there* was a white cloth-sided display booth chocked full of Indian artifacts and sculptures, almost a yard sale of prehistory. While I stared, a couple of Hispanic men in cowboy gear came over with a rubber-tired steel dolly and transported the carving to the booth. I wanted to ask this young woman why they hadn't helped her unload it to start with, but when I turned she was gone, the white minivan disappearing around a corner a block away. *Oh well*, I mused, *this must be the direct Western way of getting things done – without ceremony.*

I wandered around the Plaza, tuning out the joyful hubbub and the enticing odors, but kept looking at the one real building across the street on the north side of the Plaza: the four hundred year old adobe palace where a Civil War General, one Lew Wallace, while Governor of the New Mexico Territory, had hand-written the famous novel, *Ben-Hur. I saw the movie*, I thought, *but never read the book*, thinking back on the famous chariot race sequence. I was impressed that the man had written such a magnificent story by hand. I imagined long nights with a quill pen. Or did they have steel points then? No printer, not even a spell-checker! *There's a lot of history around here, maybe thousands of years of it.* The Message came to mind. *A lot of history and some mystery, too.*

After an hour the sky was dark, but the Plaza was aglow with arrays of festival lights, accented by the raucous strains of a mariachi band playing classic Mexican and American songs from the bandstand on the north side of the square. More odors of cooking food wafted through the air, some meaty ones of beef and pork, some other pungent ones I couldn't identify, and I was getting hungrier by the minute. By now a few hundred people milled around, their conversational noise adding to the air of fiesta. A convoy of low-rider cars, their boomboxes sounding a deep *Thump! Thump! Thump!* drove slowly around the two open streets, providing a primitive accompaniment. I shrugged it off; I was young once, too.

Buying a beer, I used it to wash down some delicious but unknown concoction of fiery chili peppers, chunks of beef and hot tortillas. From time to time I checked on the Indian artifact booth and the heavy "carving" I'd helped unload, continually strolling the Plaza looking for my contact. O.Z. orbited past me a couple of times, a couple of *chicas* on his arms, smiling and acknowledging me by a nod, but with a shrug that said, *Still no sign of any guy with a blue shirt and white pants.*

The Message had made that clear: *Go to the Plaza in Santa Fe for the Summer Solstice celebration. There you will meet a man wearing white pants and a blue shirt. He will give you what you need to know.* If I could trust an enigmatic e-mail message, believe it enough to travel halfway across the USA to check it out, I could afford to hang around the Plaza until something happened. The multicultural Southwestern ambiance itself was enjoyable enough to justify the trip; I'd always enjoyed my trips to "The Land of Enchantment." Sometimes, it truly was just that!

An hour before midnight the sky erupted with lightning flashes, the winds bringing a surprisingly cool breeze along with an intermittent drizzle, not even enough to bring out the umbrellas, a little bit of wet only serving to enhance the party atmosphere. I made another round of the plaza, dodging this and that partying couple or inebriated group of celebrators, occasionally whiffing various mixtures of smoke, legal and otherwise.

Nearby a couple were arguing about the lively industry of new prophets making a living from ominous events yet to come. Something to do with Mayan and Hopi prophecies of the end of the world. I was just happy that mankind was still plodding along on a mostly upward path, even though terrorism had threatened us all for a while before being slammed down fairly hard.

Thankfully, the prophecies of wholesale supernatural disaster just hadn't ever panned out and probably never would. But sometimes they could be fun to read about. Over the years I had written more than a dozen articles about the prophesied end of the world. Who knows? Maybe one day one of them would come true, but then who would be around to appreciate the warning? An old Spanish saying came to mind: If it *is* going to happen, why worry? If it is *not* going to happen, why worry?

Que será será. So why worry about it at all?

Another beer had made my mood a little more somber, a bit lonely for some like-minded friends back home who would be having cozier gatherings this night. But such was the price of following one's own heart. Too bad the Message hadn't specified a Fall celebration, when the forests of New Mexico would be clothed in their special glory.

Suddenly, there it was, the "carving"! – unwrapped, back in the corner of the artifact booth. As if in a trance, I stumbled through the crowd to the booth, weaving in and around the standing displays of squash blossom necklaces and Storyteller pottery, to view the astounding contents of the young woman's package. Propped up in a corner of the booth, it was actually a *bas*-relief carved from a solid piece of grayish flint-like rock, its rough-cut edges indicating the slab had been crudely chiseled from a larger stone. A quick inspection showed the slab about two inches thick at its edges, tapering to a depth of about four or five inches at the very back, a roughly pyramidal shape when viewed from the top or sides. It had to have been hacked out from the edges inward. But why? And from what?

Incredibly, as if illuminated from within, occasionally the stone appeared to be of different colors – shifting, iridescent, ghostly – depending upon which angle I viewed it from. Other times it was a flat gray. Haunting and beautiful, it was like nothing I had ever seen.

And there in front of me as I bent down to look, were a pair of full-sized human palm prints imprinted in the rock, as if they had just been pressed into liquid stone only moments before, the palms themselves exquisitely detailed, the fainter imprints of the fingers only barely visible above them. If they were sculpted, it was incredibly detailed and beautiful work. Below the handprints, and half their size, a dozen or so etched or painted, primitive petroglyph figures of – *what?* Whatever the images were, their crude beauty and their primitive, almost hypnotic and vaguely geometric symbols perfectly complemented the imprints above. *My God*, I thought, *what a lovely disjointing of cultures!* What could it all mean? Certainly this was not a painting, maybe not even a sculpture. But what was it?

As I kneeled down to take a closer look, a hand rudely grabbed my left shoulder and jerked me, spinning me around to see – *a fist on its way to my face!* Trying to dodge the surprising attack, I turned my head to the right, dropping as I did. *Too late!* The fist connected with my left cheek, slamming me forward into the *bas*-relief, knocking it to the ground and banging it into the other displayed objects, scattering them around the booth. Falling, I was able to wriggle free of the man who was holding me. My assailant leaned forward, shouting something and waving his fist at me.

My first impulse was to jump up and pound on the idiot who had attacked me for no reason, but then I saw his larger friend, a rough-looking blonde Anglo, the one who had grabbed me, holding his fists ready as well. Still lying on the ground, I shook my head, rubbed my left eye socket – *blood!* – and said through clenched teeth, "Hey, man, I don't know who you are but you've got the wrong guy! I don't know you."

"Solana. You talked to her?" The dark skinned kid was raving mad. "What did she tell you about the Indian rock here? Tell me now!"

"I don't know any Solana, you punk," I yelled back, getting back up on my feet carefully, all the while eyeing Tall Guy. "And what difference does that make anyhow? Who the hell are you?" Tall Guy put his arms down and unclenched his fists. I took a look at the enraged attacker before me. About five-five and 120 pounds, the wiry youth looked to be in his early twenties, with dark eyes blazing from his red face, dark hair glistening where it protruded from his skull-covering blue bandanna. His tattooed arms were waving wildly, wrinkling his dark T-shirt so that I couldn't read the white lettering across it.

"Solana, she's my *chica*. She said a real friendly Anglo helped her unload a package right here, today!" He waved a hand around the booth. "What did she tell you about it, *gringo?*"

Maybe it was the insult, maybe the beer, maybe it was the fact that the left side of my face was hurting like Hell and I was furious, but with my left hand I quickly grabbed this punk by his T-shirt, backhanded him with my right hand, knocking him backwards. As he fell, I suddenly felt cold steel on my right forehead. "Listen up, *dude,*" Tall Guy said, holding a Saturday Night Special against my head, "This wasn't downtown in a crowd, I'd empty your head right here, right now." His accent said Tidewater Virginia; his eyes said *Death!*

"OK, *dude,*" I said, moving back slowly, holding my hands up, palms forward. "I didn't start this, OK? Your little friend down there, maybe he should pick on somebody his own size?" Tall Guy glanced toward the fallen punk, now scrambling up from piles of fake Indian jewelry, then back at me. He lowered his pistol and it disappeared into a jacket pocket. Incongruously, his scowl broke into a quick smile, blue eyes seeming to sparkle. "You're right, aren't you, dumbass?" Then his face settled back to an ominous passivity. "But get the hell away from here," he hissed. He gave a hand up to his friend, and whispered something to him. A crowd of people was gathering around the booth, and I heard someone using a smartphone to call the police.

The punk wiped involuntary tears from his eyes where I had slapped him. Calmly he said, "You're a dead man, Anglo, *hijo de zorra.* I will find you tomorrow, me and my homie here." He gave me the sign of the finger and left, Tall Guy following him. I watched as they disappeared into the night streets. Smoothed out on his muscular back, the T-shirt read, *Coyote – Santa Fe.*

As if it were a photograph suddenly projected into my consciousness, I realized that the punk's T-shirt was dark blue, and his pants, though now stained with the mud of the Plaza, were white. The Message had said a man dressed like that "...*will give you what you need to know.*" What did I need to know from a bruised and bloody cheek?

Pop! Pop! Pop! At the loud noises, I dropped to the ground, scratching my right hand on the rough edges of the bas-relief. "Fireworks!" somebody yelled. "Happy Summer Solstice!" What a way to begin the Summer!

I AWOKE IN THE FIRST DAWN OF THAT NEW SUMMER, QUICKLY checked the morning news programs on my smartphone, and did my weekly review of investments; the market's fall had hurt things a bit but wasn't financially fatal. The local Santa Fe news didn't report any disturbances at the Summer Solstice Festival, which was fine by me. I always like to keep a low profile of my own making, and being involved in a public fight is seldom good for a writer's image, unless you're an Ernest Hemingway type. And look where it got him!

After checking out of the hotel, I drove downtown to the Plaza but found all of the booths gone. The cleanup crew had no idea where any of the exhibitors were. "Solana's Palms," as I now thought of the mysterious sculpture, was niggling at my mind. Something very unusual was contained in that rock carving, but I couldn't quite place it. Taking stock of what I knew about the situation, I walked absentmindedly through the long porch of the Governor's Palace, taking in the sights of beautiful Indian jewelry laid out by the half dozen Indian vendors, hundreds of wonderful silver and turquoise designs displayed on dark blue velvet, like galaxies of brilliant stars in dark night skies. As I passed someone spoke to me. "*Señor?*" he said, "You were the one who was hurt last night by the *cholo?*"

I stopped and turned around, my eyebrows raised. The speaker was a wizened, dark-skinned old man, Indian or Mexican I couldn't tell, but apparently one of the vendors, an elderly figure dressed in a blue velvet pullover shirt and threadbare white pants, sitting on a window ledge overlooking his array of sale items on the sidewalk. Silver and turquoise jewelry adorned his shirt. I recognized a squash blossom silver necklace of intricate, almost hypnotic, design. The old man's face was shadowed by the columns of the Governor's Palace, but from his quavering voice I had the feeling that he was not only old, but *very* old. Managing a smile, I rubbed my black and blue cheek, "Well, I did hit him back, if that counts."

"You were looking at the –" he said a word I didn't recognize, one that sounded like *ah teen* "– when he hit you?" I nodded. I hadn't known there were any witnesses.

I must have looked puzzled. "You want to know more about the *atiín?*" He pronounced the word slowly, clearly. As my eyes became accustomed to the shade, his face resolved into distinctive features: the high-cheeked face was dark and ancient, crevasses of wrinkles like canyons, a topographical map of a long life spent in the wind and sun of the high desert. Eyes of dark obsidian, a deep wisdom evident. I couldn't tell his specific racial background, but Native American was in there, and Hispanic too, and more than a touch of Oriental. I'd seen someone very much like him somewhere before in my travels around the world, but couldn't quite put my mind to the exact place or time. "The relic, the stolen thing, you were looking at," he emphasized. "You want to know more?"

"Yes, I do. What can you tell me?" My hand inside my jacket pocket, I switched on the mini voice recorder that I always carry for interviews. I usually asked subjects for permission, but the old man had initiated the conversation and this was too important to miss.

"There is a valley −" he began. At these words, my heart nearly stopped, but if the old man took notice he didn't pause a breath "− a few hours driving from here. There is where the *atiín* came from. And that is where it must be returned!"

"What is that *atiín*, anyhow? And why must it be returned?" This was making no sense to me, but I decided to play along with the mystery, adopting even his patterns of speech for the moment.

"The *atiín* is a holy pathway, a thing of wisdom, from The Valley. It was brought here by those who would despoil the sacred order." His eyes drilled deep into mine, as if plumbing the depths of my soul, testing me. "The girl you helped was −" he paused "− *is* a relative of mine. But Solana does not know what evil she did, bringing it here to be sold."

The old man never bothered to give me his name, but told me that the punk kid *Coyote* and his tall friend had somehow obtained the holy relic to sell in Santa Fe to rich Anglo collectors from around the world. "To people who do not care how it came to them. And not aware of what harm it brings to those who misuse it." He told me where the *atiín* was being stored. "Not far from here, easy to get to. We can go there together, my Anglo friend, I will show you." He pointed off into the western skies, "And I will tell you how to return it to its rightful place."

"Whoa, old pal," I objected, "I'm not into transporting stolen goods."

Ignoring my statement, he said, "It must be returned to the Valley. I believe that is why you came here, to find The Valley? I can tell you the way."

Bingo!

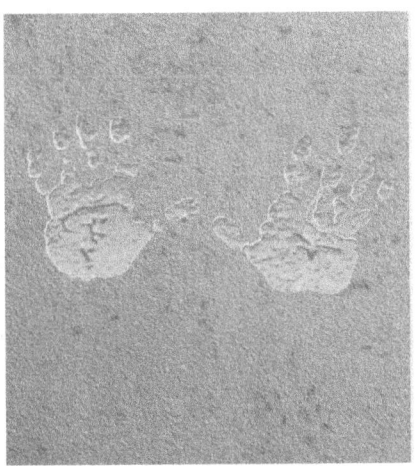

2

The next morning found me in my rented SUV, a retrieved (or re-stolen?) historical or archaeological relic ensconced behind the rear seat, under a canvas tarp and covered with my luggage. I was heading south from Santa Fe, to the little town of Bernalillo, where the old man had told me to "turn right and keep going. You will know where to go from there." I wanted O.Z. come with me but he had begged off, speaking on his smartphone to a woman. He'd had an overnight guest in his room. *The old Casanova!* I thought.

Thinking over the last twenty-four hours, I shook my head. The timing of this whole affair was exquisite, just one unbelievable coincidence after another. What if I had not seen Solana and her package? What if I hadn't stopped to scrutinize it? What if – I shuddered – Tall Guy had used that Saturday Night Special on my head? Well, at least I would now be experiencing the AfterLife, whatever it turned out to be. *But that is one thing I can wait for,* I told myself. *If it's there – and I believe it is – it's probably going to last a long time!*

Long ago in this business I learned to take coincidences in stride, as if I were being led by the Universe. If mere Chance alone had led me into some of the adventures I've been blessed to have, it is certainly a fateful Chance. Time after time such journeys have happened for me. This decision or that. Door Number One or Door Number Two? The Lady or the Tiger? So far nothing had led to Tigers or other disasters, just to interesting and profound experiences. Hence my faith in Truth, and let the coincidences fall where they may. I certainly never could have planned this course of action all by myself!

As the featureless high desert rolled past, I listened absentmindedly to the soothing instrumentals of a Santa Fe guitarist on the SUV's satellite radio, and recounted my latest steps. Last night, as darkness fell on Santa Fe, I had driven the old man through a maze of back alleys and courtyards somewhere near Canyon Road on the east side of town. He pried open a shed door, hoisted the sculpture onto his back by himself, and brought it out to my rental SUV. We wrestled it into the back storage space. Then he vanished, just like that. I had no sooner shut the rear door and turned to ask him if he needed a ride somewhere, and he was gone! Just like Solana. *Must run in the family*, I thought. *Certainly not the Anglo-American way, parting without so much as an "adios."*

My thoughts came back to the present. So, was I transporting stolen goods or merely returning them to their rightful place, as Old Man said? I decided not to worry about it; Fate or Chance had put me on this road and I was willing to go along for the ride for a while. The day was typical New Mexico – an absolutely clear blue morning sky overhead, just a bare wisp of cloudy whiteness near the western horizon. Other than the Interstate highway, the power lines and the occasional auto or billboard or Indian reservation, it probably looked this way a hundred years ago. Maybe a thousand years ago, maybe even longer than that. Mankind hadn't changed the landscape all that much. Barring more volcanic activity, the mountains here would be around when Mankind was either extinct or safely settled out among the stars in the Milky Way.

As the brown slumped shapes of the Sandia Mountains came up to my left, I made the first exit to Bernalillo, which appeared to be a collection of fast food restaurants and service stations with a small city in the distance. I gassed up the SUV and stopped in at a fast food joint for a quick burger before heading out to God knows where. While munching down on the piquant mixture of hamburger, cheese and chili peppers, I spotted a lime-green low-rider car arriving. So bright as to be nearly luminous, the metallic 1980s-era Chevrolet was chopped so low that it barely cleared the highway. In its own way, the glowing vehicle represented a kind of maniacal beauty, with so many coats of paint that the surface appeared to be inches deep, polished so brightly that an occasional sparkle of light almost "pinged" off the finish. Various flame patterns, swirling around the wheel wells, gave the rolling art show a final touch of frenetic energy.

Prowling the parking lot like a predator, the car to me represented an attitude, a threat to established order. I always figured such cars were for lowlifes who had little else to do with their drug revenues, but a couple of young Anglo girls in the next booth were *oohing* and *ahhing* over the "classic Española look" and speculating on which contest it was going to be in that day. Whatever that look was, I mused, it must be something to be appreciated in this area. But not by me, for many reasons.

On a more ominous note, the spectacular paint job was set off by the contrasting, absolutely black windows. I wondered how the occupants could see out, and if the police really liked stopping such cars because of the danger; they couldn't see if bad guys inside were pointing guns at them. The rear window was thickly lettered in chrome-bright pseudo-Gothic script: *Coyote – Santa Fe*. I felt a chill;

that was the *nome de T-shirt* of the punk who attacked me two nights before. Were they here, now, come looking for me? For the *atiín*? I tried to shake off the thought, but the car stopped and the instantly-recognizable *Tall Guy* got out, going over to look around my SUV. *Damn*, I thought, *this is getting serious*. But the punk shook his head, got back in the low rider, and the car peeled out of the parking lot, heading west. I breathed easier, glad that I had covered the *atiín* slab so well under the luggage. I decided to take my time leaving the restaurant. There was no telling what could happen in the desolate areas to the west of here if I ran into those two alone. The maps didn't show any towns of any size for the next hundred miles, and I didn't have a gun for protection.

But somewhere out there was where I hoped to go. I thought back on the words the old man had told me. "Turn right at Bernalillo. You will know where to go from there."

After killing an hour poring over a newspaper and consuming several more cups of coffee, I headed west, hoping the whole thing wasn't a wild goose chase. At least *Coyote* and his pal hadn't come back this way looking for me again. I never had received any directions from that guy, and hoped I never would, blue shirt and white pants or no. In the back of my mind, the old man's image coalesced. I never did learn his name, but he'd been dressed in a *blue velvet shirt and off-white pants*! I sighed; was that the standard dress code out here? *At least he's given me fairly specific directions so far!* I wasn't sure what might happen next.

The four-lane divided highway unrolled over the Rio Grande through a thicket of trees called the *bosque*, and then out past a monument park named for the Spanish *conquistador* Juan de Coronado, who had come this way in the early 1500s. And not a happy camper was he, I remembered. He went on a wild goose chase all over the Southwest and as far east as Kansas, looking for rich magical cities that he never found, following fanciful stories told by an old Indian called "the Turk." *Maybe better to call that a wild turkey chase?* I laughed aloud. Was I doing about the same thing, five hundred years later?

Then the next famous – or infamous, if you read the comments by local pueblo historians and politicians – conquistador was Don Juan de Oñate, another wild man. He killed and mutilated and enslaved so many Indians, potential slaves and prospective converts to the Church, that Spain itself recalled and exiled him from *Nuevo Mexico*. After all these centuries, Oñate yet stirred up controversy even today; the Acoma Puebloans mutilated the left foot of his statue down in Albuquerque about as often as it was repaired, to protest his left foot amputations of their ancestors. But in my view, as bad as these guys were, at least they had introduced European ideals and literacy into these desert civilizations, and probably better the Spaniards than some Asiatic warlords of the same time. I often enjoyed playing intellectual "what if?" games; alternate histories were a favorite pastime of mine, since actual history was often so brutal and genocidal. For example, there were probably none of the aboriginal English or Irish left, and about zero in any other European region either, so things could have been worse. But I knew the locals here "would always feel otherwise.

My own intentions hereabouts were a lot more modest – just get the stolen artifact back to its rightful place and not get hurt or arrested in the meantime. What I was doing would make an interesting non-fiction account, especially if I could figure out its history, the culture that produced it, and find the place it came from. Just where that place was, and how I was going to put a heavy slab back into a chiseled-out hole somewhere out here in the desert, I was not at all sure. I hadn't thought to bring any mortar or epoxy.

After leaving the burgeoning town of Bernalillo, the topography surrounding the road varied immensely. To my left, southwest, the dusty desert gave way to rolling, nearly flat land, covered at this rainy time of year by thin green grass. In the far distance beyond, a stark black butte stabbed upward from the horizon. To the little boy in me, it was the perfect Western movie land and I would not have been surprised to see Indians and cowboys racing across it. Miles to the right rose the dark forms of the Jemez Mountains. Somewhere in those hills lay the sprawling atomic bomb laboratory of Los Alamos. Interesting things had happened up there, too, including a huge volcano that exploded tens of thousands of years before, lifting many cubic miles of New Mexican strata into the stratosphere, dropping it as far away as Kansas and California. But those were other stories for other times.

Further along, the highway divided two worlds – on my left, low-lying silhouettes defined distant mountains and mesas on the horizon, the greenish-velvet carpet of sage grass pockmarked with dark splotches of piñons and juniper. On my right, a series of broken mesas and standalone buttes stood interspersed between the highway and the horizon, culminating in tall mesas some five to ten miles away. The mesas themselves presented a "wedding cake" appearance – a grayish-white skirt of *arroyo*-laced, eroded softer debris reaching about a third of the way up their thousand-foot heights, topped by multi-colored sedimentary layers hundreds of feet thick in all, and finally capped by vertically-striated red and yellow stones, looking for all the world like thin architectural columns. Most buttes and mesas featured a thin upper layer of short trees and shrubs, like icing on the cake.

Somewhere along the way, after passing by numerous turnoffs to Indian pueblos, the road became a narrower, two-lane affair, and the world seemed just a bit more closed-in. And then the heat began. Weather in New Mexico is strange to an Easterner. "It's hot outside here in the sun," O.Z. had said, "but you get in the shade, and you're cool." He allowed as to how the East was strange, because he'd found that "on a hot day with humidity, you get in the shade, you still stay hot." But humidity or not, the upper 90s was still hot, even in the desert. The SUV's air conditioner was acting erratically, so I opened my windows for fresh air, but I was uncomfortably warm all the same.

Surprisingly, the paved road surface was thinning and turning dusty, gravel pinging as it was slung up from the tires. "Damn, but I need a drink," I groused aloud, rolling up the window to stave off the oncoming clouds of dust kicked up by the guy in the pickup who had just passed by me in the other direction. Too late! I licked my dry lips, spitting out the fine red mist of *tierra colorado*. Red dirt. Though the road was ostensibly graveled, the ubiquitous amber powder permeated you after a few miles. The birthplace of the dust, the flat-topped mesa away on my right, extended all the way north into the state named for the dust color, a place usually noted more for its snow-capped greenery and ski resorts.

My throat ached for the rough, cool shock of beer, my hand longing for the icy caress of a soft aluminum can. And my left eye ached, still swollen from the fist of the punk in the plaza at Santa Fe, *el Señor Coyote de Santa Fe*. By now the road was turning northwest. I passed billboards for tourist attractions – wineries, hot spring spas, state monuments – still in search of – *what?* The day was hot and growing hotter; the vehicle's A/C finally quit working altogether and I was running short of moisture and short on temper. "What I'd give for a package store about now –"

The sudden sign said "*Cold beer. Ice. Gas. Ahead.*" Hand-lettered, rusted and bullet hole-perforated, barely attached to an ancient fence post, it was still a beautiful beacon of civilization. And further on down the road, a few hundred yards beyond the sign on my right, appeared my promised salvation. A weather-beaten shack of a building, just past the exit to a nearly-abandoned pueblo village ("*No tours, No photos, No –*", its painted words faded to oblivion by decades of dust and disrepair. *Like the pueblo itself,* I thought. *Wonder what happened to the people? Disease? War? Economics? Maybe the wonderful world of satellite TV, some disaster like that?*)

The one-pump gas station stood gray, colorless, as if fading out of reality into something almost natural, ready to become a part of the desert. Or maybe fading back *into* reality? I pulled up, got out. All was silent.

The interior of the store proved to be dark as a cave, almost as if light itself was wary of entering. I removed my dark sunglasses, waiting for the few seconds it took my eyes to adjust to the darkness. Gray dry boards creaked beneath my feet. "Anybody home?" I asked.

Silence.

Gradually, shadowy shapes resolved themselves into discrete objects and I made out the ancient slide-top horizontal ice box. I walked over, sliding open the top to reveal frosty silver cylinders of an acceptable brew. Taking one in each hand, I closed the ice box and walked the ten feet over to the rough-topped wooden counter. "Anybody around here?" An empty glass on the counter told me somebody had been there, once upon a time. This century?

Silence.

Well, hell, folks. I know it ain't free." Behind me, the ice box sign said *Beer. $1.50 each.* I laid four dollars on the counter, securing it from any inadvertent wind with the glass. Turning around, I leaned against the counter and popped the top of one can, savoring the smell and the sting as a light layer of foam escaped. I drank deep, letting my dry throat absorb the tangy liquid, luxuriating in the moment.

I killed that can in three gulps, then looked around for a trash can. Nothing.

Outside, I crushed it and tossed the dead soldier into a rusted old 55-gallon steel drum that served as the receptacle for all the debris of a dying gas station.

I heard the *squeak-squeak* of an old rocking chair behind me. "Thank you. *Grácias, amigo,*" said a cracked voice.

I spun around, squinting in the bright sunlight. The voice was coming from a lean-to porch off to the left side of the station. I hadn't even seen that porch when I drove up. Just the angle I came in from, I guessed. That, and the noonday sun.

"You – you're welcome, friend," I replied, still trying to make out the dark figure sitting on the rickety porch. "*De nada,*" I repeated in Spanish, just in case the owner of the raspy voice required respect in more than just English.

I was surprised at his response.

"There is a *valley,*" he spoke softly from the shadows, his deep accent a beautiful thing, like that of the old man from Santa Fe, "a small valley. Exit a mile up on your right. An old mail box on a post. Take the dirt road into the mountains. That will take you where you are going."

I still couldn't see his face, but there was a small dark figure in that rocking chair, a bandana around his forehead like some of the Navajos wear sometimes. I saw worn whitish pants, a faded blue velvet shirt. But a face still in shadows. Could this somehow be the same old man? I felt that it was, but couldn't verify it because of the almost supernatural darkness of the shadows that hid him. Otherwise, how could he know what I was carrying, where I was trying to go? "Sorry, *compadre,*" I said, "but I don't know where I'm going. Searching for –" the words wouldn't come easily "– for a *place.*"

The tone of voice, the body language informed me that I was not to approach any closer. I shook my head. "But thanks anyway, *Viejo,*" I said, using the Spanish word for "old man". The syllables echoed in my mind: *Vee aye hoh*

In that next mile, my whole world changed.

Have you ever had one of those days when it seems you are becoming detached from the world? As though a buffer had come down between the outside you and the inner you? After leaving the one-pump station, that's how I felt, queasy almost. After driving about half a mile, I pulled over. Too much beer? I asked myself. Fear of running into *Coyote* and his pal? I couldn't tell for sure, but the weirdness wouldn't go away.

"I'm going back to ask *El Viejo* what he knows about all of this," I said out loud, turning the truck around. "I believe in coincidence, but no way anyone could know I was going to stop right there and get directions." But a half mile back, there was no station! The sign – it was still there, but the shack where I had bought my beer did not exist. A barely visible foundation protruded from the white caliche clay, greasewood bushes growing inside the outline. "This place has been gone for *years*," I whispered. "Jesus! I interacted with a *hallucination*? A mirage? A *ghost*?" Back in the truck, lying there on the seat, my beer can was still cold. At least this much was real.

Trying to remain calm in the face of such a supernatural experience, I deliberately remembered the details of other reports of this kind of phenomenon – the famous paranormal investigator, Ivan Sanderson, hiking with his wife in the Dominican Republic in the 1950s, who reported seeing a whole city that wasn't there. Then there were the two English ladies vacationing in Paris in the 1920s, and their famous trip back in time to pre-Revolutionary France, where they saw and interacted with the people there. And I recalled the TV report about some ordinary English motorists in the 1970s, who reportedly ate at a roadside pub that could not be found later. And now it had happened to me! Somehow the fact that others had witnessed similar phenomena didn't help soothe my mind very much.

Heart pounding, I pulled out the voice recorder and made a few notes, annotating the approximate location, the time of day, weather conditions, and my own state of mind. I sighed. If only I had photographed this place when I first got there, what would I have seen? This was just about too weird to believe, and without the recording in my own voice, in a few days I didn't think I would believe it either! I took a few pictures of the foundation ruins with the digital camera, and left.

True to the words of *El Viejo* in the rocking chair, hallucination or not, a bit down the road I came upon a battered mail box barely clinging to a skeletal post, its flag long since rusted away, the metal shell perforated with bullet holes. I stopped and got out, touching the ruined mailbox to be sure of its existence. "At least this is real enough," I whispered, "to attract the attention of some target practitioners." Squinting in the bright daylight, I made out the nearly invisible tracks that I presumed was the road I was supposed to take. Really more just a lack of vegetation rather than a road, the trail disappeared over a small rise to the north, in the direction of the red-striped mesa. I photographed the whole scene. If this place, too, vanished on me, I was going to dump my contraband carving and hightail it back to the Albuquerque airport!

I sat for a long time in the truck, finishing the second can of beer, finally realizing that I was waiting for something to happen. To see if the mailbox disappeared? I laughed at the thought. "It doesn't have that much material left, so if it vanishes, big deal!" The road, such as it was? "Not much there, either," I murmured, tasting the last slug of "Colorado Cool Aid" and crushing the can. Wanting to get wherever I was going, drop off the "Palms" sculpture and get back to civilization, all before dark – about five hours from now, I realized with a start – I fired up the SUV and headed north. Along what I hoped actually was a trail. Preferably with a Valley at its end.

I'd been looking for this Valley since receiving the Message a few days ago.

The Message

This is the message that started my journey, an e-mail that showed up out of nowhere on my computer screen one bright morning early back in the Spring.

You are a searcher for the Truth...

But Truth is not enough.

There is a longing that Truth cannot tell, a yearning that Fact cannot satisfy, a thirst that only Myth may sate.
There, is a Valley.

WE'VE ALL HAD THAT KIND OF DAY BEFORE, REGARDLESS OF OUR occupation, our economic standing, our race or religion – the day that starts out wrong and keeps getting wronger.

As a writer working at home, my problems started early one morning near the end of Spring. The smartphone in my rather unorganized home office beeped out its electronic warning, upsetting my train of thought. I abandoned the sentence in the science article I was writing and turned to uncover the phone from its hiding place under a stack of reference books. "Hello!" I fairly screamed, "who is this?"

I was still in my bathrobe, the first cup of coffee already ingested but not yet waking me up, in no mood to answer any calls. The voice at the other end, if it was a voice, mumbled something in a language I couldn't understand. All I could hear was one word: "e-mail." Then they hung up. My caller-ID showed only a marvelously informative message, "Anonymous."

Great, I thought, whoever *calls* you to tell you you've got e-mail? And on your private, unlisted, unpublished, un-gettable-at phone number? I walked back downstairs to get a second cup of coffee, hoping the caffeine would kick-start my brain. I needed to meet the deadline for the on-line technology article that was due that afternoon.

Eventually the Muse returned and I finished the 2000 words, spell-checked it, and emailed it to the web site that would pay me enough to buy that week's groceries.

Me.

I've been a writer for years now, earning my bread by the sweat of my fingertips, penning everything from serious poems and plays and humorous stories to technical articles and futuristic fantasies – anything to keep meat – excuse me, mostly vegetables these days – on the table. The place of my origin is unimportant; I am simply an American by birth and breeding, having lived in many places in these United States. I am a semi-Citizen of parts of the World by choice, having visited many strange and wondrous places on this globe of ours, but always returning to my cabin in the woods in the USA.

As befits one who would call himself a writer, so far in this life I have had a myriad of occupations, some short, some decades long, each grist for the writer's mill. I have performed physical labor – hard, endless, mindless toil, punishing yet physically fulfilling because the body demands we use its muscles. I have performed mental labor – all the more stressful because the mind and brain alone cannot satisfy the animal nature that requires us to work. Finally I was more or less successful in enough of these efforts to keep me relatively financially free of the trap of a routine career, even with the economic downturns, though on a necessarily modest scale.

So a few years ago I found myself at last with enough time to pursue my version of Truth. Of course I have family and friends, and they are very important to me. But this is an intensely personal story of one person, one man, and of a lonely journey to understanding. Or perhaps just partial understanding. I have learned that each person must traverse this path, alone. But there are Guides to point the way.

Part of this understanding, a major part, is this: everywhere I have ever been, and everyone whom I have ever met, especially the adventure I am about to relate, has convinced me of one important part of the Truth:

Ours is not the first civilization to exist on this planet, nor the wisest, nor necessarily the most advanced.

And probably not the last.

The other hemisphere of my understanding is this:

Reality is much broader than we have been taught.

THERE ARE FORCES AND BEINGS FAR GREATER THAN WE HAVE imagined. The universe itself is beyond our understanding, though we must endeavor to find whatever limits we have, to achieve an ever greater knowledge, a vaster consciousness.

And in our efforts to achieve this higher consciousness:

We, the human race, are not alone.

There is a Valley.

My Search.

Over the years my writing has taken me to places, to philosophies, to people who are far off the widely-traveled roads, walking paths rarely taken by most humans, those multitudes of humanity who live a kind of sleepwalking existence of work and recreation and income and debts, the daily life and death cycles of mediocrity. And these other-path people have told me of places and things – incredible stories of lost lands, forgotten nations, weird occurrences, anomalous artifacts, strange phenomena and unheard-of histories. Long ago I began to keep notes on these strange facts, file cabinets full of them, tablets of interviews and trips, snippets from obscure journals and the newspapers of small towns and villages worldwide. A nebulous network of informants and contacts formed; many of them fed me these weird bits of forgotten lore and unreported phenomena ignored or avoided by the mainstream media.

With the invention of the Internet and its multisensory aspect, the World Wide Web, many of those trailblazers soon found another outlet for their thoughts, their theories, their strange reports. The volume of information available on metaphysical subjects increased to a flood, a deluge, a virtual avalanche of facts and fancies, spewing out at me from around the world. I began to spend untold hours in front of computer screens, sorting and cataloging information until I realized there was no way to handle it all. Becoming more discretionary, I left the more public aspects of unusual phenomena to others and started delving into specific details that are available only to those with resources for actual, on-the-ground research onsite. No longer the casual "researcher" who spends an occasional weekend visiting a UFO "museum" or an Indian mound, I could afford to take the time – as well as the instrumentation, if necessary – to investigate thoroughly anything of interest to me. E-mail, the ability to contact and interview almost anyone in the world, anywhere, prior to traveling, was by now an absolutely essential element of my reporting.

And so one day toward the end of Spring in a year early in the second decade of the Third Millennium of the Common Era, I received that e-mail message from an anonymous source, one I was not able to trace. The full message continued:

From your writings, I know that you are a Searcher for the Truth. But Truth is not enough. You must find The Valley.

Go to the Plaza in Santa Fe for the Summer Solstice celebration. There you will meet a man wearing white pants and a blue shirt. He will give you what you need to know.

I wasn't able to uncover the origin of the cryptic message, the anonymous writer had covered his tracks too well. Even my genius hacker friend Kris Anson, who had founded his own software company at age sixteen, couldn't penetrate the anonymous chain-link of server computers that had handled the secret trajectory of the message across the Internet from its mysterious origin, all the way to me. After an hour's session at my keyboard, his long hair swaying to the music coming from his ear buds, Kris shook his head. "It could be anybody in the world," he said. "They obviously wanted to keep it a secret, from you, me and everybody else. It came from everywhere, and from nowhere. I don't know how they did it, but they did. Cannot help you this time, man."

That was mystery enough for me. I needed another break from a reality that was becoming too mundane, and whatever I came up with, or didn't, would be the basis for an article or a story, maybe both. I called my old investigator Ol' Zack,–O.Z– in Las Cruces, and then emailed him the Message, asked him to go to Santa Fe and see what he could dig up before I arrived.

Three days later, I was on my way to Santa Fe.

THE EASTERN SKY LOOKED CLEAR THAT MORNING, AND THE DRY piquant desert air promised it would remain that way. I would not want to be four-wheeling in *arroyos* if rainclouds threatened there. A momentary shower in the hills could result in a true gully-washer flood miles downhill. People had drowned out here in flooded *arroyos*, while fifty feet away the ground was dry as bone! The road looked clear, too. I was determined to dump this load and get back to civilization yet today. I would take pictures of "Solana's Palms" when I had returned it to its rightful place; there was no time to do it right now; I wanted to be back out of the desert before darkness set in..

Up one hill and down another, in between boulders and grease-wood bushes, I followed tire tracks along the "trail," hoping that the rental SUV wasn't getting too scratched. The trail led down into a sandy-bottomed *arroyo*, a tiny canyon some twenty feet deep and just wide enough to negotiate the truck through. And seemingly getting deeper, even though I had to shift to lower gears as the canyon floor rose. It was strange; I was going uphill, but the *arroyo* walls got higher and higher, casting deep shadows from the afternoon sun. I had to turn on the truck's headlights to make out the twists and turns and to see the occasional heaps of collapsed dirt fallen from the walls. I was getting nervous about possibly being stuck and having to climb out the back of the SUV to trek back to the highway, miles back.

An hour later, I was even more nervous, and extremely worried. First, the SUV's built-in GPS was on the blink, as if the GPS satellites wouldn't reach down into this part of the world. Then, I didn't seem to be getting any closer to any rightful place, and finally, the going was increasingly rough. "Damn," I said aloud, "I hope I don't have to back this thing out of here. Don't know if I can, and there's no place to turn around." The prospect of leaving a fifty thousand dollar rented vehicle immobilized in a ditch and hiking miles back to the highway in the dark was making me nervous. And it was getting cool down there in the gully! I kept praying that no monsoon downburst would come rushing at me.

Eventually the tire tracks I was following led up a branching *arroyo*. To my relief the ditch grew shallower and soon I could see the flat land of the mesa on either side. After a bit of four-wheeling up a low dirt ramp, the truck and I emerged from the *arroyo* and onto the top of the mesa. Checking my odometer showed I had navigated just five miles of the "trail." Now I *was* nervous. Was I out of my mind? Stuck atop an unknown mesa, carrying a stolen sculpture to God knows where? In disgust I touchscreened my smartphone but it indicated "No Service." I didn't know who I would have called anyhow, but between that and the non-functioning GPS, now I felt extremely isolated.

If I turned around right there I figured could make it back to the main road by driving carefully in the impending dark. I looked back down into the *arroyo*, trying to see in the distance the winding path I'd followed, if the deep ditch could be seen from the top here. I couldn't find it; somehow the top of the gulch was hidden from view at this angle. All I could see was identical acres, *far as the eye can see*, I sighed. *Miles and miles, of miles and miles,* as the old saying goes. I looked for the highway in the distance but couldn't find it either. I thought, *I can see how turistas get lost and die out here every year from exposure or dehydration; it's easy to get totally lost!* I could foresee an evening's discomfort, certainly getting a little hungry, but nothing life threatening. I carried a minimal survival kit with me in my backpack – matches, flashlight, lantern, sleeping bag, filled canteen, trail mix and junk food snacks. Plus my trusty digital camera, smartphone, and tablet computer, complete with extra batteries and a solar cell recharger, if I had to be away from electrical power for more than one day.

If I was indeed stranded, I could blink the headlights toward the highway, maybe get the attention of the state police. But how would that look, the great world explorer, getting lost just a couple of miles from the highway? No, I'd stick it out tonight. I had the truck for shelter, after all. No need to sleep on the ground with coyotes and snakes. *I can make a campfire, too*, I knew, thinking of my little emergency kit.

The trail continued northward, on flat land this time, so I drove among the scrub trees and rocks as long as daylight held out, certain that the SUV's dashboard compass would get me back down to the road the next day. Judging that I had about half an hour of daylight left, I started looking for a likely place to stop for the evening. To my left a dark canyon spread out as I went, now a black gash at least a mile wide. To the right lay the bulk of the mesa, flat as a table, white outcroppings of minerals interspersed among the dark shapes of the piñons, greasewood, salt cedars and some other shrubs I didn't know. Following the vanishing suggestion of a trail, I made sure to keep a hundred yards or more from the edge of the canyon. Finally the truck came to a relatively smooth, rock-free area away from trees and bushes. That way, if there were coyotes, *Coyotes,* or mountain lions, I would have at least a chance to see or hear them approaching.

The vehicle safely parked, I took a flashlight and walked over to the edge of the precipice of the canyon. At my feet was total darkness that swallowed up the flashlight's bright beam. In the distance lights flickered, what appeared to be camp fires somewhere up the canyon. Tree frogs and crickets *chirruped* from the valley below, but on my lonely mesa only the whispering winds disturbed the ancient stillness.

AT DAWN I BROKE OUT THE BINOCULARS AND LOOKED AROUND THE area, first back toward the road to find my pathway in. Strange, but I couldn't see the highway or the movement of any vehicles in the distance, no matter which way I looked. "The desert plays tricks with perspective and distance," I murmured, trying to console myself with rational explanations. "Everything's out there, but I just can't see it." For an instant, I thought of the *there-not-there* service station where I had bought two beers yesterday afternoon. I hoped that civilization itself wasn't going to vanish on me. *Or me from it.* I shuddered at the thought.

A sudden flash of light on the western horizon caught my eye. I could just make out a vehicle atop the sheer cliff that defined the western side of the valley. Lime-green, bright – *my god, it was that crazy kid from Santa Fe!* How the hell did he get there, with that low-rider monstrosity? I glanced back at my large dark-green SUV; maybe it would look like a stand of piñon from there? Or did the punks even have binoculars? Oh well, they were at least a mile away across a chasm, and no way was *Coyote* going to be driving that show car of his across the intervening terrain, even if there was a road down those vertical cliffs. I didn't see any immediately obvious pathways down those walls, unless the boys had brought rappelling equipment for themselves and their low-rider ride. So I was safe for a while, maybe for good if they didn't see me first.

The valley – or *The Valley,* if that's where I was – was a mile or more across at this point, converging a bit as it meandered northward, then becoming wider until close to the horizon when it narrowed sharply, appearing to come to an abrupt end some miles north, a view finally absorbed by distant blue mesas. Those far cliffs looked to be close to a thousand feet high, mostly a chalky white from this distance, layered with horizontal reddish streaks, strata laid down eons past. As far as I could see to the north, the cliffs were braced by a skirt of eroded soil and rocks, only occasionally meeting the floor of The Valley perpendicularly in places where accidents of geological history had left no fallen debris.

On closer inspection. the far cliff walls showed more eroded features suggestive of man-made carvings and ancient architecture. One area in particular, a bit to the north, could have been a temple carved into the cliff face, if such things were possible here in the American Southwest. If I were in the Near East, say Jordan or Yemen or Egypt, I wouldn't have doubted it for a moment that it was an ancient sacred monument. In my mind, that place became "The Temple."

From my side of The Valley, a barren switchbacked footpath led down from the edge of the mesa, through a slump of stone and earth, disappearing into a deep jumble of volcanic and sedimentary rocks, presumably arriving at the bottom eventually, probably the same thousand feet below as the far cliff walls. Thank God I didn't have the straight vertical drop that *Coyote* and his thug would have to negotiate to get to me.

The trail on my side of the valley began behind an outcropping and continued down through a small *arroyo* as far as I could see. Good! I wouldn't be visible to the punks when I started down the trail. Close-up binocular views showed a thick copse of trees, cottonwoods, crowding a rivulet of water at the lowest point of the Valley. Other than that, the floor of The Valley was much like the top of the mesa here, sandy desert with boondock dunes of greasewood, scattered piñon trees, not much color, just the baked-brown look of much of this part of New Mexico. The variegated colors of the striped mesa walls and the contrasting strip of greenery below promised a beautiful hike, if nothing else. I didn't see any evidence of human habitation from my high vantage point. Without *Coyote* and his pal in the picture, it could have been a Western Paradise. I shrugged; I was going to do my thing, and they theirs. I just hoped there would be no conflict out here, especially me with no weapon and those two apparently thieves at best, and at worst, who knew?

I made sure the SUV was secure, checked the contents of my backpack, and wrestled the sculpture out of the back of the vehicle. This time, I carefully unwrapped the ancient carving and took a few minutes to study it. I figured I would take some photos of it with my digital camera, make a record of this whole experience, write some articles or a book. Depending on how things turned out, of course. Could I get in trouble myself for transporting re-stolen ancient artifacts? My lawyer would have to settle that one for me.

The smooth front surface of the slab itself, though worn by age, appeared to have been machined, it was so nearly perfectly finished. This was impressive enough, but the exquisite palm carvings took my breath away again. They appeared to be still-living impressions from a master sculptor who had passed this way just minutes before, leaving his hand-print impressions in liquid rock. Long minutes passed as I contemplated the meaning of these ancient palm prints.

Finally, shaking myself out of a near trance, I inspected the petroglyph carvings below the palms. The deeply-etched groupings ranged from side to side across the front of the slab, in two rows of four-inch-high figures. The first was a kind of spiral, the second looked like a circle and a footprint. After that, the markings grew ever stranger, seeming to run together, mixing people and shapes and rainbow-like arches. Mysterious human-like shapes in various poses figured in several groupings, strange geometric forms filling the space around them. Other enigmas rounded out the message, whatever it was.

The petroglyphs themselves were engraved, not merely scratched in place as I had thought upon first seeing them two days before. The top edges were now smooth curves, testament to eons of weathering, but the lines themselves were still squarely cut deep down in the grooves. It looked as if somebody had taken a square-cut tool and melted the figures down into the stone, they were that good. How had the ancestral Puebloan peoples achieved such machine-like workmanship?

As I wrestled the slab to an upright position, the morning sun caught it just so, and for a moment, looking down nearly parallel with the surface, I saw a hazy, bluish, three-dimensional image emerge from the slab! In near panic, I jumped back and let go and the slab fell, slamming to the ground. Grunting, I tilted it up again, and for several minutes twisted and turned it every which way, but never could get the correct viewing angle aligned with the sunlight again. All I could see were some fine scratches, a pattern of tiny swirls on the surface of the slab. Could they have produced such a – *hologram*? Or just a hallucination? Maybe so, but the fantastic beauty of the full-color, three dimensional drawing – *structure*? – was burned into my mind. A building of some kind, it seemed; maybe a temple? Some smaller objects around it. And a group of people, in variegated colorful robes. It was impossible!

"Terminally weird," I said into the recorder, recounting the event for my records. "Either I am already working too hard, or somebody has impressed a full-color, holographic picture of some kind into this stone-age carving. Very strange." I took several pictures of the whole slab, then detailed close-ups of the swirled scratches, of each palm print and each of the petroglyphs. At times I could see the different ghostly colors surrounding each image, at other angles I couldn't. Some of the played-back digital images showed tinges of colors, the others did not. This was going to make quite an article, maybe even a book, if I could get past the legal hurdles. Too bad I couldn't take the whole thing back to a lab first and play with the lighting angles, have somebody check the groove patterns and the etchings. No doubt about it, a three-dimensional image had appeared and it couldn't have been a coincidence, not with the details and the colors. The memory of it seemed to resonate with something I had seen on a trip somewhere, strangely Mediterranean, maybe on Malta or Crete, or in Egypt.

Oh well, that had to wait. I had committed to a mission of taking the slab back to where it came from and then getting out. Perhaps I could have professional archaeologists come visit this place after I had left. I was still hopeful I could complete my task in this second day but even goal that was becoming problematical.

I recalled the old man carrying the slab on his back and loading it into my truck. But, try as I might, the stone was just too heavy for me lift alone, much less to carry. So using the hatchet on nearby scrub trees, I made up a rough *travois,* an A-shaped triangular carrying skid comprised of fresh poles for dragging, like the Indians used to make. By using other poles as levers, I was able to load and tie the re-wrapped slab onto it. I was going to have to drag the dead weight – how far? – With the legs of the "A" on the ground. I laughed out loud at myself; it had probably been a century since anyone out here had used such a conveyance. Oh, for some wheels!

With a last binocular survey for *Coyote* and his pal – I could see two figures kicking the tires of the show car in frustration, and a white column of smoke coming from under the hood; overheating? I hoped – I hoisted up the *travois* poles on my shoulders, resting on my backpack straps. In the pack I were my food, water and all my modern electronic equipment, even manual tablets, pencils and sketchpads.

The trail-head, such as it was, began behind a series of outcropping rocks and plunged right into a convenient *arroyo*, so I wouldn't be visible to those two during my trek. Thus hidden from the view of my possible opponents, and with the outrigger poles of the *travois* resting comfortably on the shoulder straps of my backpack, I began the journey down into the Valley, the crude wooden legs scraping the trail noisily.

The barely-visible trail wound down through the *arroyo*, after a while emerging into a stand of junipers and piñons. I was jubilant; with all this vegetation my old pals from Santa Fe would never see me. Within ten minutes I could not see them or their vehicle, and I relaxed somewhat.

An hour later, I was sitting, rubbing my chafed shoulders and aching arm muscles. "Gotta invent wheels," I joked aloud to myself. "Skids are for the birds."

3

The sun was at its zenith in a cloudless sky as, puffing and panting, I sat to rest, just halfway down the steep wall of colorful strata of rock. From a vantage point safe from prying eyes, I looked out over The Valley. From here the space between the mesas ranged in its physical appearance, beginning from my left as a narrow canyon, broadening to nearly two miles wide to the north, and appearing to converge once more in the distance. Through the center a small *arroyo* darted in and out of upthrust rocks and clumps of trees, in some places straight, ranging hundreds of feet wide, in others narrow and sinuous.

On The Valley floor, vegetation was sparse, greasewood bushes, *cholla* cactus, and rocky, mostly barren, ground, broken here and there by protrusions of sharp rocks and small hillocks that obscured surface details. The far side of the Valley comprised high cliffs of sedimentary layers, parallel testimonies of millions of years of slow geological activity, alternating colorful slices of the long, long history of Mother Earth. The remnant shoreline of an ancient sea? I wondered what kinds of creatures may have swum past this very spot, all those untold ages ago. And what kinds of creatures might be on this spot fifty million years from now? Humans? Something else intelligent?

The mountains in the distant east were products of the cataclysmic explosion of the Jemez caldera hundreds of thousands of years before, marking the furthest extent of the subsequent lava flood's invasion. Truly magnificent and horrendous events had occurred in this valley. Did the future hold others yet to come? The heavy burden of carved slab I was carrying figured into all of this, but I didn't know how.

Sighing, I began my meager lunch of trail mix and water. Amidst all the ancient majesty laid out before me, I, a transient human may-fly, still had to attend to mundane bodily needs. Any deep philosophy would have to come out in my notes later.

THE ROCKY TRAIL WOUND FIRST ONE WAY, THEN ANOTHER, sometimes switching back uphill, sometimes back down. Overall I was descending, but the path was tortuous and I knew I wouldn't be able to get to the bottom, drop off the slab, and get back up this day. Even when I got to the bottom I was going to have to search for the slab's origin site. An ominous mood told me that the final place I was looking for might be miles up The Valley. The trail was by now just a narrow pathway, a sharp open drop on the left, hundreds of feet down and a vertical face of stone to my right. I had to keep my gaze toward the wall and away from the precipice to my left; my acrophobia being difficult to control, my palms sweated the entire time.

Here and there pictoglyphs, "rock art," similar to the one on "Solana's Palms," appeared, though most of these were scribbled on the dark face of the rock, either with crude scratches or daubed colors, They certainly didn't look machined into the rock, like those in my slab. Some were cross-haired circles, like a sniper's scope; some were stick figures of humans hunting or walking. One that showed up most frequently was some version of a spiral. I wondered what they meant. Too bad these folks never developed a written language. Or *had* they, and was this it?

As in most places in the open Western landscape without land-marks to judge with, here distances were deceiving. What I had thought would be a short trip to The Valley floor was becoming an all-day affair. By twilight, I was still not all the way to the bottom of my mesa trail. I was tired, hungry, thirsty and extremely aggravated. "Hey, *Viejo*," I said aloud, but hopefully not loud enough to carry across the valley, "where the hell are the directions to the bottom of the canyon here?" As if in answer, an odor of cooking meat wafted up from some-where, making my stomach growl in hunger.

To my surprise, a man's friendly-sounding voice answered from nearby. "Hey man, just around the corner. I'll show you the way." Some-what surprised and more than a little wary, I dragged my primitive skid three more steps and rounded a sharp corner in the rock wall. There, in front of a cave, stood the speaker, a short, thin Anglo man, probably in his mid-50s, dressed in faded jeans and a more-faded green T-shirt, sporting a graying van Dyke goatee and a nearly bald pate. A campfire just outside the cave front reflected from his thick eyeglasses.

"I'm Judd," he said, smiling and extending a callused hand, "Wel-come to my place here." His good-natured manner set me at ease. Here was a non-threatening fellow human being, not likely to be one of *Coyote*'s pals. I breathed a sigh of relief and detached myself from the *travois*, dropping my knapsack beside it. "Hi, I'm just a weary wanderer, looking for a place to rest." I eyed the stewpot gurgling on the campfire. "And maybe a bit of hot food."

Judd asked me to sit and stay awhile. I sat cross-legged while he poured some of his cooking into two tin plates. "Tastes good," I said after the first bite of the flavorful meat and spicy green chiles. "Thanks."

Judd smiled, sitting across from me, his back against the canyon wall. As I surveyed his little kingdom, comprising a carved ledge some twenty feet square, situated at least a hundred feet above the floor of The Valley, he asked, "What brings you to our Valley, Wanderer?" I didn't know who the "our" referred to, but I could hear the capital letter in "Valley." Maybe some group owned this whole place? A cult, a commune?

"I've got to return an artifact to somebody who lives down here," I replied, thumbing in the direction of the *travois* and its wrapped package. "Don't know who, or where."

Without my noticing it, a lit cigarette appeared in Judd's hand. He drew in a puff and slowly let the smoke escape, its trajectory mixing it with wisps of smoke from the campfire. I was relieved that the odor was legal. Again, I suppressed the longing to once again participate in that addiction. I was enjoying the odor, however, the contact high.

"The Old Man?" The way he put it, it was a statement, not a question.

I nodded. "Probably the same one. I call him *El Viejo*. Does he own this valley? This land?"

Shaking his head, Judd smiled. "*Own* it? No, not in the legal sense, but I guess in a way he just might. Belongs to a lot of people, I believe. Though I'm not sure the BLM map even covers us." He laughed. A private joke? An area this big would have to be on somebody's maps. Surely the Federal Bureau of Land Management, the BLM, which appeared to own most of New Mexico, wouldn't have overlooked square miles of a spectacularly beautiful valley? Not likely.

"Who is he, *El Viejo*, the Old Man?" I asked. "And how was he able to get me this far, all the way from Santa Fe, and then get me lost? I don't understand."

"Hey man, if you're like the rest of us, you've come a lot further than Santa Fe. Know what I mean?" The setting sun pushed the shadows of the western wall over us, plunging the immediate scene into darkness, relieved only by the diminishing campfire. Overhead, the sky was turning a deep purple. In the sudden shadow, Judd's eyes disappeared behind reflected embers of the campfire. The eyes of a demon? I wondered. No, the eyes of a man, a man who possibly knew more about my coming trek than I did.

"And you're not lost. Not yet, anyways." Eyeing something in the distance, Judd suddenly stood up, dusted himself off, and pointed upward to the western horizon where the sunset was a gorgeous *serape* of pinks and blues and violet. Following his finger, I just barely make out two small silhouettes walking northward. "Friends of yours?" I shook my head. "Just some punks who followed me from Santa Fe, I think." I hoped they wouldn't be attracted to the campfire. A mile apart across a canyon was still too close for me. Through my field glasses, one of the dark figures appeared to be carrying something long. A rifle? That I certainly did not need. I shuddered at the thought.

Judd shrugged off my concerns. "No problemo, man. Everybody is welcome here, lots of folks find their way here, eventually. Even dudes like those." The moving shadows were gone. *Hope they go far away,* I thought. The darkness soon swallowed up the moving shadows and a calmness soothed my nerves. The Valley was already having a soothing effect on me, and I was beginning to enjoy that.

Changing the subject, I asked, "Can you tell me about the carvings on this slab?"

Judd whistled softly as I unwrapped the package. "Beautiful, simply gorgeous," he hacked, coughing through his smoke. "I have seen some of those markings up and down the Valley here. Some of them mark some pretty strange places. I don't know what they all mean, but that spiral there is Anasazi for 'gets dizzy here'!"

"What?" I couldn't believe him. "'Gets dizzy'? What's the deal?"

He sucked in a long drag of his potent toxin and gently, slowly, let it escape from his pursed lips. "Radon, radiation, acoustic amplification, volcanic vapors, special herbs, whatever gave the old shamans their visions, these spirals marked the places where it happened." He shrugged. Laughing he said, "Hey, no matter what your language, if you're a human being you can see that this means 'going around in circles', can't you?"

I said nothing, but looked around to where he pointed. "Hey," he wagged a finger, "the rocktoglyph language was *by* shamans, *for* shamans. Every one of them understood it. Kind of a brotherhood thing, you know. Like the picture language signs the hobos used."

"So the 'message' along the bottom, if that's what it was, starts off with 'Gets Dizzy Here'?"

"Maybe the message is, man, that *you* are supposed to find a sign like that?" I was shocked. Looking for a linear message, I hadn't even thought of that. Road signs along the way? Directions for returning the *atiín*? Ancient rock glyphs that spell out something for *me*, specifically, or for just *anyone* who happened to have the stone? How could prehistoric carvers know that the slab might be carved out of its rightful place? How could they know anybody would *want* to bring it back? But with the situation as unusual as it was, I would take any help I could get, from an old hippie or an even older Indian carving. I rewrapped the slab and laid my backpack on it.

"Anyway," Judd said, "I think I know where the slab came from, about eight, ten miles up The Valley, down there, on the far wall, all the way to the North end. You can't miss it if you stay next to the far wall over there. It's pretty well marked." He smiled a knowing smile. "And some interesting milestones along the way."

I sighed. Eight or ten miles, dragging a heavy slab on a wooden A-frame with no wheels, over a rock-strewn Valley floor? That was no pleasant though. And it appeared that no way was I going to get any straight answers from Judd, any more than I had from *El Viejo*. Oh well, I figured, I was this far so far, and my destination just a few miles more. Maybe I could even make it in one more day, if the terrain got a little flatter. Meanwhile, I needed to camp for tonight. Maybe Judd would let me stay at his place?

As my gaze took in Judd's cave site, it dawned on me that his "cave door" was round, about six feet in diameter. At my quizzical look, he nodded in that direction. I walked over and stuck my head in; strange sights surprised me. His "cave" was a metallic cylinder some thirty feet long and six feet in diameter, embedded squarely in the sandstone face of the valley wall, all the way back to a dark end. Fluorescent lighting gave it an eerie, if somber ambience. "Judd, is this some kind of construction caisson or what?"

"My friend," he laughed, "what we have here is probably the world's most expensive warren. Come on in." Head bent to avoid the low ceiling, I followed him, noting that the green metallic paint was flaking pretty badly. Where did he sleep? Surely not in this, this – *tube*!

The end of the cylinder opened up into a small cubical room cut from sandstone, lit up by an overhead fluorescent fixture about ten feet up. About twelve feet square with a twelve foot ceiling, the cube-shaped sandstone room was featureless, save for the "tube" entrance and three other identical round openings, one in each wall face. A glance at each showed that Judd – or someone – was using the other tubes as a bedroom, a storage room, and a toilet facility. Two folding fabric chairs stood in the center of the "hub" room. The smell of Judd's favorite herb permeated the place. *To each his own*, I supposed. At least it wasn't a meth lab, like the cops continued to find in too many *casas* around Chimayó, a so-called holy chapel a few miles outside Española. And also the hard-drug center of northern New Mexico.

"What in the world do you have here, Judd?" I asked, puzzled by the giant tubes and by the whole weird layout. "And what did you mean, 'world's most expensive'?"

Judd plopped down into a chair, waved for me to use the other. I did.

Man, these here cylinders," he leaned back and tapped the opening of the "bathroom" behind him, "they are the transportation containers for the first big H-bombs built by the United States." He smiled again. "The devices got lugged around in these things."

Stunned, I gulped and said, "Good God, the bombs were that big? Why? And how did you –?"

Judd became serious, not at all the joker he had been. "How did I come to have the cases? Hell, they sold them off as surplus in the late '60s. I got 'em cheap, brought 'em up here, dug out the sandstone, put 'em in." Pursing his lips and shaking his head, he said in a very low voice, "We made 'em this big so we could knock out Russian cities. Don't know as how I ever really liked the idea of doing that. Military targets were one thing, but..." An intake of breath, followed by the now-familiar smile. "But, we didn't ever have to use 'em, did we? The threat was enough, wasn't it? And now, the babies themselves are dismantled and gone, and all we got left are their steel wombs. Make a pretty good condo, don't they?"

I wondered how all of this had been done, how any equipment could have made it down the steep walls I had clambered down today. Helicopters? Another way in, from The Valley floor? But I didn't pursue the matter; that they were here was good enough. With any luck he'd let me camp out here tonight in the safety of his H-bomb caissons. The irony wasn't lost on Judd, I noticed. He was visibly anxious, waiting for more comments. I had a few.

Outside, by the light of the campfire, we talked well into the night. I kept trying to figure out how Judd came to be here, at this time. *Waiting for me?* "Could be, my man," he whispered, picking up on my unasked question. "Could certainly be."

"Are there others here in The Valley?" I asked. Judd nodded.

"And are they waiting here, too, just for me?"

My host shrugged and shook his head. "Friend, there are others who live here from time to time, like I do. They have their reasons, I have mine. I come here when the feeling tells me to come. I am sure that the others do, too. After all," he puffed on his cigarette again, "we are all human beings, with needs and desires. And we have to work, too, some of us. But when we are called, we come. So here we are. Think of it as pay-back, or pay-forward." He looked long into the velvet night. "Man, no telling how long all this has been going on." Between his fingers, his small cigarette pointed toward my slab. "What you've got there, that slab, maybe you could figure it out, might be able tell us all something."

"Not exactly *El Viejo's* commune, huh?" I stood with the fire to my back, waving my hand out toward the infinite darkness of the open space beyond. "And why a valley? Wouldn't a nice oasis serve just as well, or a cool forest?"

"Friend, it is what it is. One time, I had the same questions you have now. I have often thought, in the thirty years I've been coming here, that maybe The Valley is some kind of natural amplifier, a place that makes it easier to understand some natural laws that we overlook in towns and cities. Saints and shamans all through history found their special lonely places, usually high hilltops or caves or valleys. Could be a purely natural phenomenon. I mean, it could be simply that The Valley is a natural waveguide, channeling in charged particles, ions, from the Jemez Mountain forests." My puzzled look made Judd slow down and explain.

"It's well known," he said, "that winds, sweeping over the conifer needles, will pick up the excess electrons that tend to congregate at the sharp tips. Well, if those winds flow down the mountainsides in the evening – colder air falls, hotter air rises, you know – then this place could get filled with electrical charges. Negative ions stimulate the human body metabolism; that's why it feels so good and fresh in a forest, or on a beach, where the ions are most numerous."

"You *believe* that?" I asked. "So because of some wind-swept pine needles, *El Viejo* brings people out to the middle of nowhere? Sends me a mysterious e-mail to travel to an unknown place to steal an Indian artifact and take it back God knows where?" I nodded at Judd's H-bomb condo, "And has you make yourself an impossible fusion bomb hideout in a sandstone cliff?" I shook my head. "This is too crazy, Judd, ol' buddy. Think of something else." My rational side was kicking in now, and I was momentarily irritated with myself for being stuck out in a strange place with a strange companion and an even stranger mission. Hell, with *Coyote* and Tall Guy out there, I didn't even know if I would live through the night!

Judd sighed. "Listen, I try to find rational explanations for the rational side of my brain, just to justify to myself what I do here. I mean, on the natural side, lots of things might be happening. Along with the ion-winds, maybe the Valley's walls set up standing waves that acoustically influence the body and the mind along the way. Maybe some of the Valley's geometry was carved in ancient times to enhance some natural phenomenon. Or maybe it's all natural, the combined effect of winds and plants and minerals and dust." He threw his hands back behind his head and lay back to view the stars overhead. "I just know, the other side of my mind knows, that this place is enchanted, strange and beautiful and is an important part of my life – the spiritual side.

"Like I said, I come here when I feel I should, and I leave when it feels right. Sometimes I wander in the Valley and meet the others, and sometimes I stay right here, waiting to meet new people."

"Like me?" I was calming down. Judd was right; when you calmed down you could *feel* the magic in the place, and whether or not it was natural or mystical, the feeling was all too real. *Something* was going on. And I liked it. Enchantment, pure and simple. Like the Chamber of Commerce name for the whole state, "The Land of Enchantment," the place indeed had something going for itself.

"Like you, friend." Judd sat back up and looked at me across the dying campfire. "Believe me, if you weren't supposed to be here, you wouldn't be." He chuckled. "Sometime I want to hear how you actually found us here. In my case it was something weird I stumbled across in a cave halfway around the world from here when I – but that's another story. Anyway, believe me, you are going to find out such things as you didn't know about. I damned sure did!"

"Such as?"

"Come closer to the fire, then turn around." I did. All I could see was my shadow flickering against the cliff face.

"What do you see, friend?"

"My shadow?"

Judd pointed at the wavy figure. "As you draw nearer to the fire, your shadow gets larger, right?"

"Of course."

"But *El Viejo* would phrase it, *Move wisely as you near the light; your shadow's ever larger.*"

I decided to go along with Judd's enigma game. "Which means?"

"Be careful about the truth; the closer you get to it, the more you may be blocking the view of others. Or it may be that your nearness to the truth makes your own existence that much more important, that much larger, to the rest of the world. Think about it."

It was my turn to shrug. "I'll write it down, Judd." And I did, in my tablet. It seemed to be a key to the way *El Viejo* thought, and I suspected such keys might also be my keys to understanding, maybe even survival.

After a long quiet spell spent just listening to the sounds of the desert creatures in the Valley beyond, Judd said, "You know, I used to design these things, these nukes, over at Los Alamos."

Did he ever feel guilty, any horror at what his designs could do? I asked. Burning cities, ending civilization? "Nah, not really. I mean, I was a physicist in it for the physics. We all figured they wouldn't ever be used, just threatened as a deterrent. Hell, if I had wanted to see what horrors of war were like, I could just check the daily papers, watch the TV. No way I wanted that kind of crap to happen here in America, or anywhere else, if we could help it."

"So, to stop the bad guys, we had to have the biggest stick on the block?"

Nodding, he drew in a long, long puff from his strange cigarette. "Yep, the American way. And you know what, it worked! The bad guys gave up and went away. Saved the world a lot of grief. You don't believe it, just go visit some of those so-called *enlightened* countries that endured the un-elected thugs they had for leaders for seventy years or more."

The firelight flickered, reflections dancing in his glasses, in his eyes. There was a lot of public concern recently about the possibility of small nuclear wars, especially in Asia and the Middle East. "But now that the Russkies have cooled off a bit, if we could just bottle that ol' genie back up and put it away, maybe we'd all be better off..." I didn't reply. The Cold War had cost more than brains and money, I figured. Some very thoughtful souls had been in the balance, too.

LATER IN THE NIGHT JUDD VOLUNTEERED THAT HE HIMSELF WAS walking evidence that intellect is not enough for complete wholeness – if the spiritual component is lacking, the human is not in balance. "My I.Q. qualified me for Mensa, the upper 2% of intelligence in the human race. But I finally realized that I wasn't happy, outside of my work. I truly needed something I was missing. A 'God-shaped hole' is the way one old-time revival preacher put it. I think the shape of what I have found is a lot bigger than what he would have accepted as his God, but to each his own.

"Each one of us has a special puzzle piece that we have to go out and find for ourselves, some piece of the Universe that makes us whole. Maybe I just needed a bigger piece because I was lacking more. Maybe the simplicity of revealed faith is enough for some ordinary people, but guys like me were worse off than them and we needed some concrete examples. Bottom line, I was badly ignorant of the spiritual side of existence. And so I felt bad without knowing why.

"Satisfied ignorance is the worst sin," he went on, "and much of this society seems satisfied in its willful rejection, that is, its ignorance, of the spiritual needs of human beings." Judd's eyes blazed with the reflected campfire, and it was easy to believe, for a moment, that his soul was ablaze as well. "You can see this manifested in extremely violent sports and movies, in crass and vulgar television shows, in hateful speech on the Internet, in wantonly corrupt politicians and their campaigns, in demagogues on the streets, in dark things done in dark places, and all without any shame. All these derive from the lack of a spiritual compass, in my experience."

He walked over and tapped the metal of the cylinder wall. "I believe that spiritual laws are as concrete, and as meaningful, as the laws of physics that let me build those bombs. And without recognizing and using this compensating component, mankind is incomplete, vectoring off in unintended directions. The result is evident in our society – violence, divorce, unnecessary termination of pregnancies, drugs, irreversible youth rebellion. And war."

I objected that philosophers since Aristotle had been complaining of the same things, but mankind had gone onward, and mostly upward. But by this time Judd had elevated his altered state, maybe because of the emotion of the moment, maybe because of what he was now smoking, maybe because of the enchantment of The Valley itself. My comments didn't seem to affect his discourse. I had the strangest sensation that Judd was channeling a higher power, or at the very least communing with something beyond the two of us.

"Yes, other civilizations have had similar problems, but now we have the same concerns, only exacerbated by powerful technologies that spread the effects and the knowledge of evil everywhere, instantaneously. So progress in some areas has made ancient problems worse, without any concomitant improvements to offset them.

"We understand more and more of the physical reality of the universe, but less and less of the so-called spiritual reality. With a balanced life, the wonders of technology can complement the serenity of spiritual fulfillment, enabling us to experience knowledge that many ancients would have considered magic." I sat open-mouthed at Judd's newfound eloquence. Was he truly possessed? Stoned? Or just opening up? It was hard to believe he was the same laid-back old hippie of an hour ago!

"But not all of the ancients would have thought us modern people magicians – in the many millennia that have gone before, many inventions, many technologies, much great literature and art have been created in many cultures, items that have been lost and not re-created since. Some of these were unique, some representative of other ways of knowledge, some unknowable today because the underlying science no longer exists and cannot be re-established, having taken thousands of years to develop the first time, and then along totally different pathways than Mankind now knows.

"That is why some anomalous artifacts that we see today, the physical ones, are not comprehensible." I gave him a puzzled look, though I knew in general what he was referring to – reports of machined metal parts appearing in veins of coal tens of millions of years old, evidence that ancient Egyptians had built huge power-generating stations out of solid granite blocks, alleged modern human remains dug out of geological strata thousands of centuries before even the African apes were supposed to exist. He knew I understood, and didn't stop to explain. "And yet there are also invisible artifacts, those of ways of thinking and of institutions and prejudices and mythologies, which also reflect these ancient ways of knowing." He mentioned that present-day Mankind existed over the strata laid down in the ancient past, much as the geological strata that define and beautify the walls of the Valley around us.

Judd said, "We have learned a few things over the millennia, even though many people refuse to realize it. One is, that Truth itself is fractal – no matter how you break it down, no matter how far down you go, it is still Truth; it keeps the same shape, it means the same thing. Like the mathematical fractal, Truth obeys very simple, predictable – yet very powerful – laws.

"And, like fractals, it sometimes take special powers to comprehend the whole. Anyone in the last three hundred years, since the mathematical equations of fractals were formulated, could theoretically have plotted the beautiful and complex fractal designs that we all know and love. The equations themselves are simple, yet not all the human beings who ever lived, working all their lives on the task, could have computed any one of the infinitely-detailed fractal flowers that today we can generate in a few seconds on a computer screen.

"No, it took the higher power of a computer, executing computations by the hundreds of billions per second, to generate, to reveal the colorful patterns, the infinitude of color and curvature, those intricate worlds within worlds. We are fortunate, you and I and all of us, to see figures and shapes no humans ever saw before the final decades of the last century. And while we're at it, to hear sounds, synthesized and formulated, that no one ever heard before. More than likely, as *The All* manifests its will through us, one of us or more of us, will also work out ways to smell, to touch – to *feel!* – in ways no others before us have. Such advances are happening every day, every hour, all over the world." Judd's eyes grew more frenzied as he continued, something I would have thought impossible just minutes ago.

"In a few years at most, our technical progress will be exponential and instantaneous – changing from second to second, so that we will be deluged with new information, and new knowledge, and new insight, leading us to new wisdom – every second from now on into the future. And this will take us to Transcendence, the next step in human awareness." I sat stunned, not replying, not knowing how to add anything to that beautiful concept.

"And so there may be other concepts that we can almost imagine, yet not be able to understand or fully experience, until some other higher power enables us to. Something that can act on those concepts the way that computers did on the theory of fractals."

I enjoyed the mental breather; that was an analogy I could understand – humanity might have vague stirrings of a possibility, but the concrete realization of it could only come about with better tools or better minds. Just as we had realized the dream of flight, the beauties of the fractals, the wonders of the heavens – and each time they turned out to be much more profound than the original ideas dreamed up by limited minds with limited sensory tools.

"These concepts," Judd gasped out in a last-ditch effort of will, "may involve extra-sensory powers, paranormal experiences, or traveling into the past or future, or parallel dimensions – or other things, Other Places, that we have no names for yet. But with an unlimited Multiverse out there, and with an unlimited Universe in here –" he tapped his forehead, then his heart, reminding me of a Middle Eastern Arab's bow " – we had better be prepared for unlimited danger as well as unlimited opportunity. Transcendence will not come without a price; Nature and *The All* guarantee that." He breathed deeply, closing his eyes as if trying to regain control of his maniacal mood.

As I digested the cosmic significance of Judd's expositions, he calmly changed the subject to strangenesses nearer at hand, in our Land of Enchantment. "Tales are told of the Blue Nun, who administered to the Native Americans here in New Mexico by bodily projecting herself from Spain, long before the Europeans came to this place." He smiled. "Her tales of voyages were dismissed by the priests as flights of fancy, yet the peoples here reported later that she had been among them in the flesh, a real person *apported* from Europe before the Conquistadors invaded these parts.

"Might not some of our own vivid dreams be taking us to other worlds we have not yet visited in the flesh? Or maybe we are going in the body to some of those Other Places, too, interacting there, affecting other living beings? And vice versa? And thereby assisting in the Transcendence to come?"

Judd continued, his manic pace alternately emerging, then receding, as if an unknown tide was driving him. "And maybe the Hum they hear in Taos is the beginning of a communion, for who knows if Man is the only being undergoing Transcendence? Why not the Earth itself? The ancient peoples of the West believe that the Earth Mother is a living being, more than rocks and seas. If she lives, maybe she sings in her happiness? Or in her sorrow?"

Judd said all this and much more, many things I did not understand, things I cannot remember in detail, some too shocking to pass on to the uninitiated, some merely beautiful. I never even thought to use my voice recorder, or take extensive notes, so as a result many of these observations may never be known again, maybe not even to Judd himself. But believe me, their profound relevance stunned me. For the first time in my life I felt as if I were intellectually and emotionally challenged beyond my capacities, yet still hungry for more.

For hours Judd continued to murmur or shout his versions and visions of wisdom, insight and Transcendence until the firelight finally dwindled to nothing and at last we turned in for the night. I slept on a cot in the hub room, tired and slightly dazed by the unusual conversation with my unexpected host and the unexpected intensity of his overweening philosophy.

Next morning, Judd whipped up omelets and hot coffee, which I gratefully accepted. A nearby spring furnished water for washing my face, and there were many opportunistic places for other natural functions. Clean and full, I thanked my bearded friend for his lodging and food, and his companionship. "I appreciate the insights, Judd. I really do." He declined my invitation to come along.

"No, friend, I've gotta stay here a couple more days. I feel some other folks coming, this time from the North, the other way." Judd smiled and shook my hand. "I don't see your friends up there today," he said, pointing to the opposite ridge. "Maybe you'll be lucky and get to where you're going without them. Just take care of yourself and that slab. It's unique."

"Yeah, I know. Thanks again." I arranged the *travois* and my backpack and trudged on down the trail.

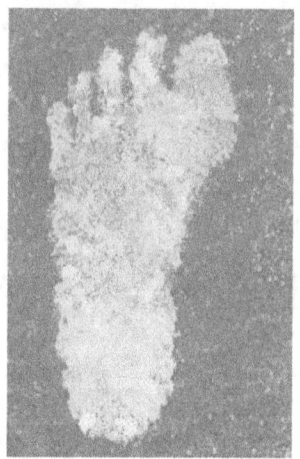

4

Two long and arduous hours later, I reached what appeared to be the floor of The Valley. I was disappointed. Other than a sparse copse of yellowing cottonwood trees set in a stony field, there was nothing. No river, not even the suggestion of a trail. I sighed, found some shade under the cottonwoods, and took off my heavy burden. After some trail mix and a swig from the canteen, I unwrapped and examined the carved slab again. Maybe there was a clue in its engravings?

The first petroglyph – if that's what it was – was the spiral. "Gets dizzy here?" I laughed out loud at my reaction to Judd's interpretation. "Maybe that was Judd's warren, UnderHill, and he was a Hobbit. And 'gets dizzy' is what happen if you hang around him too long!" I didn't smile too long, though. This was serious business. I had to deliver this sacred object and get back to civilization. I eyed the western canyon wall nervously and thought, *And not get hurt in the doing!*

The second set of markings seemed to include a footprint, maybe a hole? On closer inspection, the footprint had waves in it. A pond, a pool? If these markings were a map, maybe I should trudge northward on up the valley and find it. *If this really is a map!*

I shook my head. The other figures to the right were some kinds of geometric markings, interspersed with human-like silhouettes and stick figures. I didn't have a clue as to what they represented. With more resignation than trepidation, I covered the slab again, harnessed myself to the *travois* and headed north, intending to find a convenient trail across to the other side of The Valley. An hour later I found the first matching markings, and something else.

Simulacra are natural formations that look like other things. The Old Man of the Mountain in Vermont, the Kneeling Nun to the south of here, down below the Gila Wilderness. A supposedly world-wide distribution of gigantic lion-like faces on natural mountainsides, "The Secret Places of the Lion," according to one author. Perhaps even strange formations on Mars and other faraway places. Psychologists say that it is the merely human mind, imposing patterns on random nature. Others say nature imposes the patterns on matter. But might not it be possible that the Pattern imposes itself on all of nature, Man included? That the Pattern itself, regardless of the medium, is the message, the information?

Those were the thoughts I had when I rounded a knee of the Valley wall and first saw The Temple.

THE OPPOSITE WALL OF THE VALLEY, A CLIFF COMPRISING

sedimentary layer-cake geological strata, had been sculptured by natural forces alone, but to my mind it was an ancient Egyptian temple, natural or not. From my vantage point of about a mile away, the pre-noon sunlight accentuated shadows of vertical protrusions that looked like huge columns, a dozen of them, appearing to hold up the far wall of The Valley itself. Several doorways or arches, probably caves or dark colored rock layers, completed the illusion.

My thoughts jumped to the numerous Nineteenth Century accounts of Egyptian temples and treasures said to be situated in the Grand Canyon, but that was in Arizona, at least three hundred miles west of here. I knew that Arizona, like many other Southwestern states, had had its share of anomalous finds. Ancient Jewish weaponry and tablets near Tucson, ancient Libyan characters scratched on stones in many places, and some ever-recurring high-strangeness reports from around the Petrified Forest and the Meteor Crater. There was no reason to suspect that such weirdness would be limited to that portion of the desert, and I was finding enough mysteries right here where I was trudging. I figured that a comprehensive study of all of the reports, finds and speculations over the centuries could lead to some unified theory of what could have caused so many apparent anomalies. A great expedition by ancient Africans through here? One of the Lost Tribes of Israel? Relics of the wondrous stories told by the Book of Mormon? Something else?

Between my location and the far cliff wall, the floor of The Valley rose almost imperceptibly, and I perceived ahead of me several discontinuities that had to be *arroyos* and other cuts in the rock-scattered rise. Those might be obstacles I would have trouble with, but the stunning appearance of The Temple was something I had to investigate first. "Besides," I said aloud, "maybe it really *is* a temple of some kind, and maybe that's where I can drop this load of mine for good." I didn't want to believe Judd's directions of eight or ten miles, not in this terrain and in this heat! Not to mention a couple of hostiles out looking for me.

By high noon I was about one-quarter of the way to the far Valley wall, when the first natural obstacle came into view. An *arroyo*, a mini-canyon of its own, a hundred feet across and ten feet deep, with sheer vertical walls. A few dozen willow trees, twice as tall as the *arroyo* they were growing in, blocked my immediate view of the floor of this large eroded wash. Unhitching my load of stone, I scouted up and down the perimeter. *There!* An old cave-in on my side of the ditch formed a natural ramp leading to the bottom. On the other side of the *arroyo*, a few hundred yards north, a matching ramp would give me access back up and out.

Before beginning the trek down and through the *arroyo* I found a patch of shade under a scrub piñon tree, stopping to eat some trail mix, and washing it down with water from a full canteen, thanks to my new ol' buddy, Judd. In the distance, The Temple looked more and more like a temple and less like a natural formation. It reminded me of the great stone temples I had seen in Jordan, structures carved from canyon walls in Jordan, in deserted Petra, the "rose red city, half as old as Time," one poet had called it. I would know in an hour or two, I thought, if there weren't too many more gullies in the way. I shrugged, resumed my dragging burden, and carefully made my way down the dirt ramp, resisting the tendency to slide on the loose gravel and thick, dry dust.

Strewn with jagged rocks, the floor of the *arroyo* proved to be tricky to maneuver through. A relatively stone-free path suggested itself, leading down toward the group of tall willows, and I grudgingly dragged my load south, away from the direct line toward the up-ramp on the other side. Before entering the copse of trees, I inspected the few clouds that lazily drifted in the deep blue sky. Nothing ominous in any direction, I concluded. Especially, no thunderheads anywhere, the strato-cumulus buildups that serve to warn desert travelers not to spend much time in places where an inch of rain miles away can funnel into a deadly wall of water six feet deep, moving at fifty miles per hour. Every year, ignorant tourists and campers died in such washes, where an hour before and an hour afterwards, the ground is dry to the touch and to the sole. At least I was safe from drowning in the desert.

The smooth path was soon swallowed up in the welcome shade and profuse greenery of drooping willows, which opened into a small clearing not fifty feet in diameter. In the midst of these willows, a pool! Here, the floor of the *arroyo* transformed into a gently bulging expanse of whitish stone, topped by a depression some ten feet in diameter. There, in a pond of an indeterminable depth, what must have been spring-fed water formed a clear, deep-blue pool, jewel-like in its perfection, a sight totally unexpected. At one edge the pool drained in a thin sheet of water down into a foot-wide rectangular slot that disappeared into thick underbrush and trees.

"Man, this is a sight for sore eyes," I whispered aloud, "and for dry skin!" I laid down the *travois*, stripped my clothes, and carefully waded into the water, savoring its coolness as I immersed completely in its welcome embrace. The middle of the pond was about four feet deep, and I floated leisurely on my back, feeling cool, clean and at peace with the world. Refreshing energy seemed to flow into my being, and a stillness came over me, a quietude deeper than the natural silence of The Valley itself.

Suddenly, a woman's tinkling laughter broke the silence, "Do you like my place, here, stranger?" Surprised and shocked, I rolled over onto my stomach, my feet scrambling on the smooth stone bottom until I could stand up, my nakedness hidden (I hoped) by the water.

"I'm sorry," I sputtered, "but I didn't know anybody was around here." Wiping water from my eyes, I saw an olive-skinned young woman a bit over five feet tall, dressed in a rainbow-colored wrap much like a sarong. Long dark hair framed an exquisite face, from where incongruously light blue eyes shone forth from a delicate face, slightly Oriental in aspect, or maybe Native American. Whatever her ancestry, she was beautiful, she was desirable, and I was glad that the water hid my natural physical reaction to her presence. I gestured toward my pile of garments. "Can you hand me my clothes, please?"

She laughed that crystal-bell laugh again, and laid my pants alongside the pool, disappearing into the trees. "I will wait away, stranger. Please make yourself comfortable." I was up and out within seconds, slipping on my clothes without trying to dry off first. The quick evaporation through the fabric cooled my body even more. Dressed only in jeans, I called to my mysterious visitor. Or was *I* the mysterious visitor?

"Miss, who are you? And what is this place?"

Smiling, she walked back to the poolside and sat, drawing up her slender legs modestly with the sarong discreetly draped. "My name is

Algona, and this place I call the 'Pool of Life'. Who are *you* and why are *you* here?"

Sighing at the incredible coincidences and circumstances that had led me to this place, I introduced myself and gave a brief synopsis of the odyssey that had begun with the enigmatic e-mail the week before. "And so I really would like to take the stone slab back where it belongs, and while I'm at it, try to make sense of it and of this Valley around us. And of people like you and Judd. And *El Viejo*."

I took her cue and stretched out on the expanse of flat white stone, the high sun drying me on the one side, the smooth, cool tactile embrace of the warm stone on the other. Strange, how in this small opening, willows framed the open sky, as if we were alone together in a bubble of timelessness, cut off from the outside universe. I smelled a whiff of something burning sweetly, an almost lavender odor. Incense? A campfire? I would ask her in a few minutes, but first I wanted to know about her and why she was here. "Are you part of this whole journey of mine? One of *El Viejo*'s people?"

She ignored my question; somehow I had thought she would. "I know the stone you carry, and I can tell you where it belongs." Her voice soothed me, its lilt expressing meaning beyond sound. Her pale blue eyes carried intense information straight to my soul. *Efficient medium that, light!*

Like Judd, she told me that she too, lived outside the Valley and came here to her Pool when it felt right, when she was called by some primal voice to abandon her ordinary life of hustle and mundanity and to return to where she was needed. "I have been here several days now, expecting someone. You must be he."

I reprised for her much of the same story I had already related, adding more detail this time, and asked many of the same questions again. Who was *El Viejo*, and was he conducting some kind of initiation? Did he run a cult? How could anybody have known which path I would be taking through the Valley? Or that I wouldn't abandon the slab and the quest and just go home? What was the purpose of all of this?

Algona smiled, full, sensuous lips revealing wonderfully white teeth. "In the business world a thousand miles away from here, where I work,

I often go through routines that have been set out by others, those who formed the company and who set up the rules and regulations. Did *they* know who *I* was going to be, when I was interviewed and hired into their company, what *I* was going to be doing, even years after they had retired and died?

"No, they didn't," she answered herself. "But most of the circumstances I would encounter, most of the situations, they had envisioned ahead of time, and had set down the procedures by which things would get done. The charter of the business, like the United States Constitution, foresees the future, in a way. Somebody lays out the rules, and anybody who enters the system and wants to succeed, needs to consult those rules. Maybe that's what the Old One does here?"

I tried to be irritated at this vague response, but the circumstances wouldn't allow more than a mild objection. "That doesn't answer my question, Algona. Unlike your business office, or even national politics, I don't think we've got a set of written instructions here, to tell us which form to fill out, where to send the bills. Or how to run a government."

She shook her head slightly. *That smile, again!* "No? What might those symbols on your stony slab be, then?"

"Wait a minute, lady," I was getting exasperated by now. "If I can't read them, what good are they? And what does that say about *El Viejo?*" At that instant, that gentle odor, perfumed almost, wafted my way. From the trees? I couldn't tell. I was going to have to ask Algona or somebody what that smell was. Intoxicating, to say the least. Maybe it was just her perfume?

While I was inhaling this scent, enjoying it, Algona spoke. "Maybe you have to learn to 'read' them?" I could tell by her inflection that "read" wasn't what she meant. But she wasn't waiting. Deftly she rose, went to the *travois*, untied my treasure, carried it over, and laid it on the stony ground between us. It happened so quickly, I didn't have time to be surprised that she had handled the heavy slab without effort. Given the state I was in, that realization only dawned on me much later. She sat across from me, dipped her left hand into the clear pool of water, and with a wet fingertip, began tracing the etched figures.

"Here's a reading lesson," she began. "Pay attention." Her manner was that of someone instructing a beginning learner, but the smile she gave me was certainly not one I had ever had from my first grade teacher when I learned to read so many years ago. She excited me, as the saying goes, down to my toenails!

"First we have the spiral. 'Gets dizzy here' is one interpretation, and often used for shamanic directions. But there are other ways to read. If you lay your hand on it, perhaps there is another way as well." She took my hand – hers was incredibly warm and soft! – dipped it into the water, then laid it over the spiral. "Close your eyes, feel the meaning, let it flow into your consciousness. Be as a child, and listen to yourself."

My first thought was, "Who would have ever thought to lay on wet hands to read a petroglyph message?" But immediately upon touching the stone surface, feeling the spiral slot beneath my plan, I was caught up in a sensation, an *awareness*, that was entirely new and wonderful. *And I was elsewhere! I saw, I felt, I knew*, that the spiral meant more than 'gets dizzy here' in the intellectual sense. It was 'gets dizzy here' in a physical, an emotional, sense, an entrance to a maelstrom of beauty. The phosphine patterns in my tightly closed eyes began to pulsate, changing colors and becoming three-dimensional, spiraling me toward another level of consciousness, some place I had never been. I understood, I knew, without thinking, that this symbol was that *of the* atíín *slab itself*, a whirling gateway to a *beyond* that was outside comprehension.

For an eternity, it seemed, I wandered in the meaning of the stone, drenched in an outpouring and an inpouring of *being* such as I had never known, feeling myself stretched, convoluted, sprung out and wound up, experiencing images and visions that I still cannot express – all from this one simple symbol.

Sometime later, perhaps hours, I awoke. My little circle of paradise, limited to a bed of warm rock, defined by willow trees just yards away, was empty save for me and the – now wondrous! – inscribed slab. Where was Algona? Struggling to my bare feet, I bent over the pool, scooped up water to wash my face and to help clear my stunned mind of the remnants of the incredible visions still resonating within it.

"Stranger," that crystal voice called to me from inside the willow grove. "What did you think of your first lesson?"

"Truly wild and wonderful, Algona," I answered back to the trees. "Is there that much more in each one of those symbols? A whole new world?"

"Just come here, friend. Other lessons await."

THE SUN WAS SETTING OVER THE WESTERN WALL OF THE VALLEY when Algona and I returned to the pool. The trees were spreading their lacy shadows over the water and the broad stone outcropping that defined the clearing. I gathered up some firewood and Algona quickly set up a campfire and began roasting something over a small spit, a wonderfully delicious aroma permeating our small universe. The afternoon had been a complete marvel to me, and in the mood I was in, I could have stayed with her, right in this paradisiacal spot, forever. Overwhelmed by the visions I had experienced with the touching of the stone, again rapt by Algona's spiritual and physical loveliness, I was simultaneously sated, yet hungry for much more of each. I'd had just one kiss from her, chaste and innocent, but I was spellbound for life.

"I still don't understand, Algona," I began hesitantly, "how that stone experience worked. Is it psychedelic? Chemicals in the rock? What?"

"You must understand" she replied, munching on a piece of roasted potato, "I can't give you descriptions that fit into what you already know about physics and chemistry and the nature of the Universe. First of all, I don't know the proper words, and second, you don't have the mental and emotional framework in place yet that would enable you to comprehend it.

"I just know that this is what occurs when a person who is supposed to touch the wet stone, does touch the stone. The 'Pool of Life' gives life to the carvings, or maybe to the stone itself. Is it chemical, is it biological? Is it spiritual? Some of each? Who can tell, and why inquire? It does what it does.

"And yes, each of the other symbols can give a similar experience, if the right person touches it at the right time and place. With the right preparation."

I walked over to the inscriptions and splayed my hands over the slab. "So if I trace out these other petroglyphs now, with wet hand, I will get more information?"

"No, friend. Not here, not now." The firelight played over her face, illuminating it in contrast to the ever-darkening walls of the *arroyo* and of the far wall of the Valley. "In the morning I will show you another 'carving,' another place where you may possibly learn even more."

As she smiled, I was willing to wait an eternity of mornings, just to spend them with her.

MORNING BROUGHT A REFRESHMENT SUCH AS I HAD NEVER KNOW. Something spiritual, something physical, had happened within me, deep inside my very soul. For one thing, I was no longer sure what reality was. My situation was almost humorous: here I was, a world traveler and spiritual researcher who had given many learned talks about the true nature of the universe and Mankind's place in it, and now I was at the bottom of a sandy gulch in the middle of an unknown Valley, having to face a convoluted reality strangely different from anything I had ever expected.

My philosophical mantra is: "Reality is a lot broader than we've been taught." And the example I continually preach is: "We humans can only see the tiny visible part of the infinitely wide electromagnetic spectrum. We call it *light*. But we know that other frequencies, other wavelengths, are out there but we can't experience them with our very limited sense of vision. So, by analogy, there must be other kinds of phenomena that most of us can't experience with our limited senses of hearing, or touch, or even our imagination."

These unknown realms are, I believe, where the paranormal, the anomalies, the strangeness originate – we are vaguely aware of some of these 'frequencies' when they impinge on our known senses. But most of the time we are totally oblivious and ignorant of them, even though they permeate the Universe and our bodies and may affect our minds. Sensitives and psychics are more aware of some of these wavelengths, and spiritual teachers, shamans, and Enlightened Ones may experience many others.

We have overwhelming evidence from history that people do interact with these wavelengths, these 'higher dimensions,' sometimes for the better, sometimes for the worse. It's like having an electrical outlet available – if you approach it with the right equipment, the proper 'interface,' you have access to unlimited, useful powers. But if you don't have the proper knowledge, don't know the correct way to plug into it and how to use it, you can be killed. Electricity is neither good nor evil, it's just there. It is up to you to handle it properly so that it helps instead of hurts. So it is with the unknown psychic and spiritual laws. Like electricity, they exist whether or not you believe in them.

That has been my credo, my faith in the unseen, the unknown. That viewpoint has let me bridge the intellectual and emotional gap between the laws of science and the mass of unsubstantiated anecdotal information that constitutes the 'paranormal.' It has been my guidepost to sanity in a world that often verges on irrationality.

But now, far from the comforts and conveniences of civilization, I was finally experiencing a powerful force that shook me to the core of my existence, and all my intellectual preparation was not enough to absorb the shock. A beautiful, desirable woman, an enigmatic slab with strange carvings, a "Pool of Life" located in smooth stone in the bottom of an *arroyo*, in the middle of a Valley in a place that probably didn't exist in any real world. Yet somehow, some way, after all the overwhelming experiences, it felt as though I had always been here. It was home.

Algona sat quietly as I tried to absorb all that had happened in the last few days. Finally she rose and spoke. "Let me show you something else." I followed her back into the grove, walking beside the rectangular slot where the pool drained. A few yards into the trees, the small channel ended at an abrupt drop-off of several feet, creating a gentle waterfall. Gurgling water cascaded down layers of beige sedimentary stone, a five-foot journey ending in a basin about two feet in diameter, from where it disappeared under an overhanging rock ledge that barely cleared the water's surface.

Algona kneeled beside the basin and splashed water onto the smooth surface of the ledge. "Here is something else for you to touch," she whispered, "a place where many have come before."

Carved into the surface of the stony ledge – a human footprint, now filled with water drained from Algona's "Pool of Life."

"Wet your left foot," she directed, "and then place it in the footprint. Don't worry, it fits everyone."

Into this mysterious and wonderful odyssey, I now placed a final piece – peace?–the water-filled human footprint. "You say it fits every foot? But that can't be – we are, all of us, different people, with differently shaped feet. Different sizes."

"Try it – the proof is in the footing." She smiled at her own pun.

"But my foot is larger than that footprint," I protested.

"Wet your foot in the stream, then try it," Algona whispered adamantly.

Doubting, I did just that. The cool wetness of the surrounding stone surface was almost erotic, a smoothness almost as if alive. I experienced a momentary blurring of vision and almost tripped on the slippery surface. Steadying myself, I gathered my courage and placed my bare foot on that enigmatic depression. Astonishingly, my foot did fit! My foot was larger than the ancient footstep, but it still fit! God – *The All* – help me, it fit as if I had made that footprint myself, had displaced malleable stone with tons of pressure. In the shade – cool stone, cool water – I was sweating.

"How...?" The question died on my lips. Algona smiled.

"Reality is much broader than we are taught, my friend. Things that cannot be, often are. Things that defy logic are all around us. The first step toward understanding is acceptance. If a thing *is*, then first it must be accepted; afterwards and only afterwards, must it be explained. And, be forewarned, revelation and inspiration are equally valid tools – in the right hands."

I started to withdraw my foot from the footprint, but a promising sensuousity made me keep it there. And then, as in the petroglyph slab, I felt Life awaken in the stone. My soul flowed down into that hard surface and spread vaporously throughout the surrounding landscape. For all the unspeakable beauty, all the physical ecstasy of that moment, I shied away from letting loose of my whole being, fighting the sensation of being engulfed by the *Allness*.

I was elsewhere! Somebody else!

My resistance propelled me toward another swirling vision. Suddenly I was First Man, I was All Mankind, I belonged in a way I had never known. I saw through the eyes of another, and in his mind I could sense, however vaguely, the first stirrings of intellect, the glint of introspection, in this person who had left this footprint untold millennia ago when the surrounding region was a verdant forest on the edge of a vast lake.

It was in this Valley, or a place just like it, that First Man first came, that humans first became human. In his memory a mistiness enveloped his early life; he had not been born self-aware, but became conscious of his own awareness as he lived, developing toward the something that humans now were. My own conscious mind commented, *This was* very, very *long ago*. As if to underscore my observation, a large beast lumbered across the nearest hills, let out a bellow, and plunged into the lake. Something really huge! *A dinosaur? Impossible!* But impossibility wasn't important; what was happening here on this spot took precedence over any prehistoric animal – humanity was being born before my eyes. Before *his* eyes.

With his *eyes I made out the other trudging members of this small band of nomads who had come far, instinctively, to this Holy Place. With his other senses I felt the elated mood of the tribe as they immersed themselves in the flowing stream and springs and smelled the clear winds of peace. I felt his pride, for he knew that they would all grow into the consciousness he experienced, and then he could share with them the new world. In my mind, I wished them all well, but I was there for another purpose.*

And then the scene shifted.

I was once again becoming part of The Valley. I felt the electrically-charged winds roaring down from the far mountains, the enormous volcano that defined the eastern skyline, stroking the sky with smoky discharges; I knew of carved chambers in The Valley walls where currents collected and discharged, where men wrote stories of their homelands and their adventures and of their visits to Other Places; where sounds and vibrations focused and where other energies congealed. I understood how The Temple was natural, yet Man-made and God-

Made at the same time, and how I was to go there first; I was aware that other places in The Valley awaited me, if not now, then later; and, most importantly, I knew where to take the atiín *slab. And where to place it. And I got a glimpse, a bare suggestion, of what it could do –*

"Enjoying the feeling?" Algona broke into my reverie, dancing around me, smiling, an aura of sheer joy permeating her face as my natural sense of vision returned, overriding the fading scenes of another world. "Isn't it wonderful? I just love this place!"

My visionary trance interrupted, I was becoming dizzy to the point of passing out, and, momentarily confused, withdrew my foot. With a gentle sucking pressure and the sound of a soft sigh, my foot became free. I didn't know if it was me or my foot or the stone that had sighed; maybe all three.

My beautiful companion said, "Now you've left a portion of your soul in this Valley, forever."

Shaking all over, I sat on the damp rock and stared at her. "And will there be enough left for me?"

"Ah, but there was an interchange," she cooed. "Mother Nature always balances it all out – you left some, you received some."

Coming down from that mysterious and incredible high, I remained spiritually charged. "And whose souls might they be? Or whose soles?" She ignored the pun.

Algona stopped her swaying. Something flashed in those pale blue eyes and for a moment I felt as though all would be made clear. But the moment faded into the immediate past and was, for me, lost for all time. "Why, the souls of all of those who came after First Man, of course: First Woman, the Twins, the Aztlan, the Africans, the Asians, the Anasazi, the Conquistadores, the Anglos. And the Others from Outside." That mysterious smile returned. "And now you, my friend, the Third Millennium Man."

"But I'm Anglo," I objected. "See my skin, my light hair, my blue eyes?"

"And my blue eyes and dark hair? We are no longer Anglo or Hispanic or African or Native," she crooned, pointing up at the sky, toward a cloud bank outlined in brilliant silver. "We are all of us, Last Man, Third Millennium Man." Algona smiled that smile. "The Foot of

First Man; we are all descended from him, we are a part of him. And First Woman. It is merely a familiar impression in an unfamiliar setting – impossible by the standards of mere reason. Yet it is there, and it serves its purposes, simply by being."

"As inexplicable as a human being," I mused aloud, the ambience eliciting poetry from deep within me. "A lonely vessel bobbing in TimeSpace, its purpose unknown." I turned to Algona. "Are we merely footprints of the Gods, my lady? Am I imprinted in the stone of Time? What Pool of Life fills *us*?"

"Or could we be like the tailings of a gold mine," she replied, grinningly taking up the challenge, "shining in the recent rain, imagining ourselves as the gold, yet being the dross? We reside in a pile of waste, waiting to be buried back into Earth, while the true treasure trove has already been taken elsewhere, far away, where it is processed by mysterious means, refined into a purity we cannot imagine, and displayed proudly throughout a rising kingdom for the rest of history and beyond, shown as finery and utensils and sacred symbols made physical."

I answered, "But whatever we are, wherever we are, at least we're with our own kind."

The glistening images she was weaving suddenly faded and a colder reality sat in, something disturbing that I couldn't quite grasp. I was no longer comfortable; an unsettling aura enveloped my little paradise. Even Algona sensed it and shuddered.

I looked up. A passing cloud? A chill wind? An afternoon cloud bank had formed over the Valley, but it was not yet blocking the sun. Then, atop the far Valley wall, not too distant from the top reaches of The Temple, two small figures were making their way northward. *Good God! Coyote* and *Tall Guy!* In my reverie here I had forgotten about them!

"Algona," I whispered. "Those two *cabrónes* gave me this –" I touched my blackened cheek "– and they are carrying guns, I believe." Fortunately, the grove of trees had kept them from seeing us, down in the *arroyo*, especially if they hadn't been looking directly at us. This kind of gross reality was something I didn't need, so rudely intruding on the spiritual experiences and physical pleasures I had been enjoying the last twenty-four hours. As I watched, the two punks disappeared behind upcroppings of rock on the mesa. I hoped they would stay away forever!

I turned to Algona. "Why do we have to put up with thugs like that in this place of beauty and spirit? What about guys like them who are jealous, disturbed, who make our very existence in life a model of Hell? They are irrational, petty, violent. How do we treat them?" My sense of well-being now completely rattled, I only wanted to make them go away. *Permanently* would do.

"Every life is a lesson," she replied, nodding toward the distant Valley wall. "If the lesson is not learned by the soul inhabiting the body in that life, then consider it a sacrifice – for that sorrowful soul is there for you yourself and for all of us to learn from, an object lesson."

I frowned. "Yeah, I always thought some people existed just to show us we could be a lot worse off than we are."

The cloud bank was dissolving in a sudden atmospheric change, transforming into archipelagoes of silver-limned darkness, precursors to a desert rainstorm. I figured I should take Algona back up to Judd's for safety, then come back down and take the slab on up the Valley to where I knew it had to go. But the clouds fascinated me, and through the trees I could smell Algona's campfire, and other aromas as sweet as incense, and more intense.

Hypnotized by the spectacle of sky and smell, it was long minutes before I realized I was alone. When I reached the Pool of Life, Algona was gone, the campfire now mere wisps of curling smoke. Startled at a sudden noise I spun around to see where she was going. But breezes were kicking up, rustling the leaves of the willows and soon after only dead silence followed, the rippling pond smoothing out to its mirror-smooth state.

I suppose by then I should have realized that Algona, like that other mysterious character, *El Viejo*, would follow her own rules of protocol, of manners, of appearance and departure. I was privileged and honored to have met her, known her, spent time and emotion with her, but a simple "Goodbye, dear" would have helped! If she were leaving The Valley by a physical route (and I was not sure of that anymore; I wasn't sure of anything around this place!), I wished her safe passage and protection from the morons up on the far wall. I wasn't sure that all the spirituality in the world would stop physical violence. Or a bullet.

Would I see her again? I hoped so. With all of my heart and my soul, I prayed that I would. Rather glumly I returned one last time through the trees to locate the footprint of First Man at the bottom of the waterfall. Strange, but blowing leaves had covered all the surrounding stone surfaces from view, and I could not find the footprint impression. It was as if being here once were enough, and I had taken the First Step from the Garden. Sighing, I returned to the Pool of Life, munched a cold bit of last night's cooked food, rearranged the *travois* and began to drag my sacred load up the *arroyo* toward the ramp that would lead me to The Temple.

D ragging my heavy burden up the collapsed *arroyo* wall turned out to be quite a chore, the dry dirt resisting the weight of the poles, which kept digging in against my exertions. I was sweating in a bright afternoon sun when I finally arrived back up at the floor of the Valley, nearly collapsing with exhaustion. A simple fifteen foot change in height, a ramp not thirty feet long, and it had taken all my strength to drag the slab up. I wished I could have had the weird power that *El Viejo* and Algona had demonstrated. As tired as I was, I was also wishing I could just psychically transport the slab back to its niche, which was still miles northward up the Valley, and likewise transport myself back to the SUV.

As I rested under a spreading piñon tree, I checked out the surrounding area. In the distance The Temple maintained a stately presence in the far Valley cliff wall; strange, but it seemed to be farther away than it had when I first reached the Valley two days ago. But I was not surprised; few things in this Valley were what they appeared to be, and I was not longer sure of what was real and what was placed here for my "education," if that's what it was. All I was certain about was that I was tired, hot, and more than a little lonely after my time with the beautiful Algona.

I quickly searched the horizon for any sign of the two interlopers who might pose danger to my mission or to me. Not for the first time I wondered if they were the hoodlums who had chiseled the stone slab out of its proper place here in The Valley and took it to Santa Fe for Solana and her mother to sell. From *Coyote's* yelled questions that first night, that seemed to be the only possible explanation.

But doubts arose. How could those two know of a place like this, and how could they get by all of the strangeness that seemed to be protecting The Valley? Did Judd's place, and the Pool of Life, and The Temple, and all the other places just fade in and out, like that rundown old service station out on the highway, or were they here permanently? (I had "seen" quite a few other interesting Valley locations during my water-and-carving-induced trances; I wasn't sure that I would ever visit all of them, or any of them, but they seemed to be important for some reasons I didn't yet understand. Or maybe never would understand.)

But, I thought, the slab itself was very real, and very heavy, and had remained so. And its original location, before it was hacked out of a solid stone wall, must still be there, or I wouldn't have had to go to so much trouble to take it back. Or would I? One thing I did know, no matter how mysterious and wondrous the slab was, I was going to leave it in this Valley somewhere. Either in its intended spot or as far as I could drag it, whichever came first.

By now I had photographed the slab from every angle, recorded each of the laser-cut-looking petroglyph markings under every magnification my digital camera possessed, and from every sun angle I could arrange. Some of the shimmering colors did show up around the carvings, but I had not been able to reproduce the astonishing 3D holographic image that had jumped out of the stone when I first brought it to the edge of The Valley. By now, though, I understood that, Zen-like, I would probably have to see the images only by not wanting to; I would treat that mini-project like I did a writing assignment: throw it to "the boys in the back room" of my mind, there to be worked on by my subconscious minions, and await their eventual decision on how it was to happen.

Distances in the clear air of the high desert can be deceiving. I had originally estimated this part of the Valley to be a mile or so wide, but as the long afternoon progressed and as I continued to drag the slab and continued to sweat, growing more tired by the minute, I figured that I had at least another full mile to go before arriving at The Temple. I estimated I had come at least two miles from the eastern wall, so the Valley was about three miles wide at this point. I could not believe I'd made such a mistake in estimating the distance, but I was counting off the paces and the cold − or *hot*! − reality was that I had a long way yet to go. I desperately needed a bath; my body odor was getting downright offensive, even to myself. Unfortunately the clouds had given way to a brutally blue sky, and not a breeze stirred to take away any smells of my sweat or to cool me off.

From that location, looking to the south, the walls seemed to converge; to the north remaining parallel until they marched off into a hazy distant horizon. Too bad my smartphone's GPS had stopped working; it would have been illuminating, I think, to chart my progress on a topographical map of the area. But, I was beginning to fear, where I was and what I was doing might not show up on any map of this world.

Gratefully, I drank from the canteen I had filled up at Algona's Pool of Life. After experiencing the effect of that water when I'd touched the petroglyphs and then stepped, wet-footed, into the Footprint of First man, I wondered what that magic water might do to my insides. I had never tasted anything quite so sweet, so refreshing, and I certainly had to take care of my physical body, though I was sure by now that my spiritual body was in the first stages of a healing process. The desert is an unforgiving place, and I couldn't be sure that some of the trials I was undergoing might not end in my death or the ruination of my health. Those were a couple of dire possibilities I wanted to avoid in this lifetime; I wasn't quite ready to settle old karmic accounts with a premature passage, not yet!

I kept remembering all too many accounts of tourists from the Eastern USA who got their SUVs stuck in sand just a few miles away from civilization, who decided to trek out without any preparation, and who then died of exposure within an easy walk of a highway or a ranch. The temperature could drop as much as forty degrees as the night sky became almost perfectly dark, sucking thermal radiation right out of your body. That and rapid evaporation could cause hypothermia in the middle of the desert in almost any season. Nope, if a world explorer like me were to be found dead in a desert, I didn't want family and friends to think it was because I had been acting like a tenderfoot!

The desert sun bore down unceasingly as afternoon segued into evening. The going was a little easier as I came to what I estimated was halfway to the far Valley wall and The Temple. The sand floor of the Valley was giving way to the dusty harder surface of white *caliche*, a sun-baked concretion of sandy soil and old water. I was hopeful of making The Temple by dark, so as to have a safe place to conceal myself from predators of either the four-legged or the two-legged kind. I kept glancing at the top of the Valley wall, but never did see any more evidence of my two friends from Santa Fe.

As I detoured around a slight hill, the ruins of what had to be an abandoned Spanish Catholic mission came into view, a maze of ruined red-stone walls from five to twenty feet high for the most part, punctuated by once-excavated but now caved-in circular rooms of varying diameters. *Kivas? In a Catholic church?* The whole area covered about an acre, and I could discern from the taller ruined walls a main chapel or nave, a series of small adjoining rooms, and some outlying structures, many overgrown with sagebrush and ground covering vines.

Finding shade in the shelter of the ten-foot high standing walls of what must have been the nave, I took off the *travois* halter and sat for a snack. Soft susurrus of winds coming down into the Valley from the flatlands above whistled gently around the red stone walls, kicking up small dust devils at the corners of the old mission. I took many pictures with the digital camera, wondering who had built this, and when, and why it had been deserted. On either side of the remaining church structure stood slumped hillocks that had once been collections of bricked-wall rooms. These had to have been pueblo apartments, now collapsed into hills of dirt, covered by vines. *Strange,* I thought, *that a mission of the Holy Catholic Church once co-existed here in a Valley where other, more ancient religious experiences, of a wildly different kind, must have been prevalent.* I would bet you could write volumes about what happened when the Spanish first came to this Valley, and encountered the strangeness and the spirituality I had been finding here. What kinds of sermons had been preached, and by what Spaniard or Mexican priest? Who had lived here, and who had died here? And when?

Making my way through the piles of tumbled stone, I was especially taken by the poignancy of the *kivas*, the covered circular underground rooms characteristic of the Ancestral Puebloan peoples. In the estimation of some anthropologists, *kivas* were supposed to represent the circular appearance of the Universe as seen from a human's viewpoint. Rites and rituals and a lot of pipe-smoking had gone on inside these men-only gathering places, and in some existing Pueblos here in New Mexico and over in Arizona, such gatherings still occurred, barred from the view of the latecoming Spanish and Anglo invaders.

I found a stepped opening in the side of a large *kiva* – it must have been forty feet in diameter – and carefully jumped down, in several stages, about ten feet to the fairly unobstructed floor. Whatever roof they had placed over the top was long gone, a few long, dry wooden poles lying on the floor testimony to hundreds of years of abandonment.

Many layers of flat, reddish, flagstone rocks defined the *kiva*'s walls and the circular room featured a stone bench around its circumference. Across the room, above a gap in the stone bench, I saw a horizontal

opening about the diameter of a softball – the *sipapu*. In some mythologies, this represented the hole in the earth from which their peoples
had climbed up to this level from the Lower World. The Hopis, long-
time neighbors and longtime enemies of the Navajos, often
commented that "The Navajos are a lot like us, except *they* have one
hole too many," this often accompanied by tapping on their temple.
Once during a tour at the Mesa Verde National Monument I had seen
two Forest Service guides of different tribes almost come to blows over
this teasing tradition. I'd long ago given up on the typical white man's
view of all Native Americans as innocent inhabitants of a paradise
spoiled by the European invasion. Some of their present-day ethnic
and tribal conflicts had origins much further in the past than even
those of the turbulent Middle East!

While photographing some small stones piled up in a niche in one
wall of the *kiva*, I heard a noise. Fearing a rattlesnake or other denizen
of the desert, I quickly spun around, my heart pounding. There, sitting
on the bench in the dark shadows on the other side of the *kiva*, sat *El
Viejo* himself! "Good God, man, you scared me half to death!" I cried,
half in anger and half in relief.

"How are you coming, Anglo?" the Old One said in a low voice.
"And what do you think of this Valley?"

I slumped on the bench behind me and shook my head. In the dark
shadows I couldn't see his face, but his infinitely faded jeans, now
white, and that intensely blue velvety shirt defined his presence. He
fairly radiated spirituality and an *ancientness* I had never felt before. I
was respectful, but adamant. I wanted some answers! "*Viejo*, you old
scoundrel, what in the world is going on? How did you get here?
What's happening to me, and what are you *doing* to me? Is this place
real, or –" He didn't let me finish.

"Anglo, *amigo*," he said hoarsely, "I thank you for bringing the stone
this far. Do you want to go on?" He knew, and I knew, the answer to
that one.

"Of course I want to go on, old man," I said. "Nothing could keep
me from finishing this thing now. But first, I have a million questions
to ask and a thousand things to say." I stared at the darkness, hoping to
get some resolution before the Old One just disappeared on me again.

"Before you leave me again, *Viejo*, just tell me how you got here, how you can appear and disappear in an instant. Is it teleportation or what?" As I watched in silence, he pulled out a dark pipe, tamped down something in its bowl, and lit it. The match illuminated his shadowed face for an instant; I could see that he was smiling.

"Anglo *amigo*," he began, blowing out a column of sweet-smelling smoke, "Your Western culture requires proof, not faith. So in the last days here you have experienced the proof of just a few wonders. One proof is, I am *here* and not somewhere else. How that happens is...let me say, you need to understand many other things first, and then you will be able to understand that. You need to have faith. Faith is the transition between all that you know and all that there *is*. Faith could have brought you a thousand times more experiences than you have had, and a lot sooner in your life."

I sighed. Anything I was going to learn from *El Viejo* would be couched in mystery, metaphor and just plain vagueness. Maybe that was the way the Universe was, down deep – confusing, unreal, hallucinatory, ambiguous? Knowing that my questions wouldn't be answered unless *El Viejo* got around to them, I resigned myself to listening. Having nothing much else to do anyway, here in an ancient hole in the ground, across from an ancient old man, I just sat back against the *kiva* wall and waited for his revealed wisdom. I just hoped that it would make sense enough right away, something I could use in whatever remained of y journey here in The Valley.

"The problem has never been with your Western culture of individuality, my friend," he began, occasionally stopping to stoke his pipe. A hint of lavender, overlaid with a pleasant buttery odor I didn't recognize, soon permeated our small circular universe here below the desert floor. Not being a smoker myself anymore, I nevertheless opened myself to *El Viejo's* aromatic meditative enhancement. Who knows? Maybe I could learn his tricks and someday be able to manipulate others as he was doing with me? "To flit from hither to yon", as Shakespeare had said, "as fast as thought"?

As if he were reading those thoughts, *El Viejo* continued, "We each experience the Universe in isolation; this is usually the only experience we know, so naturally we think it is the totality of existence. But I say it is not. The Universe no more rotates around you, the perceived center of It, than do all the stars and planets rotate around the Earth, no matter how they appear to.

"But to go beyond this perception, we each must undergo the same kind of mind-change that the scientists and ordinary people of old did, when they were first given undeniable proof that old Earth was not the center of existence. What Galileo showed with his telescope observations of Jupiter and its moons. Without that mindset change, that first hint of cosmic knowledge, we could have never explored the Solar System, never sent our electronic explorers out into the void between the stars."

I was amazed at this man; one minute he was delving into ancient spiritual matters, deep in the esoteric, and the next, extolling advanced technology. Or was I missing something? I suspected that I was supposed to believe the two were the same, or at least connected. Were they?

He smiled a smile that I could see through the shadows. Damn! *Was* he reading my mind? I figured that telepathy was small potatoes, though, when compared to the disappearing service station or Algona's psychedelic wet-rock-readings!

El Viejo went on, "By analogy – a perfect analogy, it seems to me – until we recognize that we each individually are drawn toward a greater goal, we will not be able to plot outward trajectories among greater bodies than ours, in the almost unknowable voids between existence."

This was just too much! "Just a minute, Old One," I erupted, standing to walk over to him and bending into the shade, our faces on a level. "What does all this mean, *practically*? Are these just high-sounding words? How can I *practice* any of what you are saying? I can't lift that three-hundred-pound stone like you can, and Ms. Algona did back at the so-called 'Pool of Life'! *I* am not able to appear when I am needed, and disappear at will. So can your *philosophy* teach these to me? I want to know how to *do* things. I am a writer, a researcher, a man of actions, and I need *facts. Skills!* Concrete *directions!*"

"You came to this Valley all by yourself, Anglo?" he shot back, coolly. "You were not invited, and guided to this place, at this instant, with that *atiín*?" He nodded toward the upper edge of the *kiva*. "Is that not *direction* enough? And are you not *practicing* a new way of understanding? Are you not *doing* enough? Do you have the *skill* to understand what is happening to you?"

I breathed out deeply. "Yes, I *was* forced to come here, that much I give you. Beaten and bruised and exhausted, and lost, but I *am* here, now, with you. I give you that, friend." My swollen cheek had deflated a bit, but a huge bruise remained, sore to the touch. "Painfully so, if all of that force and violence was necessary."

He gave me that enigmatic lip twitch intended to pass as a smile. "Anglo, *amigo*, there is no *Camino Real* to the so-called mystic state you are seeking – each must find his own path. For some it is easier than for others." He exhaled twin streams of smoke, trails that intertwined and rose up from the *kiva*, grabbed by the wind and dispersed above our heads, into a darkening sky. "It is sometimes easier for those who already believe in spiritual realms, for they are not surprised by the –" he paused, "– the *inhabitants,* the *topography*, of the other dimensions we sometimes call 'spiritual'. But then, they often have trouble accepting that their encounters are just as natural as the sunrise, they imbue them with too much superstition. *Superstition* here meaning, 'admitting of no explanation, and too fearful to investigate.' Educated and experienced Westerners like you should have the advantage of knowing that the Universe is infinitely broad, infinitely varied, and ultimately unknowable. But for some reason you all have the most trouble." The pipe glowed more brightly, lighting up his leathery face. "I believe it is because you are seldom quiet, seldom *still*." Over my audible sigh of exasperation, he said, "Let me expand on that.

"We must all begin to learn by just being *still*. In that state we learn the natural rhythms of meditation, we feel the blood coursing through our veins, we recognize and appreciate the steady thumping of our heart's incessant labors.

"Meditation, properly performed, is the first step on the endless journey. Then will come visions, and with them dreams. As the German thinker Goethe observed, there is nothing like commitment. Once you have committed yourself irreversibly to a course, the Universe itself seems to react to your wishes. Doors open, people are met, coincidences converge in unimaginable ways to help bring about the object of your commitment.

"That great thinker recognized this, articulated it for all the world, two hundred years ago. Other prophets, ancient and new and those yet to come, call it to our attention, but most people ignore their observations because life is busy. Yet every day in each of our personal lives, such events occur, events which, were we to try to arrange them, would take intricate and god-like elegant planning, execution, and follow-up."

I was amused by *El Viejo*'s constant switching between the "ancient sage" homilies and the "modern team builder" cheerleading exhortations. "*Viejo*," I interrupted, "What do you *do* in the outside world? I mean, are you a scientist like Judd? Or a business executive like Algona? Weren't you selling jewelry there on the Plaza in Santa Fe?"

"Or perhaps *this* is my world?" he said leaning forward, hands spread wide, "and *you* are in the outside one?" Shaking his head, he continued his dissertation. This time, I would listen more closely. After all, I was going to learn by exposition, not by interrogation, for I had no idea of what questions to ask. "Do you think it requires less foresight, implementation, less caring, for *The All* to arrange that you be the beneficiary of certain outcomes? Study your physics – the energies involved are the same, perhaps even more." He must have watched my wrinkled forehead as I tried to figure out his meaning.

"For example, what combination and permutation of physical occurrences had to be orchestrated so that you would miss being hit by that cab in Washington, D.C., on the way to your first government job interview? Fractions of a second?" I stumbled back across the *kiva* and slumped onto the bench. How had he known of that incident? Just more of his telepathic skill, I guessed. That was one trick I did want to learn.

About the near-accident he mentioned, I had never told anybody about it, and hadn't thought about it in the ten years or more since it happened. I got a chill just recalling it again: Under the protection of a *WALK* signal, I was starting to cross Pennsylvania Avenue to go south to the President's Old Executive Office Building, walking around the front of a Metro bus, when something told me in an almost audible voice, "Stop!"

At that moment a yellow cab, driven by a turbaned immigrant, shot past the bus, fully ten feet into the intersection, before stopping. The driver looked at me, smiled sheepishly, and shrugged his shoulders. We both knew what had nearly happened: two more steps and I would have been hit hard, maimed, probably killed. Then none of my unique experience in the government would have happened, and none of this adventure, this journey, in The Valley would be happening. I was purely startled by *El Viejo*'s knowledge and his implication; was there really a Providence that protected fools like me? SomeThing or SomeOne that had other things in mind for my life? I inhaled deeply of *El Viejo's* smoke and calmed myself. But he wasn't through with me, not yet.

"Fractions of a second?" he repeated. "How about that near-mishap in the car when you were a teenager – at eighty miles per hour – 150 feet per second! – just 1/100 of a second more flying through the air, 1/100 of a second less braking time, and hat friend of yours driving would have slammed that new Oldsmobile through those one-foot-diameter oaken posts there on that country road, and you would have died at age 17, along with the girl who was to become your wife a few years later, not to mention your irresponsible friend, the driver." I closed my eyes, recalling the unforgettable horror of those few seconds, the car spinning on gravel, flying through the air, landing just in front of the huge posts protecting the house at that ninety-degree turn, the Oldsmobile sliding to a slow halt, its front bumper gently kissing the massive post as it slowed to a miraculous, safe stop. Unbelievably, not a scratch on the car, not an injury to three careless teenagers. And just a tiny fraction of a second had separated two possible futures, this one I was in, and another in which I had been buried for over thirty years. Until *El Viejo* described it in his own fashion, I never had realized exactly how close it had been. I was shaking from both his knowledge and from what that knowledge meant.

The ancient voice wafted from the shadows, through his cloud of swirling smoke. "Let me repeat – 1/100 of one second's difference, and you would not now be here, nor your children, nor your present wife. Hundreds of thousands of people would never have read your speculations on the future of technology, your humorous and your serious stories and articles, your researches on your web site. And a few thousand people in Washington, D. C., who took your business cards would never have met you and in turn their lives would have presently attained other directions without your input.

"So tell me, engineer, writer, researcher, explorer, in all of your physics, in all of your philosophy, can *you* account for the infinitude of circumstances that have nudged you, guided you, implored and finally *compelled* you, to be here at this time and in this place and in this state of mind?" He waved his arm slowly, expansively gesturing upward toward the sweep of the unseen Valley opening beyond. "You think all of this is *accident*, the random chances of rolling the cosmic dice and awaiting the outcome?

"Anglo, *amigo*, even each rock on the bed of the river lies in a spot where it belongs. Each of us, you and me, we are where we belong. In time, in space, in mind. And in other dimensions not measured by any standard we use."

Stunned, shaken, and now stirred, I appreciated his philosophy but I just couldn't lie still and wait for the world to work its way. "I want to believe you, *Viejo*," I replied meekly, calmly. "I really do. But that way lies passivity, old man, and the West was founded on assertiveness, aggression, novelty, individual liberty. What if humans hadn't resisted the so-called natural order? We would have stayed animals. And what if we had been totally open and accepting to spiritual truths? Which of those 'truths' were correct and which were downright evil and dangerous? The ancient cultures around the world all thought they were doing that, and they destroyed themselves in superstition and ignorance and disease and war. What is wrong with our Western way? It has brought more happiness to more people than anything in history."

El Viejo snorted, smoke emanating from nostrils and mouth like plumes from a volcano. "You are asking me, what happens if you fight doing what you know is right, and instead do something else?" He shrugged, darkness seeping into those black pools of eyes. "A rock can move? It is where it is, and external forces, geological upheavals, river currents, move it. We and I, *amigo*, we too are driven by natural forces of nature and the electric currents in our brains, and even by other forces that have no names. But in all things, excesses will be contained; forces will balance."

"So whatever we do, will be part of the balance?" I couldn't accept that, either. Human history was drenched in blood, civilizations come and gone. The brave always had to take a stand against barbarism. And until the last few hundred years or so, the brave had mostly lost.

"There *are* priorities, *amigo*. For example, we would like to make sure that when that final balance occurs, we are still around to enjoy it." I knew *El Viejo* was not going to comment further on my historical perspectives, that other issues were foremost. I shrugged; I was here to learn, it appeared, and so might as well absorb as much as possible. No use in trying to convince him of anything. What could he possibly want to learn from *me*?

The old man kept up his new theme. "Because our minds work best in a healthy brain supported by a healthy body, we must take heed and maintain our health, so that is a high priority. In our bodies and our brains, excess will be contained, but the effect will manifest itself on our minds and our souls. The healthy mind must be gentle, sweet, creative and good. Extreme states of pain, excessive time spent in sensual pleasure, excursions of the natural balance over-stimulated by chemicals and other forces, take their toll on the mind.

"To put it in Western scientific terms, we must practice *conservation of mind*. And that, again, begins with meditation, stilling the body, enabling the soul to find its place. You cannot meditate adequately on the sidewalk of a busy street. That is one reason that holy men, monks, nuns, shamans, prefer the quietude of a dark, quiet place.

"And why events such as you are experiencing are best encountered in lonely quiet places such as this Valley. Less distraction, fewer demands on your body, help produce the mystic state. It has always been this way."

Laughing, I pointed both my index fingers toward the roundness of the *kiva* wall above us. "Tell me about the Anasazi, *Viejo*. The people who built this *kiva* and the cliff dwellings at Mesa Verde, the long roads over at Chaco Canyon, all the old Indian stuff. What am I supposed to learn down here in their little smokehouse?"

El Viejo puffed a little longer in silence. "That those people were *people*, is the lesson. No smarter, no more spiritual than others, but tied down by spirituality because they had a unified world view – to them, mathematics did not exist apart from astronomy from crops from medicine from psychology from warfare – all of these were component elements of life and their cosmos, and all important.

"In these *kiva*s, they were bringing down a piece of that cosmos to the earth. But there was more than that to this geometric structure. These benches along the circumference, the sensitives sat here. In the center sat the *cacique* or shaman. He was the recipient of their meditations, their vibrations, like a psychic battery. The stones in these walls helped amplify those emanations.

"Round the whole world, stone circles were the center of worship, but it was more than worship. Like here, your famous places like Stonehenge and other megalithic monuments, layers of sensitive stones and sensitive peoples concentrated all energies into that person at the center. Sometimes this caused an overload and a death or coma; most often, though, it amplified the meditations, bringing superior insights about things of importance to the tribe: communication with other peoples, with other shamans, with Earth herself – for information from beyond the horizon. Today, remnants of this ancient practice still occur in some places where your radios and telephones don't reach. An Eskimo or Inuit may lean against a tree to communicate with another village. Ask them about that.

"Believe me," *El Viejo* continued, "in those marginal societies, if something didn't work it was quickly discarded. Only those proven rituals survived – survival of the most productive, of the fittest."

I nodded. "I will ask an Eskimo next time I'm in Alaska, *Viejo*. Are these things I'm experiencing, are they helping me be productive, one of the most fit?"

"That, friend, you will have to find out for yourself."

At that, I smiled and asked *El Viejo* to stay for dinner. He agreed. We climbed out of the *kiva*, and made camp and a campfire within the mission's walls. He produced a backpack from behind a piñon tree, and we spent the night talking and occasionally arguing. On a mundane level, I did learn from him that the mission in whose ruins we were staying, had been built by priests that Coronado had left behind during his early explorations of New Mexico, that it had existed for about twenty years before disappearing from the records of the Church.

"The priests who stayed here, they allowed the Ancestral Puebloan peoples to build their *kiva*s next to the church."

"I saw that, *Viejo*. Unusual, wasn't it?"

"*Unique* is the word, Anglo. But they were unique men, men of vision who blended into the tribes and melted away from History and from the Church."

"It's a good thing the Conquistadores never came back this way," I laughed, "or the good friars would have *melted* from frying in an *auto-da-fe*!" Burning at the stake was the usual fate for heretics who had attributed any validity to the religions of Native Americans.

El Viejo ignored the comment. "The spiritual aspects of the Valley caught them up in a realization that God is in all things. And perhaps the spiritual leaders of the Ancestral Puebloans also saw God in what the friars were teaching, and so they melded together before melting away." *El Viejo* relit his dead pipe, creating sparks that swirled over into the flames of the campfire. "See how some sparks are caught up in the larger flame, and they all ascend to great heights."

"Yeah," I remarked, "they go up far away from the source of the flame, but then they grow cold, die out, and are carried away as dust on the winds." For the first time since I'd met him, *El Viejo* laughed out loud.

During one of the interludes as the night wore on, while *El Viejo* puffed on his pipe, I walked around inside the ruined church, inspecting some of the broken pottery that lay around the dried-mud floor, finding some large pieces jet-black with exquisite white scrolling of birds and lizards. "*Viejo*, some of this is of Acoma jet," I noted, "Rare and expensive, if you scoop it all up and put it back together."

"Why do you see nobility in these long-dead shards, Anglo? Surely the most inexpensive glass in the cheapest of highway fast food diners is far more beautiful – with its uniform transparency, its cleanliness – than these simple mud-made scultpings?" He tossed down one of his own finds, breaking it.

"But – cheap glasses, *Viejo* – why they're made in a factory, by machines, by impersonal operators on soulless machines, while –"

He interrupted. "While this one," he smashed it with his fist, "this one required the labor of many hours of a person whose very life may have depended on her skill?" He spat into the jumble of still-rocking concave pieces. Walking back to where his blanket lay, he retrieved a small shot glass from his ancient knapsack. "Surely you know, Anglo, that even this cheap glass was constructed with love?

"I don't see how."

El Viejo pressed the drinking glass into my palm; it was smooth, uniform, precise. I had never paid attention to such details before, but the force of his passion increased my sensitivity.

"Do you not feel the smoothness, the precision, the delicacy of this wonderful artifact? The transference of caring from the artist who designed it, the pride with which the engineer designed the process and its machines; the precision and steady hand of the machinist who built the glass-making devices; the labor of the ones who packaged and transported this to you, all the way from –" he took the glass from my hand, turning it to look at the embossed characters on the bottom "– from Malaysia!

"Imagine, supertankers plowing the seas, navigating by satellites, people investing money in the cargo, paying its Captain and crew – an endless stream of financial transactions, physical laws and human labor, the concatenation of natural resources and human endeavors – just to bring this water vessel here at this moment, for us to enjoy, halfway round the world. Strangers, all bound by this great system – and we are here enjoying what they have done for us. Is that not *love*, Anglo? Is that not a measure of love?"

I was nonplussed, or maybe non-minused. "I – I – hadn't thought of it quite like that before," I stammered in confusion.

"Of course you don't, you're a human, like me. But only because a billion miracles a day happen just like this, all around you."

"But it's not love, it's necessity," I protested. "All those people, *Viejo*, all those resources and plans and work – they all do it because they have to, because they need to. It's not love for me, as an individual?"

"Are you sure, *amigo*? Have you ever asked them all?" He paused and puckered those ancient lips, which slowly worked into a smile. "A wise man once said that, given enough time, it would be possible for an individual to love every other human being. But we don't have time enough, so we all do what we must. Is not the sum total of all that we all do, *love*, my friend?

"Above all else, the freedom to do what one wants – or must – do, facilitated by free trade, freely engaged in, frees every member of mankind to embody love in her work and to pass on that love to her fellows. *Work is love made manifest.* Products are the medium of transference, and love – for one's time and one's creations – love is the way *The All* spreads our love to each other."

"The Invisible Hand is more than a metaphor, *Viejo?*" I laughed. "I'll bet old Adam Smith never considered that aspect of the wealth of nations."

"There are many kinds of wealth, my friend."

We discussed other things that I won't put down here, intensely personal events, emotions and issues I had faced in my own life. Maybe some of these would be important to others, but then they were meant only for me. During this conversation, however, I complained to *El Viejo* of all the time in my life that I had wasted on trivial matters, now unimportant, meaningless, in the face of the spiritual revelations I'd found in The Valley.

He replied sternly, "Never tell me any moment is unimportant, for each is a link to the next and to the previous one. Tell me, is any beat of your own heart more important than the others?"

I smiled at that. "Perhaps – the first one?" I imagined myself as an infant.

He frowned. "Or, perhaps, the *last* one?"

"*Viejo,*" I asked, waving away the stifling smoke of his pipe, "is natural law the law of God or merely the workings of Nature?"

"There is a difference, Anglo? Can you not imagine that they are one and the same?"

"But," I protested, "the so-called moral laws, the Seven Deadly Sins, they don't find expression in the laws of nature. Surely they are just devices meant to control us."

El Viejo frowned. "Are you sure, friend? Cannot you imagine that there are direct laws of morality, or of behavior, that have direct consequences?"

"Such as?"

He held out his hands as if exasperated. "Look at the man who is a glutton. He becomes fat, miserable and lives a shorter life. Is that not consequence enough?"

"What about Greed?" I was learning my part here: acolyte to Master, pupil to Teacher. Might as well learn as much as I could. I hoped I would remember all of this once I left the Valley. If I ever did leave...

"Greed, in my experience, is the uncontrolled appetite for control – it may take the form of obsession with possessions, or for control over others. The truly greedy person is a glutton himself, and the result is a mind that is unfit, miserable and filled not with natural pleasures but with the addiction. Few gluttons die happy."

"And Lust? How about that one?" I laughed. "It's my favorite." But when I thought of Algona, all intimations of Lust seemed disgusting, a gentler feeling of desire and understanding replacing it. I did not lust after her – I loved her, deeply and without reservation. Maybe it wasn't my favorite sin after all?

"That is easiest of all. Wait long enough, and the hormones dissipate and lust itself is a memory. As long as lust lasts, it must be contained; out of the dross of animal lust arose the glimmerings of love itself. Lust is there to remind us of the origin of love, and how far we have come from the slime. To linger with lust is to return to slime and the undisciplined soul may slip and fall until time takes its toll. But always remember – the legend of the Fall from Grace replays itself within each of us so long as Lust lingers."

"Sloth?" I ventured. "That seems to me the least of sins. At least you're not hurting anybody else." I wondered how he would treat that one.

"We must all fight sloth as well – in olden times, when one had to hunt or gather or plant, sloth meant a certain death from starvation, for himself or for other members of the tribe. In these times, when the basic necessities of life are available to all with little effort, sloth wastes one's life and rots the soul. The mind is a fertile ground for creativity; letting it do nothing is the gravest sin. *The All* requires every mind to be active, creative, accomplishing."

"But what of the virtues?" I murmured, becoming very drowsy.

"Such as?"

Before I could answer I was completely lost in the scent of *El Viejo*'s tobacco, wound up tightly, while threads of information, mere wisps of sensation, drifted through my consciousness without effect; I was part of a web of life, whose warp and woof are the constructs of consciousness, of *soulness*, of inner-ness. The sense of innerness at times descended upon my troubled soul like a tranquil pool of coolness, binding me to the moment. I sensed I was receptive, only now, to the rhythms of the old man's voice. "Love," I whispered into this gentle maelstrom of magic, "and Music and Life."

Those words were enough for the old man to continue his reverie. "What is Love? Love is understanding; understanding the connectedness of all Life; understanding the disconnectedness of those who are in pain and misery; understanding what needs to be said, and who needs to be touched, and how, and when. And those times when Love is best left alone.

"And what is Music? Music is the shorthand of the soul, the emotion-catcher. Some music wends its way into our holographic memory, threading through our lives like a Gordian knot. This note wraps up that piece; this riff another string of memory; that musical theme yet another web of emotion. And music, then, is the key with which the whole symphony of emotion and feeling and dreaminess is later opened and the instrument upon which it is once again played.

"And what is Life? Life is change; life is manifestation of *The All*; *The All* desires to experience every possible state of existence; thus Death is part of *The All*, but an ending part − and we need not concern ourselves with endings, for at this moment of time, *The All* is manifesting itself to levels not seen since before the Ice Ages, before the great cataclysms, before the Early Peoples began their migrations, to repopulate what once had been teeming continents. All this was long before our time; and the lessons learned by those Early Peoples were theirs, not ours. And yet, now the pace is accelerating..."

My dreamlike state intensified; I could almost visualize details of his descriptions. I needed to know more. "What of those great races of the past, *Viejo*, the ones who came before, those whom you just mentioned?"

The old man continued without missing a syllable; he had antici-
pated my question. Or maybe just ignored it, knowing just what I
should be told and when.

"They were like us in many ways – happy, sad, thoughtful, rash,
humble, proud – in short, *human*. Yet possessed of closer contact with
the forward tides of *The All*; for whatever reasons, theirs was a life of
incessant and intimate contact with *The All*, while ours is a distant life,
an arm's-length relationship. Perhaps our fate is to be purely technological philosophers, while their ancient thinkers delved into the
Universal Law with tools of the mind and spirit.

"*The All* for its own reasons keeps us further away, perhaps for our
own good. The Early Peoples, though closer to the Light, still vanished
in the night, their innate beings becoming the seeds from which we all
sprung. Perhaps *The All* is trying this time to experience Itself at arm's
length – perhaps we have the potential to become greater than our
ancient ancestors who were in the Light and who then lost it. But I
think we are not close to where they were; maybe more in some areas
and less in others, but as a whole not as far along the path to Light.

"They came to this same Valley, this place where the sea receded,
where the sedimentary layers rose like bread in the *horno*, where it split
into two matching walls, one on either side, that we see here. To the
South, the ancient sea. And from the north, a trickle of water, perhaps
from a glacier in an ancient Ice Age, came this way, through this path
of least resistance – or was it the Path of Greatest Invitation? – and
began to cut and shape the place that we now enjoy.

"This Place called and people came; the earliest of these we have
never known. Their strange drawings on the walls and in the caverns
not far from here emanate the faintest of auras; these I call the Dawn
People, First Men. Their impressions are faint now, so many millions
of years ago that they came. It is perhaps they who left the footprint
near the spring."

I blushed at the thought of Algona there, and how I had felt about
her when we had kissed on the warm, wet smooth stones at the spring.
But something he'd said bothered me. "*Millions* of years? Look, old
one, scientists tell us that humans have been around just for a hundred
thousand years or so. How can you prove otherwise?" I didn't mention

the great reptilian beast I'd seen when I touched the mind of First Man through his footprint.

El Viejo continued smoking in silence. A roadrunner perked into camp, jerking its head this way and that. It stopped and stared at us two humans briefly, then popped into the brush, returning with a lizard in its mouth. In the easy manner of The Valley and its people, the bird soon vanished into the darkness without a farewell.

El Viejo did not choose to answer my question right then. "Something about this Valley was unique, for many peoples," he continued. "After the Dawn People, many millennia passed. Many people came here, lived here, and died here.

"The cavern walls tell of another People who ventured North after cataclysms inundated their land. And they came, and stayed, savoring The Valley, then left to repopulate their part of the world. But on the walls, they told of their knowledge, and where to uncover what they knew. This is the Place Of Laying On Hands, at the northern end of The Valley, where the *atíín* must be placed, where this final knowledge will be passed on to those who access the place with the proper spirit." I nodded, having seen the place in the vision, where the stony cliffs came together in a V shape, with only a deep, narrow crevice extending beyond.

We talked on and on, until at last a lightening of the eastern sky announced that dawn was approaching. I never did ask him how he had acquired all this knowledge about my life, whether he was reading my innermost thoughts, or if he had known about me for years before. As to why I didn't ask those questions, all I can say is that in the midst of spiritual revelation, in the fog of sudden realizations, the usual logic and reason do not always prevail. It's like the old line stand-up comics use, "You hadda been there to appreciate it."

6

Abird aloft is life fulfilled, *El Viejo* had said during that eternally long evening. As if in affirmation of a prediction, an intensely blue morning sky, unmarked by cloud or haze, painted the backdrop for a bald eagle that swooped down from above and disappeared behind a rise of small hills in the distance. Shaking off the remnants of sleepiness and the vanishing wisps of dreamscapes, I watched as the eagle soared once more back into the dome of the sky, carrying a small animal in its beak, finally vanishing in the distance as a small dot. *Breakfast!* I thought. The sun was high, around ten o'clock, I guessed; I'd slept for about four hours after the all-nighter with *El Viejo*. Glancing around, I saw, to no great surprise, that he was gone. Yawning, I re-lit the campfire, put on some coffee, and prepared for the trek over to The Temple.

Half an hour later, I hitched up the backpack and the *travois* and left the mission ruins behind. I wondered exactly how and why the friars there had "melded with the tribe," as *El Viejo* had put it. Did they discover in this Valley what I had, that the ancient past was accessible, in hallucinatory visions if not in fact? That some powers and knowledge were to be found only outside The Church and The Book? That reality was not what it seemed? I wished them well, those men of four hundred years before, wherever they were and perhaps, *whatever* they were.

In the distance, The Temple finally started looming larger, its detail becoming evident. To my disappointment, it was obviously a geological formation, and not really a replica of a cliff carving like Petra in Jordan. But a few strangely symmetrical dark markings at ground level might still be doors.

It was slow going there; expanses of cracked stones meant I had to weave my way around, much as if I were on a polar ice pack. Then the stone gave way to soft sandy ground, and with the dragging poles sinking into the sand, the *atíin* seemed to weigh a ton. By noontime I was still a quarter mile from The Temple, and once again exhausted, I stopped to rest, finding skimpy shade in the midst of a clump of brushy bushes. I took a bite of my dwindling provisions, gulped one mouthful of water from the canteen, and tried to stretch out for a rest.

"*Cabrón!*" The shout rang out, and I jumped to my feet. "Yeah, you down there! Where is my slab?" On the edge of the Valley cliff wall, a thousand feet up above The Temple, stood two tiny figures, waving their arms and shouting at me. Oh, damn! *Coyote* and his buddy, the Tall Guy! I looked around, trying to see if there was any way those creeps could get down from their high perch and down here to me. Seeing no apparent pathway that they could use, short of scaling down with a rope hundreds of feet straight down, I was relieved. I figured that if they had seen me trudging across the desert floor, and had another way to get at me, they would have already climbed down. So I was safe for the moment. But the safest situation would be to get where they couldn't see me at all. That meant a run for it, across the intervening distance to The Temple, where I could hide among outcroppings of rock that they couldn't see. I didn't want them dropping rocks my way!

I attached my backpack to the *atíin* itself, freeing me for a quicker run. Bending over as I was going to have to do if I had to run, the pack would have interfered with the poles of the *travois*. But, could I "make a run for it" with the *travois* and its heavy load? I didn't think so, and no way was I going to leave the slab behind, not after all this work, not after coming so far.

At that moment I wondered why the hoodlums didn't simply go to the place up the Valley where they had chipped out the slab, and wait for me there. Maybe they didn't want to have to carry it all the way back, just get it here and lug it back to their car, miles to the south? But as long as they were up there and I was down here, they weren't going to get it.

Hiding from their view behind the bushes, I waited half an hour before trying to escape. My binoculars showed that they were walking this way and that, still pointing my direction, the occasional obscenity making itself heard over the afternoon winds. To my left a few yards away, there was a slight depression, not really a full-blown *arroyo*, where runoff water over the years had carved a channel between the greasewood-embedded dunes. About a yard wide and a couple of feet deep, the bottom looked to be smooth and harder than the sand I had come across. Checking out its course, the channel seemed to originate near The Temple wall. If I could stoop low enough, dragging the slab behind me, I could maybe sneak up the intervening distance without being seen by my two unfriendly friends up on the cliff.

In that small channel, even bent over and scrambling as fast as I could with the heavy load, the going was a lot easier than before. My own sounds were drowning out the decreasing volume of the shouts from above. Looking up to see if they were watching me, I saw that both of them were. In fact, one of them appeared to be holding his arms pointed at me. I froze. Dropping flat from my half-crouch, I quickly undid the *travois* harness and rolled over. The pointed arms followed me. I took a quick look through the binoculars.

My God! It wasn't just his arms, he had a *rifle* pointed at me!

The muzzle flashed! They were shooting!

My world went dim and yellow, and I knew I was in mortal danger. Just like so many other episodes in my life, time seemed to stand still, the world around me growing quiet and irrelevant. My thoughts raced – where was the bullet headed? I didn't even have a full second to react, to get out of its way. *El Viejo!* My mind screamed, *What do I do?*

Hither and yon, he seemed to answer, *a small fraction of a second makes all the difference.*

In what felt like extremely slow motion, excruciatingly slowly, I dived up and out of the channel, flattening myself against the nearest dune.

Pop! Pop! Pop! Three shots shattered the silence, and my world was back up to speed. Three columns of sand spurted up in a row, "walking" the distance from the channel toward my position, the last one popping up just inches away from my left arm. Heart pounding, I tried my damnedest to wriggle deep into the ground, but the sand was only a few inches deep. If the shooter could see me through his spotting scope, through the sparse cover of the frail bushes in front of me, I was a dead man.

Shouts from above, some muffled, some obscene, told me that they couldn't see me. *Pop! Pop! Popopopopop!* The shooting began again, a continuous staccato racket, dirt and sand flying everywhere, but thankfully not anywhere close to me. He was operating at full automatic now, illegal as hell, but what did a criminal care about breaking another law? What was that compared to attempted murder?

But – what was he shooting at?

Good God – at the *atíín*! The idiot was shooting at the slab! Why would he do such a thing? But from my tenuous cover, I didn't dare try to save the package. My poor backpack was being perforated, my canteen punctured, my remaining food scattered around the channel. No telling what condition my tablet computer would be in. The slab itself took some hits, too: the canvas wrapping erupted with shards of stone, the bullets ricocheting unseen and dangerous.

Finally the shooting stopped. More shouting from above, and I ventured a quick peek with the binoculars. The shooter was *Coyote*, but now he was screaming something and waving his automatic rifle around. With a heave, he tossed it over the cliff face, where it fell hundreds of feet onto the stony ground in front of The Temple. It hit with a satisfying *crunch* and flew apart; at least I wouldn't have to face that thing again.

I couldn't see the thugs from my vantage point, so maybe they couldn't see me, either. Taking no chances that they might have another weapon ready in a few minutes, after this destructive tirade, I ran over and grabbed the remains of my backpack with one hand, the *travois* with the other, and sprinted with my load toward the safety of an overhang at The Temple. I ran as if my life depended on it, as it probably did. Heart pounding and lungs gasping for air, I nearly slammed into the cliff face.

Out of breath, but for the moment shielded even from rocks that *Coyote* and his buddy might drop my way, I leaned back against the colored stratum of rock that was my sanctuary. Looking back over the ground I had covered in just a few minutes, I leaned over to check the condition of the *atiín*. As I carefully unwrapped the tattered canvas, it dawned on me what I had done – run a quarter of a mile, dragging the three-hundred-pound slab *with one hand*! How was that possible?

Then I remembered *El Viejo*'s statement from last night. "You ask about our strength in lifting heavy stones? You have heard of 'hysterical strength' have you not?" I had, including cases where a 100 pound woman had lifted an automobile off an injured child or spouse. "Well, that proves there is no reason in physics it can't be done. There's your *proof, amigo*, since you always want *proof*. So imagine a state of mind in which you can call upon that kind of strength whenever you consciously desire it. Obviously the human body can't operate at such limits continually, but most conditions in your life don't require it. But just let your mind be open to the possibility, and your body will follow orders. It's a mental thing – you will understand it and you will use it. From now on, if that's what you want."

As I rested, a sudden pain pierced my left arm, a sharpness so intense I nearly yelped. *Blood!* Blood on my forearm! What had happened? I wiped it away with my right hand, but it kept pumping. I poked my finger into the wound, and it went nearly through my arm! I had been hit with one of those bullets, but hadn't felt it until now. Remembering my first aid, I ripped part of the slab's covering into a tourniquet and tightened it to stanch the flow. I gritted my teeth; the pain was overwhelming, wave upon wave of pulsing horror, the world threatening to go dark before my eyes. If I passed out here, I would bleed to death. What to do?

With a flush of warmness, I felt *El Viejo*'s voice, his touch. *Your mind controls your body, amigo. Now is the time to exercise that control. Now! Do it!*

I loosened the tourniquet knot and wrapped my right hand around the wound. I was right – the bullet had passed all the way through without hitting bone. *A mere flesh wound,* as the bleeding hero used to say in the old cowboy movies. But it hurt like hell. I didn't remember any of the old cowboy heroes ever screaming the way I wanted to. But I kept quiet, biting my lip; I didn't want to give away my position to the thugs who had shot me, not when they could be scrambling down a rope or a pathway, coming to find me and finish the job, or even lobbing rocks straight down on me.

El Viejo's face loomed large in my mind's eye. Following the mental imagery I was receiving from him – or hallucinating that I was receiving, I couldn't tell – I imagined healing energy flowing from the earth, through my body, through my right arm and into the bleeding mess that was my left forearm.

Like before, the world about me grew quiet and still. The sunlight dimmed, and I was in another world, another place. Maybe it lasted minutes, maybe hours, maybe days, I couldn't tell, but while I was there the pain diminished, the bleeding slowed and finally stopped, and I was able to move my arm, my hand and my fingers painlessly and easily.

Then I passed out, my last conscious thought hoping the healing was real and not a dream or I would bleed to death right here and my bones might languish against this Valley wall for a hundred years, and my soul might wander this Valley forever, lonely and afraid.

If it was a dream, I liked it: I was young and tan and lithe and walking by the stream in the midst of the Valley, sturdy moccasins smooth and sensuous on my feet. Over my left shoulder I carried the still-warm body of an antelope; I could smell the musky odor from its blood as that life-liquid ran down my arm, the smell of victory, the odor of conquest of this animal, the feeling of satisfaction in providing for the clan.

We have come so far, I was thinking in this new body and this new mind, *across the vast plains, where we fed on the large hairy beasts, food enough from one hunt to last months. Before that, many months from the dark forests, across the great rivers, where we fought other men in great battles. Far back beyond then, my grandfather told, our people had crossed a water so wide you could not see any land for many, many days.*

I arrived at the camp, where several hundred people gathered in safety, their tents strung among rocks and trees, beside the flowing water. I laid down my kill for the women to take and clean and cook. The clan leaders were gathered around my grandfather's tent, as they always did, performing strange rituals over the crates of holy relics our clan had carried and protected for long ages. My grandfather beckoned me to come over and the elders made way as I obeyed. Grandfather thanked me for the meat, then pointed down at my bloody arm, and told me to go wash it in the round pool in the large stone clearing just downstream of our camp.

At the pool, I washed my arm, my face, and finally my whole body, gently lowering myself into the clear blue water. The liquid made me tingle; taking a drink from the water around me, I felt my mind opened to all of the Valley around me. This was the place Grandfather called "The Pool of Life," where all things were possible. The clan had traveled thousands of days, from the place of our beginnings, through many adventures and many dangers, to arrive at this site. We would build a temple here, to protect this place, and to protect ourselves.

I was pleased. This is where our journey would end. This would be our home. After all the wanderings, we would settle in this magical place.

I AWOKE TO THE MYRIAD SOUNDS OF THE DESERT'S NIGHT creatures: chittering ground squirrels, the rustling and *snick-snicking* of unknown insects and who knows what else. Shaking my head to clear the mental fog, I tried to recall where I was and what had happened when I went to sleep. In the distance, a pack of coyotes yelped as if carrying on a wild party, celebrating a kill. Nearby, the unlikely chirp of crickets and tree frogs. My back was sore from leaning against cold layered strata of clay and rock, and my buttocks and legs felt every pebble and twig beneath them. I shook my head again to see what was around me, but in the distance the moonless night revealed only a soft bluish glow, sufficient to separate the unbroken darkness of the eastern Valley wall from the diamond-like stars in the velvet sky above it.

Whoa! I was still in The Valley, but *my* Valley, not the Valley of that young man who carried the antelope, who bathed in the Pool of Life, who washed his bloody arm there–! In panic, I felt for my left arm. Was it still bleeding? Was I dying here, from this gunshot wound? I couldn't see anything at all, but exploring my left arm with my right hand, I could not feel any pain, any flowing blood, any holes. This was incredible! I fumbled around in my jeans pocket and pulled out the keychain with the small blue laser flashlight. Shielding the light with my hand, in case the Santa Fe thugs were out there in the darkness somewhere, I inspected my wound, and found only faint markings where the bullet had entered and left. Totally unbelievable!

Had my attempts at self-healing, with *El Viejo*'s telepathic direction, actually worked? Directed imagery, controlling the body's natural healing abilities, but accelerating it? A distant part of my mind said, "How is this different from the hysterical strength, when you were able to pick up a three-hundred-pound stone slab and run hundreds of yards with it?" The other part of my mind had no answer, and with immense relief, I leaned back against the hard wall surface and breathed deeply.

"So *El Viejo* has taught me some really practical skills after all," I muttered. "Physical skills that have just saved my life more than once." I shuddered to think where I'd be without those abilities. *On the other hand,* I thought, *without El Viejo's "guidance," I wouldn't be here in the Valley in the first place, exposing myself to these dangers!* Maybe somehow it all would work out in the end, but miraculous healing or not, I didn't want to be shot again. It was too bad that the healing process hadn't

extended to erasing the memory of the pain. That sensation was something I would not soon forget. My arm throbbed just from the recollection.

I JERKED AWAKE AGAIN AS SUNLIGHT WASHED MY FACE, WONDERING
if everything up till now had been a dream. A quick glance at my
wounded and healed arm showed pale markings where the bullet had
come and gone, and dried blood on the ground around me told me it
had been no dream. My arm had been lying on the *atín* and the
shredded canvas covering, now stained with the dark purple of old
blood, was soaked. I would have died here, alone, if *El Viejo*'s lesson
hadn't worked. The unbidden image returned, of a broken skeleton in
shredded clothes, propped up eternally against the cliff wall. I shuddered again, then stood up to work out the cramps of a long, cold
night's repose on the desert floor.

I was able to stand up straight under the small outcropping of dark
stone and get my bearings. Peeking out one side and then the other, I
didn't see anybody coming down the sheer cliff walls, and an inspection
of the desert itself, back down toward the *arroyo* and beyond, didn't
show anyone hunting for me, either. But without leaving my shelter, I
would not be able to view the top edge of The Temple, if that's where I
was, to tell if *Coyote* and his henchman were still up there waiting
for me.

"Oh well," I whispered to myself, "I'll keep to the cliff face and
hope they can't see me. And I've got to find something else to eat." All
I had was some jerky I'd stuffed down in my jeans the day before; other
snacks were undoubtedly scattered out there on the desert floor. The
jerky was better than nothing, but not by much.

Leaving the stone slab safely ensconced under a covering of sand
and rocks, I made my way slowly along the base of the cliff that
defined The Temple, edging northward in hopes of finding a cave or a
niche where I could hide for the rest of the day. From now on, I
planned to move only at night unless I could get far away from the two
hoodlums above me. I wasn't sure I would be able to heal all the
damage they could do to me if they had another rifle. Much more pain

last night and I wouldn't have been able to concentrate on the healing imagery at all. And a trauma to the head would make it impossible. I didn't want to think any more of such dire possibilities, so I paid attention to keeping quiet and out of sight of anybody who might be looking over the edge of the cliff above.

Within a few minutes I had found what I was hoping would be there – a cave opening large enough to drive a semi-truck through, extending back into pitch darkness beyond. It must have been one of the "doors" to The Temple that I had seen from the other side of The Valley.

Back under the outcropping where I'd spent the night and left the slab, I re-assembled the *travois* as best I could and dragged the heavy load back to the safety of the cave. Although the going on the flat stone of the base of the cliff was easier than it had been on the soft sandy floor of the Valley, I kept wishing I could access that super-human strength again and get the exhausting job done without all the straining and sweating. But I had learned that the particular skill was to be used only in immediate emergencies where there was no other alternative. I supposed that the human body could only take so much of that hyper-activity without sustaining damage that even *El Viejo*'s healing couldn't help. But still, it was a temptation.

I dragged the load back into the cave about twenty feet, so that it could not be seen from the entrance. Careful of disturbing rattlesnakes or other critters that might take shelter here, I turned on my flashlight and walked slowly into the darkness. If this were a natural cavern, it might traverse a lot of the remaining distance to my destination, where I could replace the *atíin* in its proper place. And then go home.

And then go home! That sudden thought startled me. Though no one was expecting me back anytime soon, and though I had made arrangements for my finances and deadlines to be handled in my absence, I had given almost no thought to the outside world and my outside life. How long had I been here? I tried to count the days. One day in Santa Fe, one day till I left the SUV in its place, one day with Judd, one day with – the memory of Algona stirred me physically and emotionally, one day at the mission ruins, and a day of terror out there alone, being shot at. Six days! Was that all? In one respect it was an eternity, in another, just a few days' outing in the Great Southwest. But I had changed; brother, how I had changed!

The cave itself appeared to be of natural origin, but I could tell that humans had been here before. Near as I could see from the limited illuminating capability of my small flashlight, the floor had been cleared of rocks, and the ceiling, some ten to fifteen feet above my head, showed the telltale black soot of torches. Whether the marks were from yesterday or a thousand years ago, I couldn't tell, but now knowing something of the mysterious nature of The Valley, nothing would surprise me.

Near the entrance the cave smelled of *caliche* dust and bone-dry vegetation. I wandered back several hundred yards until the daylight from the cave mouth was no longer visible, mustiness permeating the depths of the cave. I found nothing unusual, just a couple of rings of rocks where old campfires had been. As I turned to go back toward the light, a faint, unusual noise seemed to be coming from further back in the cave, a pleasant tone, almost musical. I stopped and turned around slowly. No sound, no noise. On a hunch, I tapped my foot against the cave wall; immediately the tinkling sound returned, echoing briefly before dying out. A few more stomps and the tone continued, and I guessed it was some kind of resonance in the cave configuration. It is entirely possible to have a situation where almost any kind of input sound will stimulate the vibration of some rock or crystalline structure within the cave and produce a musical tone, an output sound. Even conventional archaeologists were admitting to the acoustic engineering some of the ancients had accomplished in their temples. Whatever it was, it was a pleasant harmonic tone, soothing and enjoyable, but with only one flashlight I wasn't going to venture any further into the unknown darkness.

As I rounded the gentle turn leading back to the cave entrance, the angle of the diffused light revealed what looked like bas-reliefs on the cave wall. I walked past them and looked back, but the markings were not visible from that viewpoint. Going back to the place I had first seen them, I played the light over the carvings, etchings, whatever they were.

I sighed. These markings, each about an inch high and carved into the stone wall as clearly and distinctly as those on the *atiín*, were Egyptian hieroglyphics, if they were anything! Was this another one of *El Viejo*'s "guidances," or had I stumbled on them accidentally? In truth, I was beginning to believe that nothing in The Valley happened by accident, even though there was nothing in my finding shelter in a cave that propelled me to go exploring deeply into it. Or was there? It had felt like the right thing to do, I had done it; now I was onto a possible archaeological discovery of major importance, if these carvings were what they appeared to be.

I made a mental note of the location of the markings, then paced off the distance back to my camp, such as it was. Ransacking through the battered remains of my backpack, I inventoried the electronics there. The digital camera and the tablet computer were both nicked, but functioning okay, though I noticed they did not display date or time, just like my non-functioning digital watch.

I returned to the hieroglyphics with the digital camera, photographing them from every angle. Fortunately the flash still functioned so I was able to document every one of the several dozen symbols. During my lifetime of investigations I had inspected hundreds of photographs of ancient temples, and made several trips to Egypt to see some hieroglyphics in person. Based on that rather scant and non-expert knowledge, I was convinced that these markings were the real thing, not recently hoaxed carvings.

I returned to my little camp and reviewed the photos on the camera's display screen. A cartouche, or oval-shaped frame around several symbols, indicated a royal name, that much I knew. The others, geometrical and animal-shaped, meant nothing to me. I sketched them in ink as well as I could on my paper notepad, just in case the camera got lost or malfunctioned. I would hate to lose such a treasure, the one tangible anomaly I could document to show the outside world some proof of my little adventure.

While I was at it, I typed into the tablet computer an outline of my last few days. The wireless uplink, like the smartphone, still wouldn't work, so I could not contact the outside world. What that meant, I didn't want to contemplate. I was aggravated but curious; The Valley was a strange place indeed.

Other considerations than curiosity and aggravation soon prevailed; I was getting extremely hungry. Scrabbling through the holed remains of the backpack I found a chocolate snack bar in one pocket and hungrily consumed it. Other than the half-chewed jerky stick, I was now officially out of food. The canteen was almost empty as well, having leaked out most of its valuable contents through a bullet hole near the cap. So here I was, hungry and thirsty, stuck in a cave God knows where, afraid to leave, and with a three-hundred-pound souvenir needing to be toted who knew how many more miles up a Valley crawling with a couple of guys who wanted to kill me. What a deal!

While waiting until evening so I could explore outside the cave to find a way northward in safety, I saw some dry brush around the cave entrance. Carefully gathering what I could, I brought it into the cave and fashioned a torch of sticks, bound with a strip of the canvas I cut from the slab cover, avoiding the blood-soaked portion. I went back into the darkness of the cave as far as possible without light, and then lit the torch. Now I had both a torch and a flashlight – backup! Within moments as I moved deeper into the cave I again heard the musical echoes from deeper within. The cave itself was non-descript – flat floor, barren walls, no more hieroglyphics, nothing but that incessant tone, now pulsating, becoming louder.

Making sure my flashlight still worked in case of an emergency, and that there were no branching chambers from the main cave in which I could get lost if I had to return in total darkness, I boldly walked on. The cave floor began to dip a little, and soon I was traveling down an inclined ramp, by now no longer a natural floor but definitely a human-built pavement of cut and dressed stones about two feet square, their joints lightly covered with dust. This was quite interesting – somebody had had enough manpower and knowledge to pave this place with square-cut stones, how long ago? And for what purpose?

Coming to a sharp right turn in the cave, I stopped to consider my situation. The makeshift torch still had several minutes of light left, and I was anxious to see what else might have been built back there. I pressed forward to see around the turn. To my surprise, at this point the cave became a tunnel, now completely defined by manmade stone construction, a continuous arched ceiling ten or twelve feet high, leading off into the distant dark. It reminded me of the finely finished tunnels within the Great Pyramid and other pyramids in Egypt. The atmosphere itself felt incredibly ancient, musty, as if I were the first person to come here in hundreds of years, or longer.

The tunnel was *old*, a sense of vast eons permeating the very walls. A slight depression had been worn in the floor, evidence of many visitors over many years. But more than that, I felt the absence of any human presence. I've been to ancient ruins all over the world, but there was always a presence of humanity there, perhaps arising from human DNA in microscopic flakes of skin in the cracks somewhere, maybe even psychic vibrations of the soul or the aura remnant in the stones themselves.

But here – none of that. An eerie feeling shook my spine – was this place for humans at all? What could I be walking into? I shook off the feeling. The tunnel, at least, was human-sized, and the floor flat, so it was unlikely that giant spider-aliens or caterpillars had built it – they'd've had round tubes and other creepy-crawler features. I thought vaguely of goblins and Orcs and such, but pushed the thoughts out of my mind and pressed on deeper into the truly ancient structure.

A few yards into the tunnel I stopped, heart pounding, unable to continue because of the fear of the unknown, deep here within the Valley walls. But outside my cavern, somewhere, lay two morons with maybe another gun and a desire to kill me and take my increasingly precious burden. No, I told myself, better to continue exploring here inside the tunnel than take a poor chance in the open with *Coyote* and his buddy. I couldn't believe that I would have been brought all this way by whatever mysterious forces were guiding me, just to let me die inside a musty cave.Trudging through the dust made me begin to cough, and the echo from my voice amplified and distorted the melodic vibrations that had been accompanying my footsteps along the way. The pulsating sound amplified louder and louder, until I suppressed my coughs. Something weird was definitely designed to happen to people who came this way.

At that moment, I felt a humid draft in my face, as if a window over a lake had been opened on a windy day. The torch began to waver and flicker. Damn! I didn't want to lose my light now! But suddenly, along with the oncoming wind I sniffed a telltale odor of methane or some similar dangerous gas. Afraid of an explosion, or of being asphyxiated, I threw the burning torch down to stomp it out, and then to run back the way I'd come. Too late! Burning gas *whooshed* as it ignited at my feet, a column of blue flame that shot up the side of the tunnel. Instinctively covering my face with my arms, I felt the radiated heat and was afraid I would be fried by the flames then and there.

But I was not harmed; the gas was igniting down the tunnel away from me. I stood in awe at the sight: *Whoosh! Whoosh! Whoosh!* Sounding like a giant gas furnace being lit, flames shot out of a series of holes along the top of the tunnel walls, at first with blowtorch intensity, then settling down to calm blue flames no more threatening than one's gas cook stove. Every three to four feet along each side of the tunnel, at the point where the arched ceiling met the supporting walls, a blue flame an inch or so in diameter arced out half a foot, its exhaust fumes being sucked up into a vertical circular opening in the arch. The radiant heat, though warming the air in the tunnel slightly, was not uncomfortable at all. The effect was almost psychedelic: two rows of jewel-like flickering blue arcs, converging in the distance. The tunnel continued to ramp downwards, and the eerie illumination system fairly invited me to continue. I must have triggered an ancient lighting system and then ignited it at the right moment.

A fraction of a second more, the Old One had said, *and your life would have been much different.* How right he was – I didn't think this gas lighting system would have a lot of slack in it. Had I come down with only the flashlight and not a flaming torch – asphyxiation would have been both quick and deadly. Yet the flame I carried saved me from death and then lit the way to somewhere. What an efficient way to keep out those not in the know, and to let in those who were prepared! I shuddered. Like many factors in one's life, this was one where preparation, even if done in ignorance, was surely necessary. I had to trust that *El Viejo* was guiding me, because I didn't like trusting my life to blind luck.

Figuring I had little else to lose, I returned to the camp, retied the *travois* and the shreds of the backpack, gathering up firewood in case it was needed and stuffing it into the backpack. I made half a dozen more strip-tied torches, just in case the tunnel lights had gone out when I left, or if I needed them later. Then, dragging the whole life-support system with me atop the *atiín* slab, I returned to find the tunnel still lit.

Going downhill on a paved stone ramp was quite a bit easier, and my heavy load of *atiín*-stone was not much of a burden for a while. I walked for half an hour, mentally counting the paces in case I had to return in darkness, finally coming to the end of the tunnel. The terminal end of the tunnel was one solid stone, carved conically into a concavity as wide as the floor, extending up to merge with the arched ceiling.

This had to be the focal point for collecting the incoming sounds, and transmitting them back down the hallway. And my cough – or the original designer's voice commands – could be the triggering mechanism for releasing the illuminating gas. I didn't see any obvious mechanical devices for controlling the gas flow, but it could have been internal to the concavity or to the walls, something opened by a sudden vibratory signal. Ingenious! I had never even heard of a stone-age gaslight system. I supposed there must be some pressurized gas storage system, or more likely a naturally pressurized vent inside the Temple here, somewhere. I thought, *The ancients, if that's who built this, certainly had their ways! Not our ways, but effective ones.*

Not wanting to be stuck a quarter mile deep inside a stone tunnel, I looked around to see if there was some other way out. I couldn't imagine why anyone would have built all this massive stonework unless there were a destination, surely not just this blunt end. I tapped around to determine if there were hollows behind the stones. *OK, El Viejo, guide me now, old buddy, 'cause I need some help and damned sure don't want to haul this slab back up to the front of the cave!*

Nothing came to me. No vision, no suggestion, no mental images. "Okay," I said aloud, "let's see if meditation can help." I sat in the lotus position, palms upward, eye closed, concentrating on taking the *atiín* back to its intended location up the Valley. But still nothing came. After half an hour, I was impatient and irritated. What use would *El Viejo*'s "powers" be if they didn't come through when they were needed? I sure didn't want to have to panic again to access help in getting out of this tunnel dungeon.

I ran my hands over the smooth concave end of the tunnel. As an experiment, I lit a torch and, holding it aloft, yelled into the center of the concavity. "Hey, let me out of here! Open sez me!" At the far end first, the gas jets began to flicker and extinguish, plunging the tunnel into darkness there. "Wait a minute!" I yelled again. This time, the lights began to extinguish even faster, the darkness of the tunnel rushing on me like an oncoming train. Oh damn! I had consigned myself to the dark again. How was I going to drag the *atiín* back up and out, while holding a torch?

As the wave front of darkness approached me, I turned my brushy torch on its end to spread its flame faster, and grabbed onto the *travois* so I wouldn't lose it if all became black. The last two gas jets above me held off the pitch blackness beyond. "Oh boy, I muttered, "I wish they would give written instructions for this place." It dawned on me that the hieroglyphics I had photographed probably *were* the directions, if I knew how to decipher them. Next time I would certainly try harder.

As I hitched up the *travois* and prepared to hike back from this dead end, the remaining gas lights extinguished, leaving a faint smell like burnt grass. Then, the familiar *Whoosh*-ing noise made me spin my head around. The right side of the wall moved slightly, as if it were a door caught in a draft, one side protruding out half an inch from the perfectly flat wall. But this "door" was a dressed stone, six feet square! Cautiously, anxious lest I trigger some booby trap, I pushed one finger against the stone door where it was tilted inward from the wall. It moved as if by magic, and I could see another gas-lit hallway beyond. With more faith than caution, I carefully dragged my load through the doorway and into an ascending passageway identical to the previous one. Surely, if all of this were just deception, intended to kill me, I would have been dead long before now.

Once through the door, I pulled out the notepad and drew what I hoped was an accurately scaled sketch in case I had to retrace my steps. One of my lifelong nightmares was being trapped in tightly sealed places, unable to escape. I tested the door again, and it was still movable. Maybe just the second set of voice signals had ignited this corridor, and the resulting air pressure from the ignitions had moved the delicately balanced stone. But I had not activated it by touch, when I was searching for a way out. These ancients had some acoustic secrets I wanted to uncover, but at another time when my life was not at stake.

I remembered reading about the "voice of Memnon," ancient mega-statues in Egypt that would sing when the sun rose. Modern investigation of the ruined statues revealed some small chambers where some kind of apparatus had been placed, apparently by priests of old who wanted to impress the populace. But when I visited the site, it still wasn't known exactly what devices had made the statues speak. Old Heron of Alexandria, the greatest engineer of his time, it was suspected, had had something to do with it, maybe with siphons and valves, but nobody really knew.

But with hundreds of years to work, and with thousands of tinkerers and inventors to experiment, the ancients could have come up with a lot of things since lost in the dusty halls of history. Unlike today, the ancient engineers and scientists had no mass-produced books, so that one fire or earthquake, just one invasion or plague, could wipe out a city or a guild of specialists, and the knowledge would be extinguished because it only existed in that one place, maybe in just one person. Somewhere in the fires of Alexandria or Constantinople or Persepolis, we lost the documents, the papyrus scrolls that would have given us the exact methods used to construct the Great Pyramid and what its true purpose was. Who knows what machines and methods they used to manufacture and polish the giant stones used in Egyptian pyramids and temples and statuary?

And who was the unknown genius who designed the 2,000-year-old Antikythera computer, the gear-driven calculator that showed the positions of sun, moon and planets, even eclipse predictions, dug up from a sunken Greek ship over a hundred years ago and not recognized for what it was until fifty years later? And recent publications talked about the fantastic optical and precise machining feats of the ancients that had been lost for thousands of years, their clear remains true evidence overlooked in museums all around the world. I determined to write another book about truly ancient technology sites – *this one!* – *if* I ever got out of The Valley and back to civilization.

Searching my memory, I also recalled many reports of eternal flames in ancient temples and tombs. If the stories were true at all, they may have been gas or electrical lighting. But whatever the technologies of the other places, the reality of the illumination system here was quite impressive. I didn't know if archaeologists would ever be allowed in this place by whoever had brought me in; if so they would literally have a field day. But then, a couple of low-rider bums from Santa Fe had removed an even greater treasure somehow, and had carried it out of The Valley. How they did that, how they knew about this place and how they were allowed to deface it, to destroy something in The Valley, was a mystery I couldn't comprehend.

THE TUNNEL WENT ON FOR AT LEAST A MILE OR TWO, ALTERNATELY rising slightly or descending slightly. The structure never changed in size or character, the uniformly dressed stones fitting as if laser-cut; the bare stone walls unmarked by hieroglyphics. The gas lights continued to burn on, dispelling the mustiness, whether by the flames or ventilation I couldn't tell. The slightly increased humidity felt good to my dry sinuses and drier skin. I figured that anybody with the knowledge and skills to build all of this fantastic construction would be smart enough to make it comfortable. But all the time I was concerned, not knowing if there was a destination, or if this was a shortcut between points in The Valley's cliff walls.

The answer to this puzzle was no longer academic, but was becoming a matter of survival. By now I was quite hungry, and had used the very last of the water from the canteen. At one of my frequent stops for rest, I tried to assess the situation – was I going to continue on in hopes that I was closer to the other end of this tunnel, or should I try to head back? Counting my paces, I had traveled some four thousand, which made it about two miles so far. Surely with all of the work that had gone into digging this tunnel, then dressing the stones and putting them in place, for all the expenditure of effort, they had intended some great purpose. I was praying that it opened out into the world soon, and I hoped they had also planted a garden with fruit trees and a nice spring, otherwise how there could be any food involved in such an ancient, sterile place, I didn't know. I just hoped to find out soon. The humidity gave me some hope of success.

Overhead, the gas jets flickered once, then changed colors briefly, greenish-yellow flames replacing the blue for an instant. Without warning, (unless the color change had heralded it) the atmosphere in the tunnel began to change, subtly at first, then significantly. A bitter-sweet aroma, slightly citric in flavor, permeated my nostrils, and the overall effect seemed to invigorate me. My hunger pangs quickly diminished and my mind became clearer. Was this another ancient invention, a "traveler's aid" device to help pilgrims or acolytes along as they trod the stone floor? Or was it attuned to the individual?

Whatever the intent, the strange odor refreshed me, and I stood up to renew the trek. I picked up the pace of travel and felt almost as if I could trot along, the *travois*-load of slab a minor counterweight as I leaned forward into the wind. Wind? I stopped and looked around. The gas jets were blowing in the sudden draft, flickering ominously as if about to be blown out. I checked my backpack for the makeshift torches, and clicked on the flashlight for added comfort. I wouldn't be going without light, but didn't relish the idea of being surrounded fore and aft by absolute darkness, if the tunnel lights went away.

The wind velocity rapidly increased, until walking into it became difficult, maybe thirty miles an hour or more. The good old gas lighting held on, though the flames themselves were now blown away from their overhead exhaust vents. At least the same wind that was causing that would keep the exhaust fumes away from me. What could be generating such a wind? I wondered.

A few hundred more paces, difficult ones, given the opposing wind, and I saw the answer: my beautiful tunnel, all manmade and symmetri-cal, opened into a vast dark cavern. I dragged the *travois* out of the tunnel exit and looked around. The tunnel entrance itself was framed in the same dressed stone, set in a natural cave wall. The light from the tunnel only lit up ten or twenty feet of the natural cavern floor on either side, and my flashlight could barely penetrate the darkness. From the faint images I could make out, the far wall of the cavern must have been at least a hundred feet away, and the ceiling at least the same distance. To my left and right, in the flashlight's beam, moist stalactites bore evidence of a living cave, further enhanced by the definite increase in humidity. Good! At least there must be water somewhere. I could survive, uncomfortably perhaps, for several more days without food, but not nearly as long without water. If need be, I could exist on moisture soaked up from cave drippings until I just turned around and walked out back through the tunnel. But the prospect of hauling the *atín* back all that distance was not appealing.

I took off the harness and tilted the *travois* up next to the tunnel entrance. The gas lights within were still burning, giving me confidence that at least I could leave the same way I'd entered, and return to the cliffs and into The Valley whenever I wanted to spend a few hours walking again. For the moment though, I wanted to explore, to find a larger source of water than dripping stalactites. I stood still, listening for drips, for anything that might tell me where to look.

A distant murmur made itself known over the sound of my own heartbeat, a hopeful hum, as of water flowing. I lit one of my torches by touching it to a gas jet inside the tunnel, and walked straight ahead toward what I hoped was clean water. Just fifty feet or so from the tunnel entrance a stream burbled as it emerged from under a rock shelf to my left, continued for perhaps a hundred feet, disappearing under another shelf to the right.

With great relief I submerged the taped-over canteen into the water, filling it and then dropping in a sterilizing tablet to take care of any unwanted bacteria. A flicker of white moved under the water surface, and several fish of unknown variety shot toward the place from which I'd filled the canteen. These appeared to be blind fish, a common variation for fish born and living in the blackness of caves, reacting to vibrations in the water, searching for food without need of light. I smiled. Whatever kind they were, they would taste good over a fire; say, the fire from the torches at the tunnel entrance.

An hour later, they did. *Three blind trout*, I thought, *who didn't know fishhooks and tiny pieces of brush from struggling insects!* I savored the taste of hot food, carefully wrapping one of the fish in canvas and stuffing it into one of the remaining pocket of the backpack. Although I would go fishing again before leaving this area, I wanted to make sure there was food for at least one more day in case anything else happened.

Exploring the immediate vicinity around the tunnel entrance for a few paces in all directions, I found nothing but some sandal prints, presumably from other visitors long ago. The cavern walls around the tunnel entrance were bare and natural. "Why did they build this extensive tunnel," I said aloud to hear the sound of a human voice, "just to go from the cliff face at the Temple back to this cavern?" Not much in the way of echoes answered, so the cavern must have really been long, without end walls to bounce back the sound waves.

Exhausted from the walk, satisfied and drowsied by the hot food, I went to sleep just inside the tunnel entrance on the paved floor, using the rolled up backpack as a pillow. I seemed to hear *El Viejo*'s voice from days before, "Dreams, as we know them, are milestones of the soul's desire."

7

I was tired, deadly tired, pain-stricken, making one reluctant step after another, the load across my shoulders becoming heavier and heavier with each passing moment. We had waited almost too long, and I was fearful that the journey would end in tragedy, not the joyful resurrection it was supposed to be. But we had so much work to do, and Father would not leave his work to enter this world until it was almost too late. Now I was physically exhausted, having to carry him these last thousand paces, and I had to rest.

Carefully, I removed him from my shoulders and sat him up against the wall of the holy passageway.

In fear and earnestness I prayed aloud that the gods would give me strength. Of a sudden, I felt the aromas of the gods and my prayers were answered. The Breath of Life exhaled from the living stone, replenishing my energy, refreshing my mind, relaxing my soul. As I watched, Father stirred again. I saw that he, too, was receiving the Breath of Life: his pulse quickened, his breathing became deeper and slower, his face more calm.

Rested, I scooped up my father, this time cradling him in my arms for the short distance that remained. Tunnel lights warmed us as we went, until we emerged from the tunnel into the Place of New Life. I looked down at my father's still visage. "It is not too late, Father, you will be saved. We are here."

To my left and right, jets of flame erupted, lighting the way to the Place of New Life. I took my father to the small stream and laid him by its side. With scooped hands, I washed his face, his hands, his feet, his arms. After a while he awoke. "Narsensi, my son, you have saved me once again," he said. "And for this, I thank you once again."

Leaving him for the intensely personal ceremony and ordeal to follow, I returned to the tunnel entrance while Father bathed himself completely in the stream. Hours later he came to me at the tunnel entrance, almost unrecognizable in his new youthful appearance. He was trembling from the experience, but finally gathered himself and smiled. "How wonderful, Father," I said as I kneeled in front of him, "that our gods allow us to live again and again."

Father spread his arms wide and bowed in return. "How wonderful, indeed, my son." He gestured to the tunnel. "Shall we now go and return to the work? We have so much to do, so much to teach."

"Surely, Father," I replied, still in awe at this resurrection, this renewal, although I had witnessed it many times over many centuries, "and much to remember, much to record for others."

I AWOKE, REFRESHED AND RELAXED, THE INTENSE EMOTIONS OF THE dream stubbornly refusing to fade, as if it were a true memory and not just the result of my greasy fish meal of the night before. "The Place of New Life?" I said aloud to myself as I stretched. "If that's what this cavern is, I guess it *was* worth constructing a paved tunnel to. But how did my old friend, er," I tried to remember the name from the dream, "*Narsensi?* How did Narsensi get lighting in the cave out there?" I took the remains of a torch and walked about halfway to the stream, hoping to set off another automatic gas-jet illumination system if I could. But nothing worked. What was the difference between the dream and now? Maybe the devices had failed in the centuries since they were set up? No, that couldn't be, at least wasn't probable, so long as the complex sound-activated system was still working in the tunnel, over all that distance. No, something else...

The weight! Narsensi was carrying his father! Maybe there was a weight-sensitive mechanism somewhere? Under the dust around the tunnel entrance, I spotted one foot-square stone that was slightly raised above the rest. I stepped on it, but nothing happened. *I need more weight*, I thought. How about the *atiín?* Dragging the *travois* over, I laid it on what I hoped was the trigger-stone, and then stood on top of it.

Voila! Dust erupted from the sandy floor visible from the light of the tunnel, and beyond into the darkness. I smelled the methane-like odor and wondered when the jets would ignite. *Fwoosh!* A sheet of flame shot from the tunnel mouth, singeing my legs, but then the gas-jets in the cavern floor lit off, two by two, into the darkness, and immediately the cavern was a wonderland of light all the way to the stream.

The sudden brightness illuminated the cavern in more ways than one: I stared in awe as the far wall revealed an incredible panoply of carved bas-relief statues, fifty-foot high carvings of men and women and gigantic animals reminiscent of the style of Ancient Egypt that I had seen, yet strangely different. Looking upward, the ceiling itself would have put Michelangelo to shame – in the shimmering gaslight I couldn't tell what they were – *carvings? Reliefs? Three-dimensional photographs?* – but in all their flickering glory, *beings* of many kinds hovered over a representation of a globe of Earth below, though an Earth with unnerving differences in the continental shapes.

Stunned, I almost fell backwards as I tried to take in the beauty and yet the *different-ness* of the scenes before me and above me. What *was* this place? Majestic and beautiful and different, awe-inspiring and discomfiting, all at the same time.

I walked the pathway to the flowing cave-stream, the practical part of my mind hoping to see more fish I could catch for future meals, while at the same time viewing what the dark had kept concealed: carved thrones and chairs around the stream opening, smooth-topped couches of solid stone intricately inscribed around their bases. And most fascinating of all, myriads of brightly-colored hieroglyphics covering every finished flat surface, extending to the walls, up around and past the gigantic statues, up to the ceiling. Over untold ages, the geologic processes of the living cave had obscured the details of some of these figures with interlacing veins of spidery mineral tracers and with stalactites growing down from the ceiling, merging with the smooth stone blocks of the wall, limning the bodies of the ancient sculptures with bright mineral traces.

"Wow," I breathed, "somebody really had something to say, and they said it all over the place!" My digital camera recorded hundreds of shots, the telephoto lens hopefully capturing details from a hundred feet away

Narsensi's lighting system didn't extend lengthwise in the cavern, to my left and right, but just illuminated a tract some thirty to fifty feet wide. I expected to be able to find other triggering stones, or acoustic actuators, that would light up those regions as well. There was no telling what other wonders lay beyond, but for the moment I was totally content to remain right here, awe-struck at the wonderful *alien-ness*.

After a while, even in the midst of that cathedral of an ancient and mysterious civilization, I still had to answer Nature's demands, and soon I caught some more blind cave fish and cooked a large meal in the flames nearest the tunnel entrance, savoring the odor, all the while wishing for some spicy sauces but grateful for the food in all its blandness. This time, I wrapped and stored away four more fish, enough for two to three days of subsistence eating, if it came to that.

While digesting the meal, I recalled the dream. Was Narsensi's father physically regenerated by something magical or chemical in the stream there? Or was the dream strictly metaphysical, and the resurrection that of the spirit, of the soul? I was grimy and sweaty after the travails of the last two days, so I determined to find out for myself. It was too bad I couldn't read the strange markings on the walls, which were probably detailed step by step instructions for the procedures. No Rosetta stone lay at my feet, so I would have to take my dream on faith and duplicate it as best I could.

At streamside, I splashed my face, then my arms and my feet. I stripped off the rest of my clothes and, careful to stay away and not to pollute the stream, scooped up water and poured it on the rest of my body, making sure it poured onto the cavern floor away from the flowing water.

Would it work? Did the old stream still maintain the magic I had seen in the dream? Or did you have to be a priest or have some secret knowledge to be regenerated? And what was the nature of the *ordeal*? I laid back on the ground and waited for something to happen. I didn't have to wait long.

The first sensation was almost like being sedated for surgery, a weariness, a drowsiness beyond belief, yet not quite unconsciousness. Then it hit, hard: intense *pain*, a deep burning, shaking waves of horror that swept over the boundaries of feeling, tides that washed deeply into my innermost *being* with a hurt, a severity I had never felt. I wanted to cry, but could not make a sound, wanted to move, but was paralyzed. The world became dark and for a long time I was afraid that all the lights in the cavern had gone out and I would be lost in this black hole of a cave for all eternity, wracked in incomprehensible pain. Was this truly Hell, the place of darkness and pain? At that moment I would have believed it.

An eternity or two later, I was released from the rack and cross of pain, and shaking mightily, rolled over and sobbed until I could cry no more. The gas jet lights closest around me had indeed gone out, but in the distance, toward the tunnel, the plumes of flame still lit the other side of my underground world.

Shaking with release from the supernal waves of pain I had experienced, I got to my feet, gathered up my clothes in the darkness and stumbled toward the welcome light of the tunnel, where the *atíin* still lay on the trigger-stone. I laid down, head on the backpack pillow, and went to sleep again.

This time I did not dream.

WHEN I AWOKE IT TOOK ME SOME MINUTES TO REMEMBER WHERE I was, what I was doing, what had happened. With relief I rolled over and stood up, peering out into the cavern, it's weird and wonderful colors and carvings standing out as if just recently created and painted, notwithstanding the veins of mineral growth that obscured some of them.

Remembering my painful time at the stream, I looked down at my naked body in shock: all my scars, from childhood to adulthood, were gone – the scar tissue on my left knee, from a motorcycle accident, not there. My bullet-shot left forearm showing no trace of even the palest scars. Even my vaccination scar was gone, the skin there smooth as a newborn's. "Damn, this did work!" I shouted, quickly checking other parts of my body.

Familiar sun-damaged skin spots were gone; well-known wrinkles around wrists and feet, now smooth as new skin; swollen knuckles, a missing fingernail, were all good as new. My appendectomy scar was gone, as was, unfortunately, evidence of some other early childhood male surgery. I groaned. Had an appendix grown back again, too, just like other parts I lost as an infant? Though I had no mirror, I could see from my reflection in the stream that my face looked younger, all of my gray hair in the beard and on top was once again the bright blonde of my youth.

I wondered about the white splotchy birthmark on my back, whether it would still be there, but couldn't bend around to the correct angle for a reflection to see if it was still present.

I wondered, was this water a DNA treatment? A fortuitous mixture of DNA-repairing chemicals, some kind of telomerase protein compound like scientists had been working on at the University of Texas, where human DNA might be able to reproduce itself perfectly, over and over again, for all eternity, giving the prospect of actual physical immortality?

The realization was profound – could this have been what old Ponce de Leon had been looking for? A Fountain of Youth, but thousands of miles from where he had looked? I could imagine that, if this were all real, that stories of such a stream, a fountain, could have spread from here throughout North America, to all the tribes. And that an ignorant Spaniard, hearing the incredible tale for the first time, would go in the direction that the aborigines pointed, just not far enough. By several thousand miles!

I'm glad you didn't come here, Ponce, my man; you and your Conquistadores would have ruined this place as surely as Cortez did Tenochtitlan, down in Mexico, and your buddy Pizarro did the Incas! Although, I continued my train of thought, *stopping the Aztecs' bloody sacrifices wasn't totally "ruining" the place. If only you had kept the codices, Cortez, and some of the temples. And Pizarro, you old hoodlum, if only you hadn't melted the Inca's golden treasures!* What histories, what knowledge, what understanding, the human race had lost to greed and ignorance and superstition. A story repeated in absolutely every place Mankind had ever conquered; no race was innocent, no nation totally absolvable. But this place, this place, it was immaculate, untouched.

I was certain this cavern had never felt the armored foot of the Spanish conquerors. The sandaled feet of those Catholic friars, now *they* could have walked here. Though even their history too was tainted with blood, stained with ignorance, blackened with intolerance. Or maybe this cavern was the reason that the local good fathers had abandoned their mission and taken up with the locals? Why worry about striving for eternal life if it was already here, right in front of you, in the physical reality? I sat for a long time, pondering the meaning of this place.

What if other people had been using the cavern's rejuvenation process for centuries or longer? What would they be doing now? Who would they be? The rich? The famous? Somehow I didn't think so; fame would be dangerous if you were living forever. Riches, though; riches would be useful, if carefully concealed and carefully used. What would these people do with all of those endless years? Who could they be?

Maybe *El Viejo*? The sudden revelation almost literally floored me.

Could *El Viejo* be one of the original settlers of this Valley? Hundreds, if not thousands, of years old? Was this the big secret of The Valley here, why *El Viejo* had e-mailed me, to come here, find this place, be rejuvenated myself? Was Judd one of these immortals? Algona? I smiled at the memory of her; I sure hoped she was one of them. I would search for her for a lifetime, or longer, if need be. And I loved the idea of being with her hundreds of years.

But why would *El Viejo* choose me, of all the people in the world?

Why me? has been the cry of every thinking person throughout all eternity – why was *I* chosen for this? Either the good experience or the bad, the miracle or the catastrophe, each individual feels like the focus of some cosmic circumstance that forces the situation.

In my case, I felt only gratitude to *El Viejo*, whoever he was – *whatever* he was! Gratitude and contentment. I was very thankful for whatever had led me here, and for the changes it had already wrought: I possessed a physical energy I hadn't known in years, an intellectual fierceness I had never felt, and a spiritual vitality both satiated and yet aware that much more, much more, awaited beyond – just beyond – the far vistas of my experience, in a warm misty *somewhere*.

TIME DIDN'T EXIST IN THE CAVERN. I LOST TRACK OF HOW MANY fish I caught and ate, because every waking moment I spent exploring up and down the unlit portions of the cavern. In both directions, for the several hundred yards I walked with my torches, the far wall was covered with more hieroglyphics and gargantuan statues. I couldn't illuminate the ceiling with the torch and my flashlight didn't help much either, but I felt certain that the strange ceiling figures near the tunnel were continued on down the length of the cavern as well.

This place felt incredibly ancient, and I could not decipher the meaning of the markings or the significance of the statuary, nor the reality of the weird creatures on the ceiling. Or especially the strangely-oriented, unsettling globe of the near-Earth they surrounded. Such a continental configuration had to be at least tens of millions of years old, and who – or what – could have known and made such a display?

Days must have passed, but I made no progress in understanding the panoply of mystery before me. I photographed and sketched and made notes, taking particular care in going over my map of the location of the place. I wanted desperately to bring skilled scientists back. This would be an earth-shattering archaeological discovery, if only I could make it known. In the meantime I reviewed what I knew about the place.

First, The Valley was physical. I was here, I had driven miles to get here, had trudged miles across it and through it, had met people who live here at least part of the time. Got wounded here in The Valley; almost got killed here. And this cavern, it was here, too. I was living in it and had been reborn in it, physically and probably spiritually. Could I bring others back here? That I didn't know, couldn't know, not yet. Would a person have to be especially spiritual (I hadn't been), or at least especially inquisitive (I was, and still am), to be allowed into The Valley? The two hoodlums from Santa Fe, though, they too had come here, and they damned sure weren't spiritual pilgrims on a quest. Were they part of a larger picture I couldn't see yet? A picture that started with the *atiín*, orbited around it, devolved into it?

Thinking back over the incredible experiences that the stone slab had got me into, I wondered exactly what the *atiín* itself was. An artifact from the ancient past? A technology I didn't understand? Or just real magic? I smiled at the thought. Sir Arthur C. Clarke, the world famous science fiction writer and futurist, once said that "Any sufficiently advanced technology is indistinguishable from magic." I could certainly vouch for that, but maybe "magic" described it better? I said aloud, "Maybe it should go, 'Any sufficiently advanced *magic* is indistinguishable from *technology*'?" My laughter carried far down into the darkness of the cavern, echoing back faintly from the far wall, distorted, mocking.

As I unwrapped the bloodstained canvas from around the *atiín* slab, I saw that the rock surface was likewise stained, the palm carvings, especially. Thinking back on Algona's oasis, with my experience of touching the slab's spiral, and then with the footprint in the rock, I wondered if my own palms might fit here. I left the dried, caked blood in place and slowly lowered my hands into the carved recesses. I smiled as the familiar "opening" sensation returned. Why wasn't it been obvious before now? Why hadn't I thought of this, using the sacred stone itself, its palm prints? No telling what I could have learned already.

But this time the experience was different, a powerful pulling sensation as soon as my palms touched the stone. I thought I would be dragged into the stone itself! This was not like the easy visionary sensations around the Pool of Life, it was much stronger, much more intense.

In a timeless moment, something strange happened. As if in a dream, a vision, a hallucination, I found myself walking farther up the cavern. Dazedly, I realized that the cavern was now fully illuminated. There were no stalactites; the place looked brand new. To my right was another tunnel entrance, almost identical to the one through which I had emerged into the cavern. I looked in. A shimmering transparent curtain of strangely swirling colors blocked the view. Without hesitation I stepped through, into another world.

And what a world it was: I stood in a transformed Valley, a bright flatland of brilliant green grass, the distant cliffs dark blue against an azure sky, larger shapes farther still. But in that sky, an incredible sight: giant bright arcs from horizon to horizon in all directions, colorful glowing ribbons overhead as wide as the Moon's diameter, diminishing in width in the distance. Criss-crossing the hemisphere of the heavens in all directions like bright bands of Christmas package wrappings, they blotted out over half of the visible sky, yet their own light seemed to make up for the blocked sunlight. What were they? And what for? Natural? Man-made? God-made?

In the distance stood − a city? Enormously tall, wavering images reminiscent of towers, spires, even geometrical shapes I had never seen before. I could try to describe one of them as, *a perfect cube with seven triangular sides*. Somehow that phrase bubbled up from memory, an old fantasy story, but now it made perfect sense. These solid figures could not exist in my own world and I had trouble focusing my eyes on them.

And between me and that distant horizon city, half filling The Valley, untold numbers of shining wispy shapes flitted past, barely visible, almost like heat waves, though brighter. Living beings? Holographic images? Something else? I just didn't know and couldn't tell. As

I walked from the cliff behind me, through the ankle-deep grass, looking in all directions to take in this marvelous scene, I knew that I was still in The Valley, but where *was* The Valley? What were these flitting shapes? That gigantic and beautiful city far away to the East? Those literally incredible shapes?

And above all, literally, those bright bands across the sky? I stopped in my tracks as something dawned on me – the crisscrossing sky-bands were of colors different from any I had known, yet so achingly familiar I hadn't noticed it at first. *New colors*! An amazing concept, yet there they were, hundreds of strange new colors. And I knew their names: *ocha, purah, enmir, lysia, nesar, sameem, ytrus, esmahn...*

Shaking my head and closing my eyes tightly to escape the weirdness all around me, I thought, *New colors? Yet I know their names? How can any of this be happening?* Immediately my analytical mind kicked in: if one's retinal sensitivities are adjusted, and if one's brain is attuned to new frequencies, of course there could be new colors. Why not? After all, the electromagnetic spectrum encompasses far more than the tiny portion we call "visible light," going off in both higher and lower frequencies, up to infinity, down to zero. And our brain has conveniently assigned certain bands of frequencies the arbitrary sensations we call *colors*. It's just that on Earth we don't need to sense those other frequencies, those other colors, and so our evolutionary path limited our vision.

This was the analytical portion of my mind speaking, but the artistic and spiritual portions also opened up as my eyes opened wide, and immediately all parts of my mind and my soul stared at the sky, drinking in the delicious novelty of the new palette of vision.

And as I stood there in awe, a faint aroma of lavender tobacco wafted its way to my nostrils. I turned to look for *El Viejo*, but I was still alone on that vast plain of grass, the vast towers and spires of the beautiful city in the distance no longer of interest. For then I began to sense other parts of my brain, my mind, my soul, *opening, unfolding* in waves of pleasure and sensation beyond all experience. I possessed new senses, far different from any of the multiplicity of those we know in ordinary life: vision, hearing, touch, smell, taste, motion, acceleration, bodily orientation, muscular state, temperature, and other more subtle ones recognized by physiological and neural researchers.

It is important to the meaning of my adventure that I relate something of how this sudden revelation of a panoply of new senses impacted me. How can I begin to explain?

I will try to describe how some of these new senses feel, how they may be partially imagined, if only by analogy. Imagine that I have come upon a "Country of the Blind," to use the H. G. Wells story premise. Imagine that I am trying to explain to an eyeless man in an eyeless society, the concept of *Vision,* with all of its power and utility, to a person who has never known it, who lives in a society that never experienced vision and has no references to it whatsoever.

Perhaps to begin, I would inquire of my host, "Do you know the difference between what you call *The Cold* and *The Warm?*"

"Yes," might be the reply. "Most of the time I can feel The Warm when I leave our home fire place. But sometimes it is not Warm, just Colder when I leave."

"Believe me," I would tell that person, "when I tell you that what you experience as The Warm is just one small aspect of what we others – with the sense of *Vision* that you don't possess – we call 'radiation'. The origin of this 'radiation' is a great fire located very far away, that bathes the world with its Warmth. But, and please believe me, this 'Warmth' has many other aspects, properties that *Vision* enables you to experience. Chief among these is the ability to determine, without touching, that other objects exist elsewhere in your environment. And how distant they are, and other surface characteristics that they possess, whether they are smooth or rough, wet or dry, large or small, stationary or moving. And how to recognize other people, even from many steps away."

The visionless man might say, in absolute shock, "You mean, I do not have to walk and touch them, yet can still experience them? Know what they are? Like trees and stones? And many steps away?"

"Yes, and other people, too, without their speaking or making sounds."

"This '*Vision*' is a lot like sound, then? I can tell *you* are near or far by your voice."

"Something like sound, but much, much more. It would be to you as if the trees and stones themselves had voices, everything – mountains, rivers."

"But if everything had voices, how could you tell which was where? You would be overwhelmed. And – what are 'mountains'?"

I sighed. "Mountains are like very large piles of earth and stones that rise from the ground, like a large rock or a tree does. But mountains are much, much, higher, and millions of times larger. *Vision* enables you to experience them, though they may be thousands of steps away.

"But let me explain something else. *Vision* allows you to comprehend and experience almost an infinite number of other objects – people, animals, trees, rocks, rivers – because some of the radiation that you experience as 'The Warm' bounces or *reflects* from these objects, is focused onto parts of your eyes, and then is interpreted by your brain. From these reflected radiations, which we call *light,* you can sense how far the objects are away from you, and can deduce something about their size, their texture, and even the materials of which they are made. The brain separates certain bands of these lights as *colors.*"

The blind man thinks on this a while. "I do not comprehend, nor can I imagine, this sense you call '*Vision,*' or how this *light* is perceived by the brain or these *colors* you speak of. It all sounds like some kind of magic to me, fantastic magical powers that mere humans cannot experience."

I nod and feel pity for this man. "Believe me, it is probably the most powerful and universal of human senses. Those who are deprived of it suffer greatly."

"Suffer?" the blind man may retort. "How am I suffering if I have never known or used this new sense of yours? I do suppose that your so-called *Vision* would be useful in avoiding collisions, allowing me to walk faster, and maybe avoid holes and stumble-rocks. But I cannot imagine anything else about it that I would find interesting."

I could not begin to explain to this man the glories of a clear night sky. From his primal experience of '*The Cold,*' I could not think of where to start to explain to him far distant glowing objects, no way to talk to him of stars and Moon, nor of the images of the vast Universe uncovered by Hubble telescope or the space probes. Such concepts would forever be beyond my ability to relate or his to imagine. And this doesn't even include basic visual concepts such as reading and painting. There would be no method to make him understand how much he would be missing, and never even know it, never even conceive of it, even though he was communicating with a sighted person.

Thinking of the frustration arising from this brief exchange, I ask you now to imagine new and different *Parasenses* as far beyond *Vision* as *Vision* is beyond the experience of the eyeless person in this dialogue. Imagine a society built upon such senses, as far advanced as a sighted society would be over this Country of the Blind.

By analogy, the best I can do is try to describe the utility of these senses: Imagine seeing the magnificence of a world based on hundreds of primary colors, each as vivid and beautiful as the pitifully small number of individual color bands of a rainbow. The closest I can describe without showing you through new eyes is a sheen, an overlay of indescribably delicate and surprising shades that begin their beauty about where the glowing strangeness of Maxfield Parrish paintings leave off, in the merest suggestion of what lies beyond. And extending beyond in literally unimaginable flourishes of new colors.

In the same manner as *Vision* enables us to perceive our location in the surrounding physical environment – and gives us the auxiliary skills of reading, painting, watching entertainment – so the next level of senses, the '*Parasenses*,' enables us to perceive our 'location' in each unique Universal You, that is, our TimeSpace coordinates and our relation to the nearby and faraway parallel worlds. With *Parasenses* you involuntarily identify the *texture* of these adjacent Realities, the *transparency* of alternate timelines, the *viscosity* or "stickiness" of past and future events, their permanence or transience, whether they are virgin events or if they have been affected by travelers from other worlds or other times. Again, keep in mind the parallel to the blind man. This is as close as I can come, but it is as far from totality as that blind man's understanding of *Vision* after I tried my best at explanation.

One identifiable group of *Parasenses* has to do with the ability to

transfer among the infinite branches of the Universal You, to experience life therein, and to make certain choices as to Time, Space,
dimensional preferences and other unnamable parameters. Some of
these transfers are physical, and some are mental, and some – well,
some transfers entail other kinds and classes of experience that are
beyond my ability even to recall now, much less to explain. But I know
that they are out there, and that for a short time I understood this and
sensed those abilities, and now they are gone and I feel as though I
have been blinded, or worse.

And I further sensed that there are whole spectra of other
Parasenses beyond even these, senses that even I could not experience,
any more than a bacterium can experience the joys of a symphony
orchestra. Let me tell you, there is a whole Universe out there, a Multiverse actually, and we here are like those men in the example of Plato's
cave: our backs are to the true openings of the Other Worlds, and on
our pitiful cave walls we see only the merest shadows, bare glimmerings of what Reality lies beyond the narrow cave opening of our earthly
senses. That old boy had a lot of things wrong, but his cave-shadow
analogy was just about perfect!

And yet we have *Mind*, an integrating sense that enables us to
search for these other senses, and perhaps someday to find them. If
you do, I hope you don't lose them as I did, for the sudden lack is close
to fatal.

These limited descriptions and analogies are about as comprehensive as the attempts to tell that blind man about the whole experience
of *Vision* – it is just not possible. But now also imagine a sighted person
losing all vision, and trying poignantly to recall all of the nuances of a
sunset, of a Monet, of the faces of happy people and the ambience of
pleasant places. Though some of the memory may remain, the natural-
ness, the immersion in another world, all of that is gone.

Now you may know some of what I felt while traversing the grassy
green field in that Other Place, and what I sensed over there, and what
now lies just beyond my own imaginings, and what creates in me a
yearning I never knew I could feel, an emptiness and a longing to
return and be immersed in all those marvelous new senses and new
feelings. And yet, among the yearnings for that Other Place, these new

senses are the least of my desires. For while I was there, I met Another, in Whose Presence all these new senses amounted to less than nothing.

This is how it happened. Of a sudden, one of the myriads of moving bright wisps departed from a vast group, approached closely, then slowed down and stopped right in front of me, taking solid shape as I stood, open-mouthed and afraid. I can't tell you what the shape resolved itself into, only that it can't be described in any human language, although I can never forget every detailed aspect of its appearance. "Giant Humanoid," "man-shaped, larger than man-sized" are the only descriptors that fit, though that is like saying a child's mud-doll is related to a Michelangelo sculpture, or that the Taj Mahal is a "white building," denoting nothing of its majesty. Likewise a beauty, an unbelievable living *essence* instantly permeated my entire self, down to my soul.

This *Being* emanated such an aura of power, of beneficence, of pure *love*, so overwhelming and so intense, that I fell, trembling, sobbing, to my knees. The *Being* looked down at me and reached out an arm and touched the top of my head. The feeling was greater than an electric shock – more of a *cosmic shock* – something that flowed into my brain, my body, a fulfillment I had never known, a *completeness* I was not even aware existed. And a message flowed into me, too: *Don't be afraid. You are not alone. You will understand. Someday, you will know. And you will join me.*

As a blubbering puppy loves its master, so I trembled in absolute awe and love and respect and fear at the physical and emotional touch of that *Being*. All I could say, when I recovered enough to speak through my sobs, was, "Are you God?"

No, came the answer in ways I cannot describe, *I did not create all of this Universe. But I live within it, and it lives within me. As it does within you. You will know, someday. And you will join me.*

And then the touch was gone, and the *Being* became as a vaporous whirlwind, and vanished in the distance, among the wispiness of glowing vapors that flitted here in The Valley. An enormous vacuum encompassed my soul, the absence of a *Presence*, and an emptiness I never knew possible. Shaken to the root of my being, I stayed there on my knees, head down, tears flowing, under the broad new-colored stripes of a strangely banded sky, in a cool place of brilliant green grass.

AND THEN I WAS BACK, BACK IN THE CAVERN, PULLING MY HANDS from the palm prints of the *atiín*. "*My God!*" I burbled through my choking throat, "What was *that*?" Falling backwards against the cave wall, I could barely breathe. I replayed the scene over and over in my mind. And each time, the memory of the *wholeness*, the *purity*, the *majesty*, poured through, followed by the emptiness when the *being* was gone. Like the legendary nicotine addict, I was hooked on what I had felt, and the withdrawal pangs were unlike anything I'd ever felt. How could I live anymore, knowing what I was missing? It was a physical longing, but worse than that, a mental, emotional, spiritual, even a *life-force* longing, because I would gladly have given my life at that moment to stay in such a Presence.

⚜ 8 ⚜

A long, long night followed, in which I tried rationally to explain the encounter with the *Being*, as I now thought of him. An advanced life form, perhaps? Evolved from humankind or on a parallel path, or something ancient? The cynical part of my mind said, "And what if he is the evolutionary equivalent of a beautiful plant, something to draw in the bugs to pollinate it. Or, like a Venus Flytrap, having you over for lunch?" *I don't care*, said the other part of my mind. *For that feeling, I would happily give myself up, even as food.* This battle of mind versus soul kept on until physical and psychic exhaustion caught up with me and took me to sleep.

HOURS LATER, I AWOKE, STILL TREMBLING FROM THE VISION OF Heaven I'd experienced. It must be Heaven, I thought. That is what everybody has always believed in, and I was there. Why didn't I stay? Fighting back the emptiness, the craving, I forced myself to eat more dried fish, which I heated in an overhead tunnel torch flame. I wondered if the opening to "Heaven" was physically accessible somewhere in the darkness of the cavern. If I wanted to, I figured, I could walk with my hand sliding along one wall until I came to another opening. But would it be the correct one? Would it open for me that shimmering surface part for me, if I were not attuned with the *atiín?*

At that moment, still overwhelmed by the fading sensations of my previous journey, I sighed and returned to the *atiín's* bloodied palm prints, and placed my hands down into the texture of another world.

Again, immediately I felt drawn into the stone, then found myself walking down the cavern once more. I smiled; this time I would know what to expect, what to look for, what to appreciate. And more than that, I would find the Being *again and ask him more questions, and hope for that touch of salvation and love.*

Without being aware of traveling, I found myself once more in front of a shimmering screen, and with joy plunged through it.

Into Hell.

This was not The Valley of Heaven, but a noisy, ominous, terrifying place of horrific presence. Yes, the walls of The Valley were in their same places, but the Valley floor was not grass, nor even broken rock and desert, but an evilly-shimmering crusty surface smelling of sulphur, spewing dark, vile gases from the many large cracks that ran from horizon to horizon. *And the sky!*

My God, the sky was a new, unknown color! But a putrid one, as vile as deep purple, and scratched across its dome as though attacked by giant claws, raged mismatched tendrils of other unknown colors, equally sinister. Yet I knew the names of these colors, too: *vyllu, karett, nayt, enuh* – the dark, hideous colors of Hell. This was not a place for human life, this strange, savage, uncaring world.

Fearing for my life and my soul, I turned to escape back through the portal to The Cavern, but enormous dark shapes blocked my way. Instinctively I knew that these shapes were powerful Beings, too, but I did not want them touching me, contaminating my soul, feeding on me. Large, dark insectoid eyes followed my every move, faceted orbs darker than the shadows within their hoods, yet possessing an eerie radiating blackness, as if to suck from me any light, any brightness I may have had. These unsentimental eyes, less caring than those of an earthly insect, looked down on me – *through* me! – from twice my height. I was helpless if they wanted to harm me, but in my panic I placed one foot in front of another, breaking my near-paralysis and moving toward the tunnel entrance in absolute and total fear.

In strange slow motion I passed among these half dozen dark entities, their psychic stench a retching of the soul, the *coldness* of their being enough to chill me in places I had never known existed. In that moment I knew that they were *Absences,* vacuums of existence, polar opposites to the *Presence* I had known in the first journey through the curtain.

Safely back within the tunnel, I ran and ran, weeping at my narrow escape, praying that those Dark Ones could not come through as well. It seemed that I ran on and on for days, maybe years, a small Eternity of mixed fear and relief.

NEXT MORNING, I AWOKE TO THE FAINT SCENT OF LAVENDER, AND A strong smell of pipe smoke. *El Viejo* laughed aloud. "*Amigo*, have some coffee. Looks like you could use some." He pushed a tin cup toward me. A coffeepot sat on the small campfire that crackled at the tunnel entrance, its smoke wafting off in the ventilation system inside.

I was exasperated. Grateful to be away from those horrible *Absences,* irritated that I hadn't been warned of them. Though all I said was, "Hey, old man, show me how to travel the way you do, and I wouldn't have to be trudging in and out of mile-long tunnels, dragging that rock with me." The coffee was exquisite, a blend I hadn't had before. Definitely not the usual commercial crap.

My mentor smiled, slurping his brew. Nodding at the bloody *atún* slab, he laughed again. "Been traveling, have you? Met any interesting people?" I groaned, exaggeratedly at first, and then for real, as the memory of the two encounters hit me full force once more.

"Old One, tell me what that Heaven was, where that was. I have to go back." The emptiness, the lack of that *Presence,* was taking hold, making me tremble in fear. And I couldn't shake the memory of the second place, either. I could only realize that other people, the prophets of old, must have experienced both of these places in the past, and tried to tell the rest of us about it in their religious teachings. I guess, at least since I was an adult, I had never thought of either place as *real.* But, oh God, real they were, and even more real than our own world.

"Just another place, *amigo*, one of many *places.*" He smiled. "You did go to more than one, no?" At my shudder he remarked, "I thought so. Usually happens in twos. Sometimes a good place is first, sometimes it's last."

"Why were these visits so different?" I had to make sense of the experiences, and I was sure that *El Viejo* would know, if I could ever get him to tell me directly. "Those two places weren't like those visions of the past couple of days, where I experienced somebody else's life. These both happened to *me*. And I want to, no I *have to,* go back to that good place."

"Not yet, my friend. Not until..."

I was sitting up now, the coffee cup trembling in my shaking hand. "Why not? I want to be with that *Being,* he was unlike anything I've ever known." I suppressed the thought, *and so were those dark ones.*

The old man held up his left hand, waving it about. "Other people have had such meetings, such encounters, and have told about them, written about them. They lived without going back, and so will you." He puffed that lavender tobacco. "Some of their stories, you know, they changed the world. Maybe yours will too." It was a question, not a statement of faith.

I groaned. "I know I will live, but God, *Viejo*, knowing that such a place and such a Being exist, I don't know if I can bear not going back." *And please, tell me how I can avoid returning to the dark place!*

El Viejo said, "Did one there not tell you that you would join him some day?" I nodded. "And did he not say that you would also understand?" Again, I nodded.

"So, why do you fret so? In good time you will understand, and you will join that Being and others, of your own accord, as equals."

"Equals? *Me*, like *that*?"

"It will be so, *amigo*. In ways you can't imagine. Patience."

I knew I was not going to get the step-by-rational-step explanation I wanted; the old man never gave me such a Royal Road, *uno Camino Real*, as he had said. "So, tell me what I need to know, so that I can get started on that path right away." Vividly, the glowing dream returned to my vision; but this time I held it back. The nightmare of the Dark Place balanced it quite well. Maybe it was better for me to stay in this world, at least until I learned to control where I was going to wind up!

This session with my guide, *El Viejo*, was going to be a long, strange journey, I knew. "Start with the *atíin*, old man. What in the hell happened when I put my hands there?"

"*Amigo*, blood on the *atíin* triggers a physical translation to other times and places. That place you loved so much, and others like it, have existed for untold ages. Your own blood, on the palms of the *atíin*, and your palms there, too – how much clearer could the message be?" That ancient head swung slowly, side to side. "A message to last through all time, to be understood for all time: *Put your hands here!* Regardless of the language or the culture that found it. If they still had hands, they would be men! With blood!"

"*Viejo*," I choked on the realization, "you mean that ancient blood rites to propitiate the gods could have started with something like this?"

He swallowed the last bit of coffee and set the cup aside. "Mankind ever finds ways to generate horror where there is first hope. Look at your world's great religions. The wars they fought, when most all first preached peace. The hatred practiced, when most all taught love. Many religions eventually recognized the power of blood rites, but most of them wrongly. It was one's *own* blood essence, not that of others, that takes them to other worlds, to see the truth." A great sadness welled up in him, and I could see it take hold of his facial muscles, though he never cried. I could never imagine *El Viejo* crying, though the look on his face was worse.

"Such a sad path they took, using the blood of others, the blood of innocents, when all the time the power was in their own hands. Literally."

His far stare meant he was not to be interrupted. We both sat in silence for long minutes. Finally I spoke up, "Is it a DNA kind of thing, then, that interacts with some technology in the *atiín* stone, is that why the sensations were so powerful compared to the water I used at the Pool of Life?" *And why, oh why, did I ever go to that Dark Place?*

My mysterious friend lit up his long pipe. Again, that faint scent of lavender – I wanted to ask him about his tobacco but didn't get the chance. "You, my friend, want a technological answer because you are from a technological society – you have a hammer, technology, so every problem looks like a nail, needing a technological solution. I have to tell you, *amigo*, and you have to understand this – there are other ways of knowing, other ways of, of, *constructing* such a thing as this *atiín*, such a place as this cavern – and other people in other times had their other ways to do this. And some still do, even today."

I was fascinated but increasingly frustrated by his usual style of answering with enigmatic allusions. "I don't have to go into the advances we've made using the science and technology all around us, *amigo El Viejo*. I wouldn't've come to this Valley without my SUV and radio and recorder and smartphone and tablet computer and binocs. Not to mention all of the medicines I've used over the years to save and prolong my life."

El Viejo shrugged. "Then the nearest I could come to explaining it to you would be for you to immerse yourself in the latest theories of physics, and even they might be inadequate to what you have witnessed here in The Valley. Do not even your own scientists postulate other worlds that overlay this one, shadow worlds of another eleven dimensions? Or twenty-six? Maybe an infinite number? Even complete other universes where other possibilities have real existence, and where the probabilities of *this* world never happened?

"And so, occasionally in human history – *this* history, *this* world – other people made their ways to this place and other places like it around the world, and they found a way out, or a way over, to the next world. You saw a glimpse of two of those worlds today, the one that you loved so deeply, the one that disturbed you so much."

"Yes, it did," I answered. "Strange webs crisscrossing the sky, and colors I did not recognize, and impossible shapes that my eyes would not see. And the feeling I got from that Being. So many things I didn't understand." *But I don't want to know any more about the Dark Place, except how to stay away from it!*

El Viejo smiled. "So you could not even grasp the meaning of things you saw, and felt and touched? The evidence of your own senses? You were over there, and you did not understand. And yet, now you want me to give you concrete scientific answers that lie within your understanding, limited as you admit it is."

"I think you want me to believe that this *atiín*, and these carvings," I waved toward the constellations of hieroglyphics all around us, "are gateways to other worlds?"

He nodded. "And to other times. And to other *possibilities*, as well."

"How could that be? These are the scribblings of stone age peoples."

"You are sure, my friend? You are content to believe that what you have experienced, even your own rejuvenation, that these are simple primitive things your own science and philosophy can explain, can replicate, can utilize? If they can, then you take me to where I can experience all that you have experienced here. Where would that be? Over in Los Alamos, not far away? I don't think so." He grinned. "Up in New York City? Not in your wildest dreams. You cannot, I tell you, because your society and your science have not traveled this way, the way that this Valley shows you.

"I will tell the scientific part of your mind this: there are energies stored in these stones, in these carvings, in that *atiín* you have carried so far. These energies enable a person who is, is *attuned*, to access certain *other* energies and thus be made aware of – but not always *transported* to! – other realities that exist in TimeSpace itself, in the multiple infinities that we can comprehend.

"It is as if the consciousness that you now think of as yourself is actually just one 'solution' to an infinite equation, and that the real you, the 'oversoul' if you like, the Universal You, is the true sentient being, and the *you-here-now* is just one small cell of that Universal Being. The *atiín* and other gateways merely allow you to sense those other 'you's' in those other places and those other times and other possibilities."

I was somewhat prepared for his exposition. "So I was a pre-human when all of this was on the edge of a sea?" He nodded. "And some kind of Atlantean refugee when my escaping people came this way? And I will be one of those future people out there, too, with the weird skywebs and all that? And I am also in alternate possible worlds, with alien beings and other histories?" *Please tell me that I am not in that Dark Place, not in any form, not any part of me!*

"Yes, you are in all those places, *amigo*, all those and more. And there are other realities beyond all these, realities that even I have not experienced." The pipe's bowl ebbed down to a glowing ash; he emptied it into the fire. "I would not be surprised if some kind of existence extends both outward and inward, for infinity in all directions."

THE NEXT FEW HOURS, THE REST OF THAT ENTIRE DAY, EL VIEJO AND I spent in deep conversation, as if he were a counselor attempting to bring a drug addict through a particularly rough withdrawal sequence; *cold turkey* would be the appropriate phrase for it. Which, in many respects, was exactly the truth. Some of the topics, as before, were so intensely personal that it would not be helpful to anybody else for me to discuss them here, as they would have little or no influence on my story of my adventure in The Valley, of what I learned there, what I became there.

But sometime during the evening, some interactions truly relevant to the universal human condition did arise. I asked my wise friend, "I wonder sometimes, if I couldn't have learned some of these life's lessons elsewhere, in some other way. Maybe in one of the *ashrams* I used to frequent, or from a book, or at one of the holy sites or churches or temples I've been to." I yawned in exhaustion, stretching.

"I mean, is my enlightenment only to be found here in The Valley, amidst all of these weird tunnels and caverns and parallel worlds?"

He was silent for quite a long time, an unusual length of pause even for *El Viejo*. "You misunderstand, *amigo*. You were not brought here solely for your own need for enlightenment and understanding. You came for the needs of The Valley!

"You were chosen by the forces in this Valley in some mysterious manner that even I do not comprehend – as you said, perhaps a match of DNA? Of life experiences? Genetic necessity? Other factors that are unknown, even unknowable, to us? – to bring something to The Valley, and to leave something here. And perhaps take something away?" He shrugged. "How am I to know what it was you brought? I have been in and out of this world and many others for thousands of years, yet all I can tell you is that I cannot express in human words what took place in your selection or your, your, call it – *education*."

At this point, I had to jump in. "*Thousands of years?* You have lived this long, and traveled among the worlds, and you're still a –" I couldn't find the words. But *El Viejo* just smiled again.

"Still a poor old man, a peddler of jewelry? Is that what you wanted to say, *amigo*?" Ashamed, I nodded. "Then, what would you have me be?"

I thought for a while. "Look, why aren't you one of the world's great religious leaders? Or one of the wealthiest people? You could own a whole continent by now." The possibilities swirled in my imagination. "*Viejo*, you ought to be a political power, a world-renowned scholar –"

He cut me off with a hand gesture. "Little one, when you were a child, you dreamed of eating all the ice cream and candy you could get your hands on. But when you finally became a man, did you immediately go out and eat all that ice cream and candy? Did you purchase all of those childish toys you always wanted but never had?" Shaking his head, he murmured, "These things you speak of – money, power, fame – what makes you think they are desirable to ones such as we have become? Compared to what you have experienced, compared to what you now *know*, those things are just the same as those dreams of ice cream and toys." His arms opened into a wide span, taking in the cavern and the outside world and the infinity of other universes. "Why limit yourself to playthings," he asked, "when you can have all of *this?*"

Chastened, I sat silent among my thoughts. He was right, of course, but I still would have enjoyed some of those wildly materialistic perqs, the worldwide fame, the respect of billions, for at least a little while, before I totally matured into the realities of the Multiverse. I smiled inwardly; maybe one could be the equivalent of a teenager in this arena for a few centuries first? I didn't dare propose any such thing to *El Viejo*, of course.

El Viejo caught my impish intention, ignored it with raised eyebrows, and continued along his chosen path of revelation. "Suffice it to say, as I have said before – *reality is much broader than you have been taught.* For example, this civilization is not the first one on this world, and it will not be the last. Understanding reality is the key to enabling you to become something much greater, in that you will become aware of what you already are. This in itself will give you abilities that you will not comprehend any more than you can comprehend why you are already able to create new art, new poetry, new music, new stories, new ideas. You will just be able to use the new talents in the same way.

"These new abilities will manifest themselves in you, for your use, once you understand that you already have them, just as sports training releases new powers in the men and women who bring them out from within. I stress, *Recognize these talents within yourself, let them surface when you need them – and they will always be with you.* They are much more valuable than political power, or fame, or wealth. These latter things, they can be hindrances. Many of the philosophers and prophets have recognized this, and said as much.

"As you once heard in that Mexican bar down in *Ciudad Juarez,* 'Ace, don't sweat the small stuff!'" He smiled at my shocked reaction to that statement. How had he known about that confrontation with an attempted pickpocket, something that could have led to violence, had not my friend interceded? He evidently had some kind of overview of the threads of my life in some manner, through some faculty. I wanted to ask him how to do that kind of investigation, but never got the chance. I figured it must be one of those powers that you pick up as you mature into the true knowledge of reality. I am looking forward to that particular power. I think.

In spite of my obvious introspection, *El Viejo* went on without a pause. "In the extreme circumstances you have experienced in The Valley here, you have been shown, a step at a time, that you are more than you knew you were when you first came. Already you are more than you were; already you know more than you did. Already you can do more than you could. The encounters with *Coyote*, the wounds and the bleeding, the blood and the visions, the encounters with the other worlds, they were all necessary steps in your self-realization." He puffed a small cloud of smoke chuckling. "Like your first exercises in a gym, when you exercise dormant muscles, you feel a little pain. The same thing applies here, too."

He saw my grimace, as I thought of the blood rites of the Aztecs, the Phoenicians, the Roman crucifixions, and the bloody perversions found in other ancient religions like the Celtic and pagan. "Yes, friend, others have sometimes misunderstood the power of human blood and suffering. Many have shed much blood in vain, sacrificed for naught, but only a Few have known the true power and have used it well and properly." I let those thoughts go. I was on my own path here, and if I trod in holy footsteps that had preceded me, I was very proud to be walking such a way, particularly if I knew where truth and error lay, even if the journey caused me physical pain. I could even understand, now, how bloody evils had been perpetrated by well-intentioned people, though I could not forgive them.

"Look, *amigo*," *El Viejo* continued, his eyes focused on something beyond this world, "to be excellent in sports, you train and train and train your body, right?"

"Of course."

"And to achieve intellectual greatness, the mind must be trained and trained and trained, right? Not many people get there without learning from others, but most any mind can be trained far better than just being left to itself to be educated by trial and error."

"Too obvious, my old friend. What's the point?" I knew some response was called for, but could not always tell which way the old man's zen-like parables would go.

"Well, what you call your spiritual side, your psychic talents, they must be exercised again and again, too. Even more, since you have not been using them much at all, and they have atrophied over the years."

"Psychic exercise? That's what this Valley is for?"

The old man closed his eyes and sighed. "No more than the Earth was put here for showing your athletic prowess, no more than the mysteries of the Universe were created for your amusement. No, friend, the Valley *is* – it exists. It is a place. It is a, a *crux of creation*, a place where *glory* resides, a conglomeration of powers. Just as the fresh water spring does not exist for your purpose, nonetheless it is of great value and possesses properties that are life-giving – if approached properly. You know, you can also drown in a spring. Or find one that is contaminated and dangerous. You must always be careful. That is why a guide is necessary. That is why I am here."

I couldn't hold back my trauma: "But you let me get shot! And beaten! I could have died out there! And you could have told me about the experiences I was going to have – any preparation at all would have helped, old man! And I was scared to death in those other universes, if that's what they were. I mean, non-human creatures, looking at me like I was a *bug*, for God's sake!"

"You read too much meaning into what you think are looks, *amigo*. You have no idea what they were sensing about you, no more than an ant has any idea of a human scholar's abstract philosophical arguments. You have to understand – *Mankind is not the measure of the Universe.* We, you and I, we have our place in this Universe, and in other Universes of the Multiverse, but there are beings as far beyond our understanding as we think we are above the ants on the ground."

I had heard that argument before, and didn't believe it even then. "But we know we are sentient, we know that the others are intelligent. And we can try to talk with any one, any thing; that gives us a chance that the ants don't have."

"You are sure, are you? And how would you communicate with a willing ant on the ground here? All he knows about communication are chemical compound traces and some ultrasonic chittering. You could tell him about religion? Politics? Technology? Even if he could somehow desire to know, and to let you know that he was willing?

I remembered my own arguments about the Country of the Blind, when making my notes about the encounter with the Being in the Other Place. *El Viejo* was right, of course. The realizations just had not sunk into my consciousness long enough to ripen.

"By comparison, *anglito,* I think we are like willing ants for that wise one who looked at you. And even he could not distill his thoughts, his actions, into anything we could recognize or comprehend. Just the barest suggestion of his infinite intellect could ever make it through the gulf between the species. And you felt it, as love and caring on a scale incomprehensible to you."

"Maybe a few observations, or rules, *have* made it through from his side to ours, *Viejo?* Such as 'love one another as yourself'?"

"*Si´*, and 'With God all things are possible.'" The old man stood and dusted himself off. "Many prophets and sons of God have witnessed the similar Greatness, but all they could tell us were a few simple rules, commandments. They are true statements in themselves, and should be followed, but they give us only basic hints on how the Universe works. For example, that the so-called moral rules are as real as everything else."

"But are they?" I objected, as much to keep my mentor from leaving as for sake of argument. I didn't want to spend more time here alone, not with this source of wisdom close by – however tangential his reasoning. "Surely the laws of physics can be demonstrated and repeated, but the religious laws can't."

El Viejo continued to brush the dust of the cavern floor off his dirty white pants. "You have already forgotten the Other Places, the other worlds? Until you recognize that you are a multidimensional being existing in an infinite number of other places and times simultaneously, until you truly understand to the depths of your consciousness what your subconscious already knows, then you cannot possibly realize that these moral laws indeed do have immediate consequences up and down and across your spectrum of existence.

"The Universal You can be visualized, poorly I admit, like this: imagine another '*you*' to your left, and one to his left, and so on to infinity. Then imagine that same sequence of *you*'s to the right, and then to the front, and then to the rear, and then above you, and then below you, and then radiating out at every conceivable angle, until you are at the focus, the central node, of a cosmic dandelion – then add in the many separate dimensions of Time and all of the other dimensions of TimeSpace, and they all sum up to You. It is even more complex than that, but this will have to do as a beginning."

I sat back down. Yes, I had seen that myriad-branched structure of Me-ness in the visions or actual experiences, if that's what they were. "But along those, those, lines of Other-Me's, they gradually morphed into other creatures, things that couldn't be Me." *El Viejo* just stared, silently. "Oh," I said in sudden realization, "those are so far away from me that I am no longer their main component?"

He nodded. "And this You that is right here, right now, is a part of them. And a part of others. There are other intersections as well, where many other components meet, and form other beings." His pipesmoke traced trajectories as he waved his hand about, attempting to describe the indescribable. "Relationships exist for which humankind has no concepts, much less names. We ourselves are the intersections of other phases of existence of other beings, and so it goes, an infinite web of intricate complexities.

"And yet, arising from all of this, though we are parts of something greater, you and I are also individual souls of *The All,* a part of the Truth.

"And arising from this universal web of Truth and oceans of existence, mankind perceives 'voices', 'visions', apparitions, hallucinations, delusions, channeling, all of the psychic powers you have heard of."

"And teleportation–*apportation?*"

"With training – *exercise*, we have called it – you are able to access these other actual physical dimensions consciously, physically, to coexist with your other self there for an instant, and then bodily apport back from that other dimension to this one, but displaced physically."

That one floored me – a rational explanation for an impossibility! A way to teleport without crossing intervening distances, without violating any laws of physics.

"And with more – *exercise* – you may be able to access the temporal space of another part of You."

"You mean, visit the past?"

"Or the future. Or even sideways, into those parallel worlds you visited, places with different histories. What is real in one world, may not be real in another."

I was stunned, floored. I waved my hand around us, indicating the caverns, and said, "The mesas outside, the vast expanse of The Valley? All this is not real? I can't accept that. I believe this Valley was here before Man and will be here after Man is gone."

El Viejo took another puff. "Ah, Western Anglo. The Multiverse does not rotate around this particular timeline, no matter how real all of this seems. Other places are just as real in every sense. But they are no more centered on this place, around this particular TimeSpace, than the stars up there rotate around this Earth, though our senses tell us that they do.

"When you apport through the other components of existence that are parts of You, each place you arrive at is real in every sense, as real as this one. And each Universe you share during your travels has its physical laws and its psychic laws, very much like the ones here." His face disappeared in a cloud of pipe smoke. "Those distant ones you saw, the ones that scared you so badly, those are places where our laws have changed enough to make a noticeable difference."

"And so there I see Beings who live in a different plane, colors that don't exist here, music and sounds and smells and other senses outside our normal existence?"

"Sure, *amigo*," he said softly, grinning. "Where do you think all those artists and writers get their crazy ideas?"

"YES," THE OLD MAN SAID LATER, "SOME PEOPLES IN THE PAST, OUR past, came into the cavern and found their way out to other worlds. Some of the truly ancient ones, many of the Aztlan, a number of the Anasazi. Many of them, in fact."

"Why wouldn't they leave records so everybody could come over?

He snorted and choked on his smoke. "Think of the absurdity of what you just said, my man. And then remember the hieroglyphics all over this cavern. Someone left most of the story here, if you could but read it."

"But I mean, what a great gift to humanity, other worlds to explore, other places..."

El Viejo cut me off. "Anglo, this place was a new world to Europeans lately, and to others millennia before that. Many people came looking for wealth – gold, slaves, agriculture – or to convert the heathen. Exactly zero of your ancestors came over to live with the aboriginals and learn their ways. Well, maybe in the early years, perhaps a few.

"Not that your people were any worse than mine. Like all humans all through history, we fought and killed and enslaved and plundered, even had cannibals like every other primitive human society. It's just that we kept almost no written records of these thousand-year wars, and anyhow the world doesn't pay much attention to the campfire tales of old Indians.

"So why should one group of people, who want to escape privation and oppression from their own or other races, why should they open the golden gates to the ones who could come and harm them?

"So that a few wise enough could follow, just a few, they set up mazes and traps and puzzles in a few obscure places where the *atiín* doorways are easiest to access. They, or someone, wanted those few wise ones to search, to understand and to find. You have been one of those, and one of the successful ones."

He laughed. "Can you imagine a troop of Conquistadores tromping down that tunnel? Or old-time cowboy outlaws? Or a bunch of drunken college kids?"

Actually, I replied, I could very well imagine just those scenarios. "Or maybe a scientific expedition of archaeologists and anthropologists?"

"Even worse!" he laughed out loud, turning to throw more wood on the fire. The sudden aroma of burnt cedar was a welcome contrast to his lavender tobacco. "Well, not one of those kinds has ever made it through here." That enigmatic smile again. "We keep it well hidden, don't you think?"

"Hell, I had a hard enough time getting to The Valley and into this cavern as it was. Without the messages, the disappearing service station, all the clues, I would have never known to search for this place, much less drag a three-hundred-pound slab all this way."

SOMETIME DURING THAT DAY IN THE DARKNESS OF THE CAVERN, MY exhaustion caught up with me once more and I slept, my dreams alternating between Heaven and Hell. I realized in that dream-world that our present Earth was somewhere in between.

When I awoke, I was alone again, as usual, though this time the lavender aroma was still fresh and strong. I washed with water from the Spring of Rejuvenation, trusting that I would not keep on getting younger and revert to my physical childhood. But apparently the treatment only worked when it was needed; maybe only one 'inoculation' per decade would take? I just knew that I wanted to come back here again, some day in the future before aches and pains and wrinkles and infirmities once again limited my life. With another blind fish in my stomach and several more in my sack, I felt prepared for whatever might come.

I never did discover any way to bring up the illumination of the rest of the cavern, and I didn't want to trust my remaining torches to potentially hazardous explorations of other tunnel entrances, especially given my recent experiences. So either the ancient illumination system was in disrepair or was denied to me for some reason I didn't understand. In either case, it would be suicide to try to explore beyond the range of my torches without knowing if there were an exit back to The Valley, so I decided, reluctantly, to re-trace my steps back through the original tunnel and take my chances outside. Besides, I was anxious to see the old familiar blue skies of Earth – assuming I wasn't now in one of *El Viejo's* accidental alternate worlds.

With my renewed body and abundant energy, the return trip went quickly and uneventfully, the gaslights turning off behind me as I went. How did this system know I was leaving, and how could it extinguish the jets, pair by pair, as I departed? It was an interesting engineering problem, but one that paled in significance compared to the wonders of that cave stream and those unimaginable statues and carvings, and the dreams, the visions, or the actual parallel worlds I had visited!

Several hours later found me back at the cave entrance where this stage of the adventure had started. I rested my *travois* load against the cave wall, and checked my digital camera to ensure that the hundreds of images were still there, still physically recorded and not merely psychical recollections. To my relief, the display screen played them back, tiny representations of incredible wonders of workmanship and ancient mysteries. Too bad I hadn't taken it to those other worlds; I wondered how those strange new colors would have shown up. Even now, in my memory, I cannot quite recall their different beauty. And I would have liked to had any kind of photo of the wonderful *Presence* that so changed me. On the other hand, I certainly did not want to have any images of those *Absences* I'd encountered in the Dark World.

I had filled several digital memory cards by this time, amounting to some five hundred pictures, going all the way back to that first night at the Santa Fe Plaza. I was surprised that *El Viejo* himself showed up in several of the pictures; I still didn't know if he were just some phantom of my imagination, or an apparition from another world. Whatever he was, and whatever this place was, these pictures would form the basis of a great photographic essay book. The rest of the world would know what I'd seen, and maybe greater minds than mine could explain it all. My tablet computer's wireless link stayed dead, though – *no wi fi in The Valley!* –and that was a pity. It was just too bad I couldn't use it or my smartphone or something to let me send all these images out to the world immediately, and to distribute real-time streaming reports on my unbelievable experiences.

Outside, to my relief, The Valley was still *my* Valley – broken rocks, sparse bushes on a sandy desert, the Mars-like landscape so dear to my memory, now laced with the moist desert fragrance that said the annual monsoon rains had visited The Valley sometime in the last few hours.

And with Earth-type, human-adapted colors, though now draped in semi-darkness, a bright crescent moon rising over the eastern mesa. The desert was unusually silent this night; I had no idea of the time, or even the day. None of my digital equipment had worked since I'd left the highway, days before, en route to the mesa that led to this Valley.

Knowing that I had several more miles northward to carry the *atiín*, I decided to continue on that night while the darkness provided me with cover, the mooncast lighting up the cliff wall just enough for me to go on in safety. Surely by now *Coyote* and his buddy must have given up the chase and walked back home. Since I'd stayed in the Cavern at least three or four days, by my recollection, and since hotheaded punks usually wanted immediate gratification of their violent impulses, they should have been frustrated a long time ago. Or so I hoped.

As I moved northward, staying close to the cliff, I found myself being a lot noisier than I liked. The *travois* legs *skritched* incessantly, and in the semi-darkness I frequently stumbled over small rocks or stepped down into erosion channels cut into the sandstone base. I ventured further out into the desert floor where I reduced the sound of my passage, at the expense of softer soil that increased the friction of the legs of the carrying apparatus. In a way, my little bit of noise was a warning for the critters of the night to get out of the way, and this was good for me and for any rattlesnakes nearby. In this less than satisfactory mode I was able to travel a mile or more before the eastern sky glowed pale azure.

Up against the comparative safety of the cliff wall, amid a collection of large boulders, I quietly cleared out an area of small rocks, swept it quickly with my flashlight to check for other critterly occupants, then took refuge from the oncoming sun. Sleep was easy, and this time, thankfully, dreamless.

9

A wakening a few hours later, judging from the sun's position I estimated the time to be around 9 AM. The campsite was still deep in shadow, the boulders shielding me from a direct line of sight from the top of the mesa. Not that I really expected any more trouble from there. I nibbled on cold fish and drank deeply of the canteen of water from the Place of Life. I thought it strange that taking the water internally didn't have the rejuvenating effect of a bath in it, but that would have to remain one of the mysteries of the Valley until somebody told me or I was able to comprehend it myself. "Just chalk it up to magic," I chuckled, remembering Clarke's famous phrase about technology and magic. Based on what all had been happening in The Valley, though, I now truly believed in "sufficiently advanced magic."

I rested several hours, jotting down more notes in my rapidly-filling notepad. (I didn't trust the tablet computer enough, in this weird place, to keep all my notes just yet.) What had I learned, or more precisely, what did I *think* I had learned, so far? Apart from the fantastic experiences in the parallel worlds, aside from the deeply-held philosophies of *The All* that *El Viejo* insisted were the Truth of the Universe, all I could prove to anybody else was what was on the digital photos. That, and of course how my own middle-aged body was suddenly a lot younger than it had been, my scars and wrinkles and circumcision gone. Would that evidence stand up to scrutiny? I was sure my friends and family would attest to a change, but would even the testimony of my physician be enough to prove my unbelievable story? I wasn't sure.

And the photographs? I could hear it now: "Computer trickery! There is no way any advanced ancient civilization ever existed in northern New Mexico, so all your so-called 'photographs' have to be fakes! They aren't even on real film, so they were easily faked by computer!" And if I asked anybody to read the markings, if they could, the answers would be, "Well, obviously whoever made these up didn't know the proper grammatical forms of Egyptian Old Kingdom writing, so they are all-too-evident forgeries!"

No matter how I tried to argue with myself, I knew it would be worthless to try to publish anything in the professional archaeological journals. The best I could do would be to publish the pictures and my story in one of the numberless small presses and hope to find a sympathetic hearing, maybe eventually touching one professional archaeologist or anthropologist out there who would believe and who could help. Though I was not certain that I could ever find the road that would bring me back in here – assuming I would ever get out.

As the day wore on, I scouted up the Valley about half a mile, looking for an easy way to drag the *atiín*, leaving behind that precious cargo behind for the moment, safely stowed under brush and rocks. I didn't see or hear anything from the cliff tops so concluded that the hoodlums had gone away for good. But before acting on that supposition and making myself a target again, I wanted to locate a secure place to run to and hide if I were wrong.

No other caves presented themselves, but another *arroyo*, formed by runoff from a cleft in the cliff, revealed a spring-fed pool and a formation of whitish sedimentary stone of the same variety as that at Algona's Pool of Life. I felt relieved at finding water again; the canteen could only hold a day's worth, even if I rationed myself strictly. Moreover, the twists and turns of the *arroyo* substantially hid the pool from line of sight from the top of the mesa, so it was about as safe as I could get if attacked from up there. It was only a few hundred yards from the base of the cliff wall, so it would not be much of a detour. Certainly not the miles I had walked to and fro in the tunnel and the Cavern inside that mesa. "But who's complaining?" I whispered to myself, looking at my young skin, feeling young strength in my entire body. Offhandedly, I wondered how long the rejuvenation would last. Funny, but that was the first time I'd considered that eventuality, the possibility that the effects might wear off. But Narsensi's words reassured me and I felt I'd added another twenty years or more to my life. If I were fortunate, like *El Viejo*, maybe I would be able to add thousands of years to it. Maybe.

By mid-afternoon I had retrieved the *travois* from its hiding place, returning to the *arroyo* and the spring just as evening shadows darkened the area. This was all for the good, I thought; darkness was my friend that day. I sincerely wanted to make a fire and heat up the wrapped fish but there was still the possibility of attracting unwanted attention if the bad guys were still around. An unsettling thought hit me: what if, in the days I had been gone, they had come down to the Valley floor itself, looking for me, waiting to ambush me? Could that have happened? No, I argued, those guys probably didn't even prepare minimally for this trip, certainly not to the extent I had. Or had they? If they were the original thieves of the *atiín*, surely they knew what they would be getting into when they returned. Wouldn't they?

I shook off the thought. Prudent precautions are one thing, but paranoia leads to panic. Making sure that the immediate vicinity was indeed vacant of bad guys and other predators, I was able to hole up in a convenient cleft in the rocks, the *travois* load acting as a protective shield in front of me, covered with brush. With any luck, any human passersby would not notice me in my hidey-hole. After a less than satisfying meal of cold fish, I laid back to get some sleep, hoping to awaken during the night and continue further northward. But a torrent of thoughts, of feelings, of expectations, raged through my mind and sleep wouldn't come. What was the true meaning of The Valley and of all the sights I had seen and events I had experienced? I pondered these over and over again.

Intellectual deliberation didn't seem to be leading me anywhere except deeper into an unknown mental maze, so I figured it was time to access the more mysterious means of knowledge available here in The Valley. Sighing, I began to meditate the way *El Viejo* had shown me, waiting for an answer, praying for more guidance.

In the darkness, in my tired mind, finally a vision came.

It has been a long journey, but we have survived. Far from our beloved homeland, away from the cataclysms that destroyed our homes, we have arrived at this beautiful valley, where we will stop awhile and rest.

The dragon-prowed boats, the flying bags of silk and cotton, the copper-hued temples, now all gone, perhaps to be found once more by others, perhaps not. My only concern now is to survive, help my people survive, help our ways survive. But I suspect that our old ways may not propitiate the gods of this new land. We will have to explore this new land, uncover the new gods, discover these new ways that will let us live here with respect for the new places we have come to find.

We have traveled over endless seas, over vast lands, into darkened forests and desolate flatlands, over snow-capped mountains, now into this Valley. We find ourselves strangers from a strange land. We have made our way here, carrying the few treasures remaining of our civilization. Vividly I recall details of the journey, some triumphant, some very sad. My vision lifted, quickly carrying me across the years, the centuries, that followed. *Members of some of the clans, along the way, stayed with the native tribes they encountered, stopping out of weariness, or out of love and friendship, or of desire to assist backward peoples.*

These lost clansmen often became shamans and healers, their legacy yet to be uncovered and understood, still lost in vast caves and mute stone constructions throughout the vast northern continent that would one day be called North America by other explorers. The ones who came here became, eventually, the predecessors of the Anasazi, and remnants of their thought, their religion, are embodied in the very landscape.

They carved mountaintops and moved rocks, creating high mounds of earth,, revealing the alignments of the moon and stars; they laid out their mysteries in vastly long roads, the remains of a few still evident in the much-newer constructions built over them at Chaco Canyon and in a hundred hidden canyons, caves and arroyos throughout this region. These ancient ones found and marked the secret places of the lion, surveyed the energy flows, tapped in to the sources of Earthpowers, attempting to undo their own mistakes and to help others avoid them. Eventually some of them found the true meaning of The Valley, finally taking their peoples and departing into the myriads of worlds accessible through the curtained tunnels of the Cavern.

The vision was fading now, and becoming half-awake in that dreamy state, I reflected on what I had seen. Worldwide, legends persist to this day of peoples emerging from a lower world, or returning to one. Were these ancient ones here in The Valley a people who had escaped from other worlds into this one? The thought chilled me. Yet, *El Viejo* claimed that each of those other places, those other possibilities, was just as real as our own, and that some of us flitted between them unconsciously, like a butterfly winging from one flower to another, never realizing that each bloom was a world unto itself, rooted to one place only, while the butterfly was free to roam as it wills, touching first this bloom, then that world, then that flower, another time, another world, another history, another manifestation of *The All.* The butterfly, unknowing, lives in a broader existence, where rooted worlds, though beautiful and productive in themselves, remain forever doomed to experience only one location, one reality, one existence.

Whence does a butterfly alight, and brush its wings in innocence?

Other legacies of these early peoples are so subtle, so evanescent, that few Indians and no white men even know of their existence. An anomalous artifact, the occasional screw found in a fifty-million-year-old coal deposit, the very large or very small skeletal remains, all are easily dismissed by professionals who, like Galileo's critics, refuse to "look into the telescope." What they already know is not there, cannot be there, so they simply will not look. It will take a series of discoveries, and a willing cadre of young archaeologists and other scientists, to overturn the present paradigm and restore the knowledge of our true origins to the world at large.

Wispy remnants of the vision persisted, echoing in my memory. *Others have gone other ways – some said they would find a safe place and from there come and map the world again, discover its new configuration, find us and unite us all again. But, because so many perished when the Gods struck, I do not know if we will ever replenish the Earth.*

All I can do is work to provide food and safety, to write of what knowledge remains, and to tell stories of our journey for our children to hear.

FULLY AWAKE, HAVING TAKEN CARE OF NATURE'S NEEDS, I harnessed myself up to the *travois* and headed northward under the midday sun, searching for the landmarks that would locate the final resting place for the stone slab that had changed my life. I knew that my destination was the far northern end of The Valley, where the two mesas converged; there, a thousand foot high cliff bore the ragged wound from where the *atiín* was torn.

I tromped for hours, one foot in front of the other, dragging my increasingly heavy burden along wide swaths of barren flat whitish rock, into narrow *arroyos* I could barely wedge myself and my load through, and finally along the very foot of the layer-cake cliffs. Nervously, I kept a look out and upward for my nemesis, *Coyote*, and his weapon-toting pal, Tall Guy. *The idiots who shot me!* I recalled grimly. *Yet without that blood, I would never have traveled to – to those Other Places.* Given the choice back then, I would have opted not to be shot. But with the knowledge I now had, I had to admit that the pain had been worth the price of admission. I smiled to myself. On the other hand, how about something civilized, like a simple finger prick for a blood test? Wouldn't that have worked just as well? Something told me that the way the blood was delivered might have been a factor in the transitions as well. Maybe extra adrenaline, too? Some other blood chemicals released by pure panic and fear? I knew that I would never get around to testing these hypotheses. Once was more than enough! This soliloquy did remind me, however, to wipe my dried blood off the *atiín* after I had put it back into its location. Who knows what would happen if somebody else tried to take a trip to the Other Places with my DNA? I just didn't want to know.

Wham! Something large thudded just feet behind me, barely missing the *travois*, and rolled down the slight rise to my right. "What the Hell?" I screamed out, spinning around to see a head-sized boulder bumping its way down the vertical cliff. Immediately I looked up, and there at the edge of the cliff wall, saw two silhouettes throwing things down at me! Cursing, I ran away from the cliff, toward a jumble of large rocks that had separated from the cliff and fallen centuries ago. With *thuds* all around me, I took shelter in an overhang amidst tall boulders where I hoped the hoodlums couldn't reach me with their stones. I was in a veritable forest of jagged rocks, smooth stones and compacted soil, the occasional juniper bush jutting precariously in defiance of its lifeless surroundings.

"*Cabrón!*" the wind carried their angry voices, "We see you down there, and we're coming after your *pinche* butt! See you soon!" Daring to peek around the edge of my protective rock fortress, I saw them each toss a final boulder in my direction and then disappear from view. Their missiles missed me by several feet, but either one of the fist-sized rocks could have killed me easily, or injured me severely if I were less lucky.

After getting over the surprise and shock of the attack, I was puzzled. Had these two been hanging around The Valley for almost a week now, just to get at me? Did the *atiín* mean that much to them? How much did they expect to sell it for anyhow? I didn't think the Santa Fe solstice festival booth would have been the optimum venue for disposing of such a valuable artifact. But what did I know? Just that I was not going to let them get it again. The thought surfaced, *What's to keep them from taking it out again, after I have returned it?* I knew that such vandalism could not be allowed to happen again, not this lifetime. In any event, all I could do was what I could do. I felt certain The Valley could take care of its own, and I was certainly one of its own by now, if anybody was.

Breathing deeply, I was grateful not to have been hurt by these morons. I assessed my situation. They didn't have any more guns, or else they would have shot me right off, rather than try to drop rocks on me. That was a positive, at least. If I could stash the stone slab somewhere, then I could probably run away and hide until they decided to call it quits and leave The Valley. Obviously if they found me they were intending to kill me, the rifle shots from days before and the thrown rocks just now were ample evidence of that. And just as obviously, they must know a quick way down from the clifftops, or they wouldn't have warned me by threatening me as they did.

I looked around among the boulder field I was hiding in. They would come here first, for sure, so I couldn't stay here or hide the *atiin* anywhere close. On the other hand, with my heavy load I wasn't going to make it very far away before they arrived, not if they did have a fast route down the cliffside. I had to think.

I made a quick decision. I untied the stone slab from the *travois* and stashed it in a crack between two halves of a split boulder, a stone taller than me. After I was through, even from close up only the edge showed. With some sand from around my feet, I disguised the slab even further, blending it into its neighbors as if it had always been there. *Good!* Without knowing exactly where to look, they'd never find it. I made sure I could re-locate this treasure again, taking long, detailed looks at the surroundings and imagining the whole scene from above, like a treasure map. I made a couple of X-marks on nearby boulders to remind myself, and rapidly took a few pictures of the area as clues for when I did return.

Then I tied another heavy stone to the *travois* and ran like mad through the narrow passageways of my forest of rocks, tracing backwards occasionally. Along the way I removed the heavy stone, replaced it with a smaller one, and made for the center of The Valley, far away from the ancient treasure I had stashed. I figured that the hoodlums would see the *travois* marks and in their rage not notice that the track furrows, where they appeared, were not as deep as before.

Half an hour later, panting and exhausted, I rested behind a large *piñon* tree. I unloaded the *travois*, threw the stone as far away as I could, then dismantled the faithful A-frame that had accompanied me on my incredulous journey. I took the cord wrappings and stuffed them into the ragged backpack, then laid the framework poles in separate locations some yards away from my sheltering tree. If I had to, I could reclaim the pieces again and have a working sledge within an hour. If I didn't return, no one would be able to tell that these innocent pole-pieces had been an essential tool in my travels within this world and other places.

Evening shadows grew from the western Valley walls, absorbing the light, coalescing with subordinate shades of trees, bushes and rocks. I had kept up my eastward trajectory until I was now in an *arroyo*, in a corner washout overhang, hidden from the view of anyone who was not directly in front of me.

I had stashed a pile of hand-sized stones for throwing in defense against my two stalkers, for I was sure they would be following me, *travois* tracks or not. I munched on cold dried fish, the last in my back-pack, not daring to start a fire. The night was long and strangely muted; the usual evening winds did not appear, and the thermal radiation from the heated *arroyo* walls kept me a little bit too warm. I knew that by morning the heat in these bare surroundings would be given up to the infinite dark sky, and all would be cool again. I listened and waited, wanting to sleep but jerking myself back to consciousness with every whispering noise that wafted down my little canyon. And so it continued, a long warm night of tension that slid finally into an uncomfortably cool pre-dawn.

At daybreak, they attacked.

I was dozing off, standing against the back wall of my tiny washout hideaway, when *Coyote* yelled, "*Ven acá*! He's down here!" Shaking my head to throw off sleep, I jumped forward, right into the open space of the ten-foot-wide *arroyo*. There, a dozen feet above me, *Coyote* stood grinning, a large stone in his hand. "Got you, *cabrón!* Now I'll kill you and get that slab back!" As he yelled, he threw something at me. I rolled to the left, jumped back to my feet and threw one of my own arsenal stones at him. *Splat!* An extremely satisfying sound to me, it must have hit him directly in the face. *Coyote* screamed in pain, staggered toward the edge of my little canyon, and fell.

On impulse, I ran to catch him, to break his fall. I was partially successful, holding my arms out and intercepting him before his back slammed against the ground; but his weight, falling as far as he did, jerked me down with him. I heard something crack, and wasn't sure if it was his bones or mine. All I knew was, he was unconscious and bleeding, flat on his back, and my arms were pinned beneath him. I slid them out, and felt excruciating pain in my right shoulder. *Damn, it was dislocated!*

Behind me, the crunch of footsteps announced Tall Guy's arrival. "Hey man," he said slowly, unbelieving, "why would you catch a guy who is going to kill you?" I turned to see him approaching, a large wooden stick in his hand. I recognized it – one of my *travois* pieces! The irony was lost on me at the moment; my right arm was useless and I felt faint.

"Don't want to hurt anybody, man," I mumbled. Shaking his head in sympathetic wonder, Tall Guy swung his club at my face. I didn't even have time to duck before the world went black in pain.

I AWOKE AWASH IN WAVES OF TORMENT, THE BLACKNESS GIVING WAY to the dancing flames of a campfire. I was leaning against the *arroyo* wall, sitting in a forced position, my legs straight out in front of me. The left side of my face was swollen and bleeding where Tall Guy had cold-cocked me, the throbbing pain matched by its malevolent cousin in my right shoulder. Other relatives of that throb told me my hands were tied behind my back, and my feet tied in front of me, my boots now gone. *My travois cords,* whispered a cynical part of my mind. *Should have burnt them, and broken those poles!* I was naked, save for my undershorts.

Against the opposite *arroyo* wall, twenty feet away, sat *Coyote,* looking about as bad for wear as I figured I did. Tall Guy was bandaging him with what looked like –and were! – strips of my shirt.

My thought was that they would just as soon leave a naked body out here to die, as a clothed one. Or maybe if they considered themselves merciful, they would kill me first.

"Hey, Tall Guy," I burbled out, fighting my swollen jaw and tongue. I could swear that a couple of teeth were loose, too. "Can I have a drink?" The outlaw turned slowly to look at me, spitting on the ground.

"Man, you are lucky I let you live this long." He continued wrapping strips of my shirt around the battered chest of his companion. "Don't push it."

I sat for hours, fighting off sleep. How long had I been out, to have had the fight right at dawn, then to awaken at darkness? And how come Tall One hadn't fixed up his friend right away?

He must have been sensitive to my thoughts. Sometime in the darkness, while the campfire sparks were fading out, he brought over a cup of water and a piece of some kind of hard bread. "Here, man. Don't want you dying on me, at least not until I have that damned slab back for my friend here." He allowed me a couple of greedy swallows of the drink, and then broke the bread into several pieces, leaving them on my legs so that I could feed myself by drawing my knees up to my face. "Don't try anything stupid or next time I might hit you too hard." He stared long and hard, right into my eyes. I tried to recognize a fellow human being in those dark pools, but just could not. I hated the feeling of being so vulnerable, tied up and helpless, my fate in the uncertain hands of a proven criminal who had already tried to kill me twice.

"You know, I figured that you must have that slab somewhere around here, so I spent the whole day looking for it, couldn't find the damned thing. My friend *Coyote*, over there, he was alive and not going anywhere, and you were flat out on your back, so I tied you up and went searching. Couldn't find a damned thing."

From out of nowhere he pulled a lit joint and blew the smoke into my face, the unwelcome sweetness making me turn my head. "You fooled us, man," he hissed. "We chased you all day, and you hid out in a cave or something. Then we saw you yesterday morning, down in the rocks. You hid that slab somewhere else, and you ran down here to hide. I'm telling you, if you hadn't of been catching my falling friend, after you knocked him out with that rock, I would have offed you right there, beat you to death with that stick. But seeing you catch him, something made me just coldcock you." He smiled evilly. "Lucky for both of us." He stubbed the joint out, rubbing it between his fingers, and placed the remaining roach in a shirt pocket.

"Now the fun is over, dude." He gestured toward *Coyote*, who was moaning. "You tell me where the slab is, and I kill you quickly. He wakes up, we're gonna carve it out of you –" he pulled out a switch-blade – "and my friend will enjoy himself for a long time, even after you scream out your secrets."

I closed my eyes. These monsters were serious; this one in partic-ular meant what he said. But I would be damned if I was going to give them the *atíin*, not after what it meant to me, what it could mean to the whole world! "Let me up, man," I asked. "I've gotta go to the toilet."

"No way, dude. Just go in your drawers there." He stood up and spat, leaving me to go care for his buddy. I inched myself up against the wall and stood, making motions as if to drop my shorts to do my business. "Not there, dumbass!" Tall Guy shouted, "Don't stink up this place. Go around the corner." Under his watchful eye, I hopped ten or fifteen feet into the darkness, hidden from the campfire. "Far enough!" he shouted again. "Any further, I'll come and cut off some pieces!" His cackling laughter echoed up and down our small canyon world.

I meditated for a few seconds, gathering all my strength. This was it, I decided, anger rising, heart pounding. I wasn't going to wait to be tortured and killed. *El Viejo, if I ever needed those 'powers' you told me about, now is the time! Coyote*, still wounded and not yet conscious, wasn't a worry yet, just the big one. But everything depended on my element of surprise, being able to take out Tall Guy with one unexpected body blow. If it didn't work I would be mutilated; if it did work, maybe I could get my hands on that knife and cut myself loose and get away.

I hopped back into the light, straight toward my enemies, a ridicu-lous sight in shorts, bare feet, bare chest, hands behind my back, ankles bound. Tall Guy, crouching next to his awakening friend, stared at me in disbelief. He saw my eyes and understood my intent, but before he could reach for his knife, I jumped right at him, launching my whole body to slam into his. *Do or die!* My last thoughts were of the Other Places, the infinite worlds of the Multiverse. *Universal Me, help me now!*

I will never know what happened in the next few moments. One instant, I was sailing through the air, bracing for the impact with Tall Guy, wondering what I would do next if he wasn't knocked out or too hurt to fight back. The next instant I was – *somewhere else!* – slamming to the ground with my already injured right shoulder, jerking my face back to avoid hitting my eyes against anything.

The impact knocked the breath out of me, and for an instant I lay there wondering how Tall Guy had been fast enough to jump out of my way. If he had, I was in for a painful night, maybe my last night. I opened my eyes in fear and looked around. No campfire! No Tall Guy! No *Coyote*! *Where* –? The thought died as I staggered painfully to my feet, using the rocky wall as support. Good God, I was not tied up, not bound. My right hand went up to my face. I was not even injured any more, no pain! I glanced down at my feet. No cords. Ruefully I saw – no shorts, either!

I fell back against cool stones, realizing where I was – in the midst of the forest of rocks, right in front of the cleft and the hidden *atiín*, where I had begun my escape the day before. That meant that my enemies were at least a mile away, down in that *arroyo*, one of them so hurt he wouldn't be able to get around for a while. At least he wouldn't be a threat for a few days!

But how –? As if in answer, a faint lavender scent touched my nostrils. "*Viejo!*" I whispered. "Are you there?" No answer, just the rustling of evening winds beginning to kick up through the sparse junipers amongst the rock forest. "So these strange powers *can* work, when you need them." I closed my eyes, watched memories of his smiling face, his nods. "My life was threatened, the *atiín* in danger of being lost or taken again, and somehow I solved the problem with what I have learned."

Grateful for the escape, and for the healing, I rued the fact that such powers hadn't saved me from *Coyote* and his buddy before that pole hit me up beside the face. *Or maybe it takes trauma, real danger, overwhelming fear, to unleash the potential, like the bit with the blood from the gunshot wound before?* "No pain, no gain?" I didn't like the sound of that. The human race had had too much in the way of sacrifice and pain. Part of my mind argued, *But what if it's true? What if it is necessary?* Another part of my mind argued back: *Some things just shouldn't be true!* My main mind was too confused to argue with either of them.

Coming back to the material world of consciousness, I was happy to be back where I was, but here I was buck naked and with no prospects of finding clothing. The desert sun would make life unbearable in a few hours, and I didn't relish the idea of walking barefoot and naked in the sun, much less trying to move the *atiín* another mile or two up The Valley to its home.

What would El Viejo do? I asked myself. *I know,* myself answered. *He'd teleport himself and the slab that last few miles.* Could I do that? Maybe, if my life depended on it. *Or find himself an Anglo fool to carry it up there?* I was fresh out of new foolish Anglos, and could not figure out any logical way to employ the two dangerous fools I had left back in the *arroyo*.

"I wonder what it looked like to Tall Guy?" I smiled at the image of the criminal, bracing for the impact of a body against him, feeling only the tied cords – and an empty pair of undershorts! – meekly plopping against him. I could hope for his heart attack out of fear, I supposed. But that would have been too much to ask for.

Leaning against the cool stone surface, I continued that thought. What if the two thieves knew about the powers the *atiín* possessed, and were wanting to use it for themselves? For all kinds of evil purposes? Had they taken it from The Valley here for that purpose? But if that was their intent, why did they let Solana put it on display for sale in the Plaza at during the Summer Solstice Festival?

As I wondered about these contradictions, a series of scenes came to mind, not quite the vivid visions of inside the Cavern, but more like memories I was sharing: *Coyote showing off his "find" to his attractive girlfriend without telling her how he'd stolen it; Solana in turn mentioning the artifact to her aunt, who would be putting up a booth at the Plaza; arguments between Solana and Coyote over displaying it in public; finally, Coyote's consid-*

erations of how much money it would bring if it could be sold to some rich Anglo New Age jet-setter at the Festival.

The "memories" faded into darkness and I was left wondering. In my exhaustion, I tried to rationalize this information. The sequence of events could explain parts of the mystery, but how did *Coyote* find it in the first place? And then take it away, and how would *El Viejo* know? And what — as tired as I was, I couldn't finish the thought

Sleep came, and I did not dream.

I AWOKE TO THE WARM, WELCOME SCENT OF *EL VIEJO'S* PIPE, AND wondered if my recent unpleasantness – the flight, the fight, the weird jump through space – had all been a dream. But when I rolled over to face the respectable campfire, the old man wasn't there. Just a skillet full of frying bacon and eggs, a full pot of coffee and – I don't know why I should have been surprised, given all the miracles of the last few days – a new pair of jeans, a shirt, shorts, and socks, neatly folded and stacked on an adjacent boulder, the pile topped off by a pair of new hiking boots. I had no doubt they would be a perfect fit. My backpack was there, too, I saw with great relief, immediately taking out my digital camera, flashlight, and binoculars. For some reason, *El Viejo* hadn't seen fit to replace the shredded pack with a new one. I laughed aloud, "I guess miracles do cease at some point." At that point, the wave of odors of cooking food and coffee melted away my wonderment.

After eating and dressing I decided to take a look at my favorite stone slab, to try to concoct some way to transport it the remaining distance. But when I brushed off the sand from the cleft of the hiding place, the *atíin* was gone! My heart sank! Had the jerks come back and found it after all, right here in front of me? If they had, why hadn't they killed me then? "Now, what do I do?" I spat in disgust.

El Viejo answered from behind me. "Don't you think you have worked enough, my friend?" I jumped, scared out of my wits. I would never get used to this way of doing things.

I gulped, taking my head in my hands. "Look old man, I am truly grateful for everything, but can't you just knock before you come in?

My nerves can only take so much." Actually, I was very relieved at everything he had done for me, and now he was here. I figured I would need all the help I could get, with the two criminals up and around by now, and the slab itself gone.

Ignoring me as usual, my mentor poured himself a cup of coffee and sat with his back against a large stone. "I thought, why let my *amigo* work so hard, when we have two healthy – well, at least *one* healthy – backs down in that *arroyo*, who could do the work for him?"

"And so, you let them come and take the slab?" I asked. It didn't make any sense. Why would they have left me alive? But, then, this *was* the way the old man worked – in mysterious ways, his wonders to perform.

"Something like that," he replied. "Anyhow, you and I can take a leisurely walk up to our destination, and talk along the way. I am sure you will be happy when we arrive, with those two doing all the work."

"*Coyote* can do work? He can walk? I thought he was out for a few days?"

El Viejo just shrugged. "Here in The Valley, things are different," he said. "Maybe *Coyote* knows a few tricks, too?"

I had thought nothing more about *El Viejo* could surprise me, but here I was, surprised again.

I packed the newly-arrived cooking implements in my backpack, hoping they wouldn't fall out through the holes, and then accompanied *El Viejo* northward, staying close to the cliff walls. I could sense from his familiar body language that the old man was in an answering mode, rather than a lecturing one. Since I had an unlimited number of questions, and I sensed also, very limited time, I felt an urgency to understand more while my mentor was in the mood.

"Why *Coyote*, *Viejo*?" I asked first. "In the balance of *The All*, why is there somebody like him? The rest of us have enough to fight in our battles with Nature and with our own natures – greed, sensuality, hatred, all the excesses. Why is there somebody like *Coyote* who seems to bring out the worst in us? Why is he here in The Valley at all?

The old man huffed and puffed as he walked. Maybe tobacco affects even immortals? If so, why did he keep on chugging away at that ancient pipe? I shrugged. Who would ever know the true thoughts of such a being? "*Coyote*," he drew out the name in an accent I hadn't heard before, "*Coyote* is first a symbol, a manifestation supplied by *The All*, as one who merely represents the problem. *Coyote* cannot plant, he may only cultivate, at best; you must plant, and you must harvest. You supply the seed; he will nourish the seedling and he will help you until you harvest the bitter fruit that comes from being out of balance with the will of *The All*.

"You supply the kernel of fear; *Coyote* helps you find the patch of ground where it will flourish, and he will work to make sure that you assist at every step of the way. You yourself can terminate the process at any time; but you must remove the source of fear, the kernel, and dispatch it to the rainless desolation above the valley. There it will wither and dissipate and neither *Coyote* nor anyone else will be able to revive it."

In the far distance, at least a half a mile away on the floor of The Valley, walked two men, a tall one and a short one. Between them they carried a heavy load – the *atín*! I hoped they couldn't see me in the shadows down here. "But I see *Coyote* now, *Viejo;* he's not a symbol but a man, an angry man, shouting at the sky, as he shouted at me. He has attacked me, hurt me. Tried to kill me." I recalled the horror of being shot, the miracle of healing myself through what *El Viejo* had taught me. The strangeness of my attack on Tall Guy at the campfire.

"And did you ever fight back?"

"Just the once, when I jumped at his friend, in the *arroyo*. And I did hit him back when he first attacked me at the Plaza in Santa Fe, too. But in my dreams, when I am offered vengeance, I can't bring myself to strike him." *El Viejo* didn't respond for a while, and we kept up the pace. Far ahead of us, the two criminals lugged their heavy load and disappeared around a bend in the cliff wall.

My friend picked up the conversation. "What would you do were *Coyote* taken ill at this moment, fallen helpless, his tall companion gone? Go scramble up and have at him? Get back your pride, hurt him? Kill him?" *El Viejo* hunched his shoulder and spread his hands wide in an unmistakable Mexican pose. "What would you do, *Señor*?"

I thought back on my unthinking, involuntary attempt to break the hoodlum's fall into the *arroyo* yesterday, but I was sure my old friend knew of that before he asked. I replied, "Yesterday I nursed a bruise, old man, and my left eye and jaw were swollen; he or his friend shot me last week, tried to kill me; then yesterday hit me up side the head with a pole. If you hadn't helped me heal myself I would have bled to death from the gunshot wound there against the cliff, under a rock, like an injured animal. And last night, if I hadn't been able to, to –" I couldn't find the words to describe my flight through space.

"*Apport* is the word, *amigo*."

"–*Apport*, they would have butchered me in that *arroyo*." At the memory of my miseries, my blood rose again, anger surging. Seeing the idiots in the distance again added to the flames. "Of course I'm angry, but I don't think I could take him now; his friend is bigger and meaner than I am." I kept thinking of the handguns I keep in my home for protection. I realized that if I'd been armed I would have killed the short man, maybe both of them. The sudden realization struck me, probably harder than *Coyote* or Tall Guy had. *I would have been a killer, if I could.*

But now I was so happy that I wasn't a killer, even if that meant the two enemies were still a threat. With an exposure to the infinity of existence that every individual possesses, I couldn't see myself being responsible for terminating millions upon millions of alternate *Coyotes* and Tall Guys, no matter what their offenses. Or is that what happens? Maybe just one facet is terminated, and the rest continue? Do they overlap, take up the slack, or what? I wanted to ask my friend, but I knew that if such distinctions mattered, he would tell me before I asked.

All that conflict must have shown in my face, in my body language. *El Viejo* said, "A better violence is violence postponed; the best violence is the violence never done." He drew a deep whiff of smoke from his pipe, letting it out slowly, its wisps curling upwards to oblivion. I knew that I had not formulated the correct question; his answer, though, applied to unasked queries. "You *apported* to accomplish two things – your own escape, but also to prevent injury to your enemy. You conjured up the courage within yourself to help yourself. You unlocked another power you always had.

"But you want an answer to your question about our friend up there," he said. "So, consider this. If trickery were even distributed throughout the world, then the world would be full of mischief and we would be hard pressed to recognize it. Eventually we would come to believe that *The All* itself was party to evil, and had thrust it upon mankind. By condensing it into recognizable form, we are able to realize it, to contain it, to define it, and perhaps one day even to convert it.

"*Coyote* is the way *The All* has of saying, 'Here is what you should *not* be; so look at his life and count yourself fortunate that you are not he.' How many times have you stopped yourself from a selfish or unwise action, only because you could suddenly see a sorrowful soul like that in your own actions, a miserable wretch whom you knew who could perform that action without reflection?" I nodded in acknowledgement; *many times*, I admitted to myself. *Too many times*.

"Well, you have learned what was intended – look at the wonderful gift that sorrowful soul has given to you – preventing you, by example, from behaving in the same manner and bringing misery and suffering upon yourself and others."

"But he is a *man*, *Viejo*," I protested. "*Coyote* is a human, not just a symbol, or a bad role model. A punk from Santa Fe, and he hurt me and shot me and he and his murderous friend are after me because I took back his archaeological relic." I wanted this old man on my side, sympathy against these devils.

What I got was, "And so are we are all human in this Valley, my friend. And so are we all."

As we walked on, *El Viejo* kept chatting. "Politics and international relations might seem far removed from the lessons of The Valley, my friend, but they are important indeed. No nation remains untouched, for very long, by the realities of the outside world, and that is why it is important that the whole world become aware, so that no one will rise against his neighbor. This is why education and democracy are so important. In all of history, representative democracies with a free press and free economies have never warred against each other. They haven't been perfect, nothing human ever has been or will be, but their histories are so much better than any kingdom or aristocracy throughout history, that there is no comparison. These last few decades, at least for those living in the democracies of this world at this time, have been among the happiest and most productive of all history, or at least history this time around. That is no accident."

"But old one," I objected, "the 20th Century saw the bloodiest wars in history."

He smiled. "I think not; per capita, the religious wars of the later Roman Empire saw more deaths and the total destruction of vast regions of the Near East and North Africa. And you yourself know of ancient wars where all the losers were slaughtered, their cultures totally exterminated. No, be gentler with yourself – the dictators and warlords of the Twentieth Century were merely the first in modern times to have access to rapid killing machines. The ancients did as much evil as they could, with only swords and spears and fire." He looked deep into my eyes. "And that brings up the concept and the practice of war itself." He sighed, "There are just wars, wasteful though the process may be. And even necessary wars."

This was going to be an interesting one, I thought, and I motioned for us to sit. *El Viejo* needed no further prompting, and we sat to rest in the shade of fallen rocks. There was no hurry; our two hoodlum friends further up The Valley weren't going anywhere quickly, and both the old man and I knew their final destination. I wasn't all that sure I even wanted to see them again anyhow. *El Viejo* re-lit his faltering pipe and wafted the smoke in my direction. By now it was just a familiar scent, a loving softness that enhanced my mood. *And probably my receptiveness, too*, I mused.

"Those civilizations that love democracy, beauty, and spirituality, must defend themselves against those who would exterminate them. The scattered oases of those who are already enabling *The Alt* to experience Itself, these places and these peoples must be protected, for the Multiverse is not yet free of conflict. Those forces that would drive this process backward must be restrained – this is the price of mankind's existence in the physical world, just as one must protect one's children from wild beasts and diseases.

"However, there are those who take this responsibility too far and make it the center of their lives. It is alright for some to do so, as a sacrifice for their society, their nation, but never is it good for the entire society to do so, for that perverts the meaning of individual consciousness, and the struggle of *The All* to know Itself.

"Witness the societies founded on blood – the sanguinary temples, spectacular architectural beauties stained with sacrifices by the tens of thousands. Yet, though it did the victims no good, at least their sacrifices satisfied the superstitious belief of the killers that propitiating the violent gods in such a manner would protect the rest of society. Unlike the tens of millions of innocents sacrificed in the last century for the mere ends of social power and economic control."

"But *Viejo*, all empires, all nations, eventually die or change, don't they?"

"A society that has endured happily for hundreds or thousands of years, then dies, is analogous to a human being who does so. But, you may offer, what of the rejuvenation powers of the Place of New Life in the Cavern? Ah, that teaches us that a nation or a people or a whole world can be similarly made young once more, if the appropriate method of healing is used. And by this I mean a human race that learns the truth of *The All* and then returns to its self-regenerating powers of meditation and communion. So some nations may continually refresh themselves and last many centuries, happily and advancing, if they learn the truth."

I chuckled. "Something like, 'You shall know the truth, and the truth will set you free'?" I murmured.

"Exactly," said the old man. "Precisely."

WE SAT AND RESTED FOR A WHILE LONGER IN THE AFTERNOON shade of the Valley cliff, while in the distance the two thieves struggled with their load. I supposed it was *El Viejo*'s doing that they never turned back to see us following a quarter-mile behind them. Then again, if they had discovered us, *El Viejo* would be a potent adversary if they dared bother us. I wondered what limits there were to his power, if there were limits at all. Or maybe, the limits were just what he exercised. I would never want this man angry at me.

"What are you having them do?" I asked, gesturing up the trail. "Why would they be taking the *atiín* back to its original location?"

El Viejo answered, "Sometimes people are infused with strange ideas. Maybe these two ahead of us think that they if they place the slab back into its niche, they can gain the awesome power they saw you demonstrate last night?" His smile told me where they had obtained such an infusion. I wondered if *El Viejo* appeared to them directly, or just inside their heads. I asked as much.

"Friend, one does what one must do. To each his own. Don't ask, and you won't be disappointed with my answers." By now, I could have given myself that same answer. Strangely enough, through my interactions with the old man, I was finally beginning to understand his peculiar form of semi-logic, semi-revelation. The methodology was not something I had ever considered before: learning by not-asking, seeing by not-looking, knowing by not-seeing, understanding by not-thinking, a form of thought process tangential to the straight system of logic and reason that formed the basis of my mental discipline. I understood that "not-seeing" was not at all like "not seeing," a subtle and awesome distinction. I thought, *But it works all the same. I am living proof that this system works!*

And I realized that *El Viejo's* way could not be written down, nor carved in hieroglyphics – it had to be taught, one person to another, over an extended period, and it had to be punctuated with experience. *This will never be a Web-based course of study*, I told myself, laughing inwardly. *Reading is preparation, of course.* I recalled the words of an old spiritual song from my early childhood: "You must walk that lonesome Valley, You must walk it by yourself..." Could the songwriter have meant *this* Valley? The individual responsibility inherent in that old song took on new meaning as I sat with my ageless friend to drink in the draughts of his wisdom.

After a few minutes of silence, I asked *El Viejo* to tell me more about those beautiful Beings in the Place of New Colors, as I had come to call it. "How can an ordinary human ever hope to be like that? Tell me the ways."

"One step at a time," he murmured, between puffs on the pipe. "You can call it the road to glory."

I laughed aloud at the unexpected statement. "Sounds like an old revival meeting, *Viejo*. I didn't know you were into those." I was beginning to suspect that the raw emotion, the waves of spiritual feeling, that I had experienced as a child at tent revivals down South, may have been closer to the primal truth of existence than all of the intellectual education I'd had since. At least here in The Valley, I was finding a relevance that had been missing all these decades. I would have to take another look at that peculiarly Southern tradition; I had already come to realize, here in The Valley, one more aspect of the reality of re-birth after a ritual immersion in water, if it were the right kind of water.

So many truths, so hidden and so misunderstood!

El Viejo ignored my outburst, as usual. Taking a deep breath, drawing in a cloud of smoke, releasing it, he said, "Those who have been born with the 'glory' or who have unfolded their souls into it, sometimes emanate a part of it that can be seen or felt by others. The halos and shining auras of ancient paintings, did you think all these were the fevered imaginings of demented minds? No, my friend, they just painted what they saw. Even the ancient cave paintings of Europe, forty thousand years old, they show the light. 'Enlightened ones,' where do you think that term comes from?"

"I felt that power, *Viejo*. When I approached the Being of Light, I felt such overwhelming emotion and physical pleasure that I felt I was about to leave myself, exiting my body to lose myself in that Light. I experienced in every cell of my body, every fiber of my being, such joy, love, respect, fear, admiration, that all I could think of was merging myself in that Light forever.

"And when I returned, being deprived of that moment of absolute absorption left me gasping for breath, pain replacing every joy, a vacuum of deprivation where before I had been fulfilled and filled. It is worse than losing your vision; it's more like losing your soul."

El Viejo nodded. "Now you see why some have described Hell as being absent from the presence of God." The inhabitants of Dante's First Circle of Hell, I recalled, suffered that one punishment alone, for the apparently unforgiveable sin of having been born too soon. Until now, I had always wondered why that could have been so hard to bear. Now I knew.

"It hurts even now, old man. When I think about the feelings –"

"And that is, my friend, the origin of the warning that in their physical bodies human beings dare not approach God too closely, dare not look upon His face. Very much time in that condition, you would not physically survive. Just a little longer than you yourself had, and you would be unfit for any human activity anymore. This is one reason that true searchers must prepare themselves physically, emotionally, spiritually, before they dare to take many more steps closer to God, *The All*, or however you want to designate it."

I knew the truth he was speaking. All holy books talked about the fierce radiance of Gods or the gods, and how humans wilted in the nearby glory. I knew the truth, all right, but just from the glory of the fading, receding memories, I still would have given anything – *everything!* – at that moment, to return to the Being of Light and melt away in that awesome love.

As with most things near to Truth, my feelings were irrational.

El Viejo knew this. "*As with everything, time will heal the happy wound. Consider yourself fortunate. I do. Or would you rather have not met Him?*"

El Viejo smiled when I hesitated. Like people have asked about being in love: was it better to have known it and then been deprived of it, or never to have known it at all? I still can't answer that, although I do know to the depths of my being that there is Love out there, and that it can be found. And that I want my afterlife to be with it and within it. Knowing what I had experienced, an eternity of anything less would indeed be Hell.

10

The Valley began to converge, and in that last mile became a narrow canyon, its vertical walls only a hundred yards apart, still converging. The small river had long since disappeared from view, mere trickles of water emanating from beneath random rough pyramids of small boulders, fallen centuries ago. My vision of the *atiín's* proper location showed it in a bare rock cliff face, with the end of The Valley not a quarter mile away to the North, terminating in a crevice just a dozen yards wide, a thousand-foot-deep crack in the mesa lands above, with a very narrow trail leading upward within its depths. Later that day, just as the shadows of the western Valley cliffs began to cover us, *El Viejo* and I caught up with the two thieves and their precious loot.

As we rounded a pile of rock slabs, our two adversaries were not more than fifty yards away. My friend put out his hand to stop me, and motioned that I stay behind and watch the proceedings.

The two punks stood at the base of the cliff, where the floor of The Valley met the cliff wall perpendicularly. A few hundred yards to the north, as I had seen in the vision at Algona's Pool, The Valley ended in a sharp acute corner, where geological forces of eons past had caused the first rift. Here, the cliff face was solid rock, no sedimentary layers visible, and it was that same thousand feet from the floor of The Valley to the flatlands above. A suggestion of a trail, just as I had seen, began a few feet up from the floor, disappearing through the narrow cleft into the dark distance. Looking upward, I could make out evidence that this trail eventually went all the way to the mesas above, though the many switchbacks made it look treacherous and steep.

This, I thought, must be the very base level of the Valley, maybe billions of years old, with its high cliffs converging into solid rock, terminating The Valley in this sharp V. We watched as the men dropped the *atiín* between them. Its original location in the wall was about five feet from the ground level, in a hacked-out niche. The two were gesticulating and yelling.

"Put it back, *pendejo?*" *Coyote* was screaming. "Why the hell would you think I want to put it *back*? It's worth a freekin' fortune back in Santa Fe!"

Tall Guy spoke softly. I'd heard that soft voice too, but then he had been threatening to slice off my body parts to make me tell him where the slab was hidden. Now he was saying, almost too softly to discern, "The Old Man, he scares me. You know he let us find this rock. I'm afraid if we don't put it back in the cliff, he'll kill us."

"I'm not afraid of that *cabrón El Viejo, estúpido!*" the short one boasted, but I could tell in the tone of his voice that he was not too certain of his own bravado. "I say we take this damned thing back where the *gringo* stole it, and sell it at Solana's store."

"My friend," Tall Guy replied, leaning against the cliff face, cleaning his fingernails with his large switchblade, "You weren't awake last night. You didn't see that dude jump at me, then disappear – *poof!* – into the night." He took a deep breath. "I'm not going to wait and see what other powers that the Old One has. He might make *us* disappear, too." He threw the switchblade into the clay ground covering, where its handle vibrated for a while, slowing to stillness. "This is as far as I go. This is all I'll help you do. *No more!*"

Coyote went berserk, screaming as loud as he could, mixing English and Spanish curses, jumping up and down in uncontrolled rage. Tall Guy just bent over, took the switchblade, cleaned it off, and patted the shaft in his hand.

"You all through now, dude?" *Coyote* shook his head. "I don't care, man, you give me a hand and let's put this back where it belongs, and let's go back to Santa Fe. Two days is enough. I've got things to do back home." He shoved *Coyote* on the shoulder, then grinned widely.

Coyote said something unintelligible and angry, but bent over and hoisted one end of the *atiín*, Tall Guy assisting him. Much stronger than I would have guessed, they easily wrestled the three-hundred-pound slab into its position in the cliff face, about five feet up from the floor of The Valley. I wondered how it would stay in place, once situated. Maybe the very roughness of the hacked-out niche would help hold it in where it belonged? Or did they have in mind some mortar or cement? I didn't see any other tools with them.

As I watched, the cliff face seemed to *flow* around the *atiín*! The "sculpture" fit flush into the surround stone as if by magic. I couldn't trust my eyes in the shadows, but I would have sworn that the rock somehow fused itself back into the canyon wall.

The whole fantastic scene didn't seem to faze the two thieves a bit. What was happening here? They *expected* this miraculous healing of the cliff wall, as if a living creature had grown new tissue? Having thought I could never be surprised again, I almost fainted from the scene before me.

Coyote and Tall Guy continued their argument, and a small part of me wished they would come to blows. *El Viejo* saw this in my eyes and shook his head, holding up a finger to his lips, a command to remain silent.

With the short one still shouting curses, the thieves finally left the scene, heading northward, continuing their heated discussions. Soon they were out of view, taking the trail in the crevice that led upwards toward the mesa tops. We waited half an hour before making our way to the *atiin*, now so securely positioned as though it had never been removed. My heart pounded, and my mind raced. First, with the binoculars I checked the trail for evidence that our friends were not going to be throwing rocks down on us. I was surprised that from this location, little of the upwards trail could be seen within the depths of the crevice. I hoped it was reciprocal. I didn't know if my apportation skills included dodging boulders I didn't see first!

Then the realization struck. My days of anticipation of this moment, of finding where the *atiin* came from, of seeing it back in its place, the end of my journey – taken all together, they were almost too much to bear.

I ran my hand around the carved symbols, feeling a coolness they hadn't exhibited before. But I could not find even so much as a seam where the slab had melded with the rock cliff. I was dumbfounded. "*Viejo*, what in the world was going on here? How did this slab just fit back in a hacked-out niche? And why did those two criminals know it would happen? And how the hell did they ever get to this place in the first place? And find the *atiin*, and cut it out, and bring it to Santa Fe?" The old man held up a hand to silence me.

"You of all people should not be surprised any more at the miracles, excuse me, the *technologies*, here in The Valley. It goes where it goes; it does what it does. As for those two –" he gestured with a thumb northward, "– what makes you think they haven't done this before?"

What he said sank in and I yelped, "*Before*? You mean those hoodlums have done this more than –?" The question died in my throat.

"The Valley often repeats its performances, my friend. And sometimes uses the same actors."

"They are real thugs, not hired performers, right?" I didn't want to have been brutalized by mere actors.

"My terminology was misleading, friend," the old man said. "They are not conscious actors, but serious criminals. And yes, they have been here before. They may even remember doing this, once or twice previously."

"*Twice?* My God, *Viejo*, these are killers, they shouldn't be, shouldn't be..." I didn't know what I wanted to say. Who could say what The Valley should or shouldn't do? After all, I had made it through the horrendous gauntlet of traumatic experiences. Could I have done it without true criminals trying to thwart me? But it seemed so unnecessary. And so dangerous.

"Man, I don't know. I just don't know. They do all of these crimes, cause all of this pain, and they just walk away, maybe not even remembering what they have done? You call this justice?"

El Viejo stood on tiptoe to stroke the intricate carvings on the ancient slab, smiling as he touched first one symbol, then the other. "Justice, my friend, is a man-made concept. Nature is not just; in Man's eyes she is brutal, inefficient, cruel, yet she rewards the strong, the smart, the quick, the lucky. *The All* itself does not necessarily provide justice from our transient viewpoint; but it works its ways in ways beyond our understanding. We witness the end results of violence and cruelty, and think that many times there is justice for the perpetrators. There are always consequences, and sometimes we see those consequences as a form of justice. But the laws of physics and the laws of morality are laws, meaning that is the way things are. WE do not have to like it or understand it. It just *is*."

He pointed toward the converging end of our canyon, at the tiny trail that vanished behind outcroppings as it wandered upwards toward the mesalands, hundreds of feet above us. "But as far as our two unhappy friends now leaving us, they are not entirely unpunished, as you might call it. They, too, have to walk this Valley, and must continue to do it until they have learned. Maybe they will learn what you have learned, in a similarly harsh manner; or maybe they will learn something else. But, you may be assured, they will most certainly learn the most basic of lessons – of the Universal You, of the Other Places, of the Multiverse. They were chosen, too, like you. Sadly, they are just slow learners.

"You are one of the lucky ones, *amigo*; you have only had to do this *once*."

THE REST OF THE AFTERNOON, I TRIED TO FOCUS THE OLD MAN'S attentions on the immediate physical surroundings, leaving the philosophical nuances for sorting out later. This cliff, it was physical; I could touch it. At its top, some thousand feet or more above us, began the mesa lands that would stretch northward to Colorado. And somewhere ten miles or more to the south would be the trailhead that had led me down from that mesa, into The Valley, into my life-changing adventure. And there, of course, would hopefully still be my rented SUV and my way back to what I had once called civilization. I wasn't so sure that term applied any more.

This little V-shaped canyon at the northern end of The Valley marked the end of one leg of a journey that had changed my life, and I was determined to photograph it, document it, internalize it, absorb as much of it as I could before leaving. I wanted to know it, then to write about it. I realized on that day that I could never return to that place, would never be able again to find it, either on a map or a dusty side road, or by apportation. But I certainly did want to find Algona again, assuming she was still in this TimeSpace, or I was still in hers. In the meantime, I demanded answers to all of the questions bubbling up in my mind. "*Viejo*, so this place the *atíín* belongs, how did it get here? It was carved by – whom? And when? And for what purposes?"

The old man looked up at me from where he sat against a shady stone. "You must answer your own questions now, friend. You must integrate all that you have learned, you yourself must feel the wholeness of your journey." As I wrinkled my forehead and threw up my hands at his enigmatic words, he gave me that same head-shaking routine. "Think of it as a final examination before you are ready to leave this Valley."

I didn't feel as if I were ready to graduate from The Valley. How would I get answers to the mysteries of the *atíín* if he didn't tell me? In answer, I followed his gaze, from me to the carvings on the cliff face, back again. Then I understood – now that the slab was in its proper place, it should be much more powerful than it was as a broken piece, away from its position of power.

But, I asked myself, *can I withstand a power more potent than the one I experienced in the cavern?* Gulping, I pulled out a small pocketknife from the backpack, bathed the blade in the flame of *El Viejo*'s proffered cigarette lighter to sterilize it, and drew the point across my left thumb. A minute later I had rubbed blood on both palms, and slowly approached the carved palm prints on the *atiín.* I noticed that my old friend walked closely behind me. To catch me? To hold me against the cliff face? I didn't know but I appreciated his presence there, feeling much safer. Fearfully, I raised my hands in offering to the *atiín* and its ancient palm prints.

This time, the energies were overwhelming: my bloody palms were pulled toward their carved counterparts like iron to a magnet, forcibly, immediately. And immediately the vision began, this one not of simple travels and beauties. This one was of Power and History.

In overwhelming waves of sensory impressions, and in ways I realized had to be far beyond normal human senses, a history of Earth unfolded. I almost glimpsed the Powers and the Forces involved, but found myself turning my astral head away from those magnificent and powerful Beings, fearing them yet loving them, and fearful they would find me lacking. My soul filled up with flowing wonder and awe, unable to contain the massive swirling love that permeated all of my being and beyond.

And this is what I saw:

Vast eons ago, on what is now our Earth, other creatures, reptilian and even stranger, became intelligent and created world-girdling civilizations. They warred with each other, and with others from other worlds, and in terrific cosmic battles annihilated themselves. Millions of years later, our anthropoid ancestors – with the intercession of Gods? Aliens? Something Else? I could not tell what they were and still don't know what they did – began the long trek from animal consciousness to sentience, self-awareness, and souls.

Millions of years ago, just a twitch in cosmic time, human beings at various stages of awareness, of evolution, of intelligence, also built civilizations. Some were primitive, regional. Some were worldwide, technological, at our level and beyond. Some of these destroyed themselves, some were erased by Nature, but they were many.

The last great civilization before ours endured for twenty thousand years, until great geophysical disturbances rocked the Earth so suddenly that preparation was impossible, and survival a matter of time and chance. Their space explorations left evidence on neighboring planets and our own Moon. These relics may yet be uncovered in our own time, in this TimeSpace dimension.

This final scattering of civilization and the resulting diaspora of the human race happened around thirteen thousand years ago, nearly exterminating us all, and the pitiful remnants of mankind have been struggling upward ever since. The saga of these events and of mankind's rebirth are reflected in legends and myths from every corner of the globe, stories of flood and earthquake and moving skies and strange heavenly battles among the gods. Memorialized in stones and circles and pyramids, none ever wholly understood by the distant generations who followed.

And intermixed with this history, are the overlapping and anachronistic influences of those who have physically traveled the gateways between the worlds, between dimensions and times. For in other places around the Earth, in places like The Valley, in ancient and modern times, some few people found the ways to these other worlds; some took villages, tribes and even entire nations with them, vanishing forever from our history and our world. In The Valley, in its vast caverns, those who departed this way left instructions for those of us who might follow, in hieroglyphics and paintings and sculptures in the Cavern.

Others came from their worlds to ours, some of them merely human, a very few of them awesome Beings of good or otherwise, becoming the Gods of legend and myth.

And so it was, around our Earth, and so it remains in The Valley – an infinite intercourse of worlds and times and dimensions.

Gasping, I pressed my way back from the slab; there was too much information pouring in. But gently, ever so gently, *El Viejo* pushed me back. "There is more, my friend. You must feel the personalities, not just the grand scope of all history. Find the players, the men who loved and lived and died. You need their lessons. Listen, learn." I closed my eyes and once more placed my bloody hands on Solana's Palms.

In a vision more vivid than life itself, I was immersed into a battlefield, amidst screams and smoke and spears, swords and shields and headdresses. I was a warrior, my head and chest clad in bronze armor, my arms in bright brass mesh; I could feel my legs wrapped in cloth and leather padding, the sweat burning as it rolled down wounds on my legs.

There! I parlayed a spearpoint, grabbed the shaft with my left hand, bringing my short sword down through the living neck of my enemy. For a moment, I was free of opponents and in that moment saw a darkened sky in which a celestial battle was being fought. As the Gods Themselves war in the Sky, so do we down here, I thought. But my modern mind saw not gods, not cosmic dragons, but incredibly large comets, one with a tail encompassing the Moon itself; another comet further in the distance, its effusions tangling with another globe, another planet, another world. My own mind – not that of the warrior – thought, there are no other worlds so close! But there it was, fighting its own celestial intruder. And the night sky! A fireworks show of blazing meteors and bolts of lightning, a horrendous Hell of falling stars. The very noise of those cosmic battles seemed to be echoing here on Earth, in the chaos and madness of the warfare around me, the clanging of swords, the screaming of men.

And around me, thousands of warriors in battle dress, strange banners illuminated by awesome sky-shattering daggers of lightning, weapons moving in a dark ballet of death, reminding me of a movie of some dying ancient civilization, screaming and bleeding and dying!

This was happening on my own Earth, I knew, but it felt so close to that other Dark Place that I feared for my very soul.

Then the chaos was over, the scene shifting to the same V-shaped canyon at the north end of The Valley where El Viejo and I had completed our mission. Being a warrior of some high stature, now severely wounded and bleeding profusely, I was being carried from the battlefield in a litter, and finally propped up at an angle in a place of honor for consecration rites before dying. I recognized the cliff face – I was back at the atiín site! Standing atop a wooden framework at least ten feet high, a small man in a red robe was using a lightweight hammer to drive brightly glowing wedges into the stone. As he moved about his work, I saw that the palm prints of my own time were already there. I knew they had been up on the cliff face for ages before I came here. Through the curtain-waves of pain, with my unfocusing eyes about to fail, I watched as the word-maker used those glowing wedges to make a set of marks under the palms.

From out of nowhere came an attractive, dark-haired, olive-skinned woman in white robes, pouring into my mouth a draught of some warm, bitter drink, *which eased the pain almost at once. I thanked her in a language I didn't know; she smiled, and began to wipe my body with a cool wet cloth. A numbness filled my limbs, finally relieving the sharp pains in my chest and neck. I saw my arms, swarthy and hairless; my now-unwrapped legs, through the blood the woman was wiping away, were similarly dark and smooth, though lacerated. The woman, the stone-carver and all the others were of the same complexion as I – Egyptians? Phoenicians? My warrior mind could not formulate a comprehensible question that would make sense to my companions. They would think me delirious, impugning my honor as I died.*

No, I would not so dishonor my life of service. Not after the years of study in the School of Secrets, the severe discipline of the military training necessary to help fight off the hordes of refugees from the sunken lands, the incredible years-long journey from our homeland during this Twilight of the Gods, watching as the heavens themselves opened up and loosed demons on the Earth and Sky. Well, the Sky-Gods are powerful; but they have to fight their enemies, the Sky-Demons, up there in their domain; we down here have our own foes.

Our people, we fought our way here halfway around this world, and here in this Valley we will stay, even if we have to war forever against these ignorant ones. I pray that my secret books will stay in the hands of my acolytes, so they can bring knowledge and glory to my people, when there is peace once again. But now I am dying, and can fight for my people no more, nor teach them anymore. Now I go to serve the Gods I have seen in the caverns.

The priests are now lifting me upward to touch the holy hands of The Valley gods. My bloody hands, they touch the stone impressions made by the gods themselves at the beginning of Time. Oh Gods, as I die, please take my soul and my sword and let me battle for you forever!

The warrior died. I died.

I AWOKE WITH A START, PUSHING MYSELF BACK FROM THE *ATIÍN*, where its bloody palms dripped their ochre down across the symbol-carvings below. *El Viejo* caught me, preventing my fall. My chest heaved and I could barely breathe. "God, *Viejo*! Who was that warrior? Where was he from?"

"He was not the first, my friend. You could see the palms were there in the *atiín* even before he came?"

"Yes, I did see them." I leaned against the cliff face, trying to breathe, trying to comprehend that awful vision. "But they were much further up the cliff then." I wondered how long it had taken to fill this end of The Valley floor with five hundred feet of rock-hard *caliche* clay. Thousands of years, at the least.

"What was going on in the sky, old man? Comets and meteors and other planets close by?" I complained. "That never happened in any history I heard of!" Actually at the moment I said that, I did remember some incredible stories by Immanuel Velikovsky and other unconventional historians, who'd maintained exactly that. But hadn't they all been discredited? *Oh well,* I thought with resignation, *nothing else here is believable, either. Even though it is all true. Even though I have seen it with my own eyes.*

"Other times, other worlds, other dimensions, other histories. Who can say?" *El Viejo* wasn't concerned with celestial happenings just now; I could feel that he had other agendas on his mind.

"But now, you must go back, beyond the warrior, further back." And he pushed me quickly, so fast that I could not resist, holding out my hands to break the impact against the cliff face – and I touched the palm prints again. "Learn," my mentor whispered commandingly, "learn."

I was First Man. I came to this Valley when it was an inlet to the sea, a sea just down The Valley a few miles from here. I could smell the saltiness, the welcome freshness of the breeze. As my mind melded with his, I knew there would be fish tonight, and the clan would enjoy the variety. I turned and motioned for the others behind me to follow, and grunted the sounds that meant 'new food from the wetness.' Hunched and hairy, more hunched and more hairy than I, they followed me, pounding the shafts of their sharpened sticks against rocks in happy agreement.

We spent hours in the gentle surf, spearing more of the 'new food' than we could carry, throwing piles of them, flopping, on the beach. Running our sharp spears through as many as we each had fingers, we carried the treasure back to the waiting clan, and gorged ourselves on the raw pungent tissue and innards and blood of the living food.

As leader, I had only this dawn found this wondrous place, and had positioned the clan at the end of this small canyon, with walls so steep and high no enemy could climb down and surprise us, and with no way to be seen from the top. I stationed two warriors at the head of the trail that led down from the high flatland to our campsite, to warn us if anyone approached from that direction. With the end of the canyon opening to a wider valley and then to the great water, we were safe, we had food. Here we would stay while the weather was warm. We would have to find other shelter eventually, but the cold was several Moons away, and we needed the rest after our long treks and the battles on the flatlands.

Or maybe we could stay here longer, if we found a cave to stay away from the chill. I would send scouts out tomorrow; there might be openings in the cliffs down nearer the sea.

As morning came, a night-warner was shouting at me to come, see the 'new thing.' He was very loud, disturbing the children and the old people, so grumbling, I took my spear-stick to whack him and teach him not to wake the whole world and alert our enemies. But as I rounded the camp and saw what he was pointing at, I nearly dropped my spear in shock.

The far wall of our canyon was lit up by the Great Day Light. There, as high up as two hands of men, were two hand-prints, surely of the Gods themselves, that shone as brightly as the Great Light itself, two small but brilliant Lights, here in the wall of our new canyon home. Wakened by the night-warner's cries, the whole clan was now up, gaping at the miracle. I turned to Herb-man and pointed at the hands of the gods, querying him by grunts. "What is this new thing?"

"It is," he said slowly but clearly (for he, like me, was nearly erect and nearly hairless) "the blessing of the Great Light on us, his clan. His approval. This is now our land. We will stay here."

Reluctantly, I agreed, tapping Herb-man on each shoulder with my spear, designating that he spoke truth. Now I would have to find a cave for us all to live in. If none could be found, I would have to punish the Herb-man for being wrong. But, looking up at those hands of the gods, he had to be right. That was good. He was my friend, and I did not want to kill him.

Clan-Leader I was in this canyon, and in the large dark caverns where we spent the cold season, during many, many turns of the stars. We worshipped daily at dawn the shining Hands of Gods in the canyon, and in turn lived under their divine protection this entire time. Herb-man convinced me that it was these Hands that had found our cavern-home for us, though I knew my scouts had.

But who could really know? And it was better for the spirit of the Clan to believe his way.

And so it went, season after season, fat living from the sea, harvesting nuts and small game from the high flatlands, fighting off half-men and beasts without too much death and difficulty, until my two lusty sons announced for my title. The Clan had never had a contest for Leader before; until my time, all Leaders had died in battles with half-men or beasts, or in accidents or taken by the demons of sickness. Myself, I was old and weak and not desirous of killing my sons to keep my position; the clan needed all the strong young men it had, and more, to keep the beasts at bay, and the half-men and the Others we had seen but not yet fought.

I was glad to give up my position to a stronger, younger man. I could see great challenges ahead, great battles. Some of the cave-drawings the torches revealed in the cavern hinted of Great Ones that not even our spears could kill. I did not like to see these Gods of the darkness. Herb-man and his son even told me wild tales of other Gods and other Valleys they had encountered down in the depths of the cavern, far beyond where the Clan ever ventured. I did not want to see those Gods, either. Though the Good Place sounded pleasant, the Dark Place was deadly and the two men were never certain of which they would encounter in their journeys. I already enjoyed life out here in The Valley, in our canyon, on the beach, in The Great Light, with the scent of the sea and the fragrances of the rain.

And out here I would die.

So I conferred with Herb-man-son and we decided that on the day of my death, I would meet the Hands of God and be taken to the stars. My sons agreed to this and I was happy. I knew they would have to battle each other to the death, but I would be with the gods by then, and could greet my fallen son as a fellow star. And we two, we would watch over the Clan as protectors from our heavenly heights.

Herb-man-son had the women knit long ropes and a sling, and I was hoisted far, far down the cliff face from the flat land above, until I was level with The Hands of Gods. With a like sling, many seasons before, Herb-man himself had carved magic symbols below the Hands, to mark the place for our Clan, and to inform the Gods that we were their people. I ran my fingers over the deeply-cut stone, wondering how my friend had ever made such beautiful work, much better than the chipped spear points he and his family made for our weapons.

But now, it is too late for wondering. Except, I do wonder if Herb-man is with the gods in the stars, and if I shall meet him. I take the dark, serrated stone knife and slit first my wrists, then my palms. As Herb-man had done so long ago, I press my wetted hands to touch the Hands of Gods.

Far below me, my two sons reach up to catch the stream of my noble blood as it falls toward them, each hoping for an advantage over their brother-adversary. Myself, I am drawn into the stone, and go to become a star.

I died with Clan Leader, traveling with him, fading into the other world he hoped would be a star. For an eternal moment I was totally aware of both my own surroundings, in the present-day Valley, and in Clan Leader's Valley hundreds of centuries ago, the two worlds merging in a holographic perspective unlike anything I had ever known. This, I knew, was not a vision, not even a living of two lives – or a life and a death! – at once. This was a way for me to encompass the entire history, billions of personal experiences, simultaneously. *And I did, oh God, I did!*

Paroxysms of emotion swept through hidden fissures of my soul, places I had never known were there. And knowledge, a deeply personal knowledge of billions of lives – joys, sorrows, pains, triumphs, illnesses, injuries, deaths; knowledge, accomplishments, progress, decline, surprising technical developments, encounters with star-travelers, visits to the Other Places; and finally, the loss of innocence, the loss of knowledge, the loss of literacy, the loss of hope, darkness encroaching, darkness come.

All these and more flowed through my newly-enlarged soul, a soul that expanded vastly to absorb the enormity and the wonders of the human experience, the pain, suffering, along with the transient, temporary joys. And yet, and yet – through it all, in each of those individual humans, a pure spark of life, of love, of inner essence, radiated. I felt them each merge into those other worlds, becoming part of The All.

And just then, when I thought there could be no more revelation, no more experiences, just then the door opened from our small corner of The All, out into the Multiverse itself. Briefly I realized that all I had seen, had felt, had experienced, was a mere drop in a vast Ocean beyond. I felt another transition occurring as part of me yearned to step into that far Ocean and drown in its glory. For just a moment I felt new senses and understandings as far beyond everything I'd felt, as that was above my ordinary life before coming to The Valley, but –

– I could bear no more, and cried, in a million human languages: "Take this cup from me, O Lord!"

Once more I fell backward, this time literally blown away from the *atín* by the power of its visionary arts, into *El Viejo*'s waiting arms. I sobbed and sought refuge in those powerful arms. And I knew the old man had been here, too, thousands of years before. And had helped many others like me to survive the encounter.

I could barely croak, "Oh man, man, I don't think I can do this anymore." He took me, trembling, and sat me against a resting-stone. From somewhere he found bandages, and a sharp sting of antiseptic preceded his wrapping my thumb. "That was a long time ago, *amigo*," I said. "An ocean was down there, a mile or two away, and these cliffs must have been five hundred feet higher! When was that? Who were they?"

"I heard you say 'First Man,'" he answered. "But it was not in English you spoke it. More like a grunt."

I kept putting the infinite number of images, of experiences, out of my mind. That way lay insanity; much contemplation of that last vision would put me into a mental institution. Who would ever choose *me* to dump all of humanity's history onto, or show *me* what lies beyond our Universe? "I think I've had enough of our bloody stone for a while, old man, and its bloody stories, too," I muttered. *El Viejo* was finishing off his wrapping job, with a neat covering of adhesive bandages. I tried to keep the conversation on details; I simply did not want to re-visit the eternity in the stone.

"But you know, those palm-prints, they were up there on the cliff even back then. They glowed tremendously when the sunshine hit them. And, from the memories of the Clan Leader, the hieroglyphics and paintings in the cavern were there, too."

"A lot of mysteries, to be sure," was his only comment. I sighed. *Some kind of final examination this was. I didn't even know the questions, much less the answers! I just never want a re-test!*

"SO NOW WHAT, OLD MAN?" I ASKED AS *EL VIEJO* SAT, PUFFING HIS lavender-scented tobacco. It was coming onto darkness now, and I supposed this might be my last night in The Valley. I cooked up some of the canned foods *El Viejo* had conjured up out of somewhere – I didn't bother to ask – and we sat to eat. I had recovered from my trembling and was trying to absorb the knowledge that had slammed into my soul so dramatically.

"I had a couple of more questions to ask you, *Viejo.*" He cocked an ear my way, while eating a spoonful of beans. I wanted to keep off the subject of my overwhelming visions. "What was Tall Guy saying, that those two had been in The Valley for two days? Man, I was in the cavern there probably a week. And a couple of days on The Valley floor, and then another day up here. What's going on?" He knew what I was ignoring, what I had felt, had seen, had witnessed, that last time at the *atún.* He also knew the reason I would never speak of it, to him or anyone else. That shared experience, that shamanic initiation, would forever bond us and the others who had been here; and yet we would never discuss it. I prayed I wouldn't dream of it, that it hadn't changed my basic humanity; and I also prayed it would make me more like *El Viejo.* Were those two goals compatible? I couldn't tell as yet.

He smiled that same damned smile, and I knew I wouldn't get a straight answer. "My friend, my friend. Always the straight-line, linear thinker, aren't you?"

"Hey, old man, days is days. And I can still count."

"Why do you, of all people, think that you can count the days? When you have spent immeasurable time in those Other Places, and in those deep visions, and in the Spring of Rejuvenation, and in Algona's Pool, and in the Footprint of First Man, and all the rest? Are you so sure you can count the days?"

No, looking at it that way, I was not sure of anything anymore. "So, you are telling me that I zigzagged through TimeSpace, each time I went into one of those tunnels?"

He nodded.

I gave up. "Okay, so what *is* today?"

"You tell me, Anglo. You've got all the electronics."

I did, at that. And every attempt to use them to access the date and time was unsuccessful; nothing wireless was working, though the tablet was still functioning, just not displaying any time or date. "Too bad," he said, "Maybe when you are up out of The Valley, they will function again?" I ignored that, and busily began typing up fresh notes, trying to capture the unreality of the moment, the phrases that might come now but never again. That was an old writing trick of mine – do it in the heat of the moment, while the blood is high and the adrenaline flows; never try to re-create significant events or any traumatic experience solely from memory, because the conscious mind will inevitably color it, compare it, analyze it, until though the images may remain, the emotional uniqueness and significance are forever lost.

Night came swiftly, swallowing up our small canyon. The campfire flickered and glowed, illuminating the *atiín* and its carved symbols. I continued to take flash pictures – of the inscriptions, of my old friend, of the fallen rocks where we were camping. I was very careful not to touch the palm prints or the carvings again. I would try to do the rest of my research without any blood involved, or dark visions of the past. There was nothing more I wanted to know about the *atiín*, or who created it, or how. *Maybe that was the true reason for the final visions, the personal participation in the warps and woofs of the tapestry of human history? To dissuade anyone from wanting more information? Or to push them onto a new path, one where information was unimportant and experience the only meaningful measure?*

"So, old man," I ventured, "am I going to be able to go out into the world and tell the stories of my fantastic adventures here?" I laughed, "Nobody would believe one bit of it – ancient civilizations, parallel universes, flitting in and out of other dimensions, going backward in time." I chewed on my bandaged thumb, trying to ease the pain of the cut. "Or the blood. Especially the blood."

He was very quiet, shards of reflected firelight glowing in his eyes, as if he were a demon of the night world. Finally he replied. "What if there did not exist in the world anywhere a guitar, *amigo*? And what if you had just discovered one? You would want to go tell the world of this marvelous device, but you could not do it right away; without proof, no one would believe you. So first you would have to learn to play it, either on your own by trial and error, or have someone who already knows how, to teach you.

"And if you had to leave it behind, when you went back into the outside world, you would first have to create another guitar, then demonstrate to others the wonder and beauty of the fine discovery. And each person you met, each time they heard it, would have different responses – some born with inherent musical talent, those few gifted ones, might play it immediately, and beautifully. Others would have to be taught carefully and though they would be able to play other people's compositions, would never be masters. Still others would not be impelled to learn either music or playing, but merely content to listen to what others could do. And many might prefer not to hear anything at all, for new sounds can disturb people who are satisfied in their ignorance.

"By close analogy, then, all that you have learned here in The Valley cannot be properly put into words, though you will try. Nor even into music, or paintings. So your task is much more complex, much more subtle than if you were the first man to discover the guitar and learn to play it.

"As a teacher, you may be able impart the concept and a few fundamentals, but those who want to know must find their own guitar somewhere, in order to hear the music." I was thinking about his comments, having no idea how my experiences could relate to music or a guitar. But he usually had a point to make, so I stayed silent and tried to learn from this master. I knew our time together was drawing to a close, and he had so many other tricks I wanted to learn. And answers, too, if only he would just get to the point.

He picked up on my continuing frustration, hurrying his analogy. "Now, I think you have begun to realize the magnitude of your task. Concentrate on describing the music that only you have heard; let others find their own teachers and their own guitars. Those who are inspired, they will go on; the rest will wait until the music finds them." I tried to absorb his meaning. Which I think was, "Do your best to describe what happened to you; each other individual will have to respond in their own way. And don't be too discouraged at the reception you might get. A few will believe, and will find their way. Forget the others; it is not yet their time to learn."

For the rest of the night, until I fell asleep, *El Viejo* and I exchanged stories. As strange as it sounds, I never did get around to asking him exactly when he was born or what his real name was, or how he ever got into the shaman business, or which of the Other Places he had visited. *As an initiate now*, I told myself, *there are things we share that need no answers, no explanations*. Would I myself be in a similar place, talking with a new acolyte, thousands of years from now? On this world, or another?

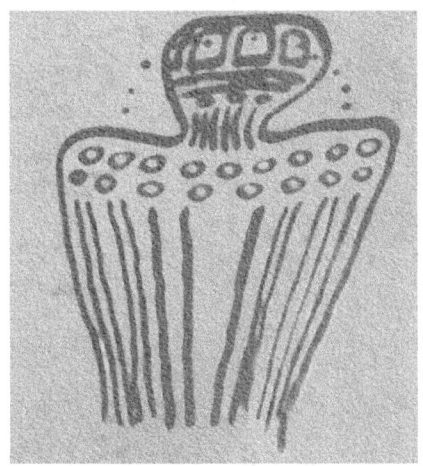

The next morning after breakfast we packed up and trudged along the steep, winding path to the top of the mesa, stopping only as Nature called and to eat or drink. The switchback trail wound upwards through the narrow crevice, and looked as though it would take us several hours to trudge up to the mesa lands at the top. This route was going to put me at least ten miles from where I had parked the SUV down south of here. A part of me worried whether the vehicle was still safe, but the prospect of losing a rented vehicle was not a high priority any more, not after the cosmic revelations of the last few days.

That was going to be a problem, I realized. How could I ever take the mundane things of daily life very seriously again, when I knew that the Multiverse existed, overlapping this world? Or would I get so much involved in the mundane world, once I returned, that The Valley would fade into distant memory? That latter thought I could not accept: I had the strong feeling that, along with *El Viejo* and others, I might be doing other things, performing other services, tasks as yet unnamed, maybe un-nameable.

I was certain of one thing: life could never be the same again for me. I was determined that it wouldn't be.

We walked silently up the trail, as the crevice itself grew narrower and narrower. Without a railing or any safety protection, we trod just inches from the ledge, and any fall would be hundreds of feet straight down to death. Strangely, my old fear of heights no longer prevailed and I was able to climb, step after step, until we had reached about halfway up the trail. Whether this was confidence from newly-found abilities, or a conviction that nothing bad could happen to me, or whether it was just that the waters of The Valley had cured a psychological problem, I had no idea. But it was definitely an improvement over my past condition. Back then, I would not have been able to make this hike at all.

Presumably our old friends *Coyote* and Tall Guy were long gone. Though with *El Viejo* nearby and with my own proven talents, I was no longer very worried about what those two might do if we did run into them. Besides, I was fairly sure that I could easily – from the collective memories of the millennia of battles I had experienced at the *atiin* – access all of the fighting tricks mankind had ever known, should it become necessary. I let that thought pass. Looking back down toward the *atiin* site, I was wishing I could have again seen and photographed the emergent holographic images that the slab produced, or the glowing hand prints, but those were just a few of the many regrets I was having at departing the mystical Valley.

The Old One told me of several other sites of caves, cliff-dwelling ruins and mine entrances. "Other peoples were here, *amigo*, and they did what their natures inclined them to do. So this is a truly physical place, to those who are only conscious of the physical world.

"As you have experienced for yourself, however, other layers of reality are superimposed on these so-called 'Holy Places' or 'Power Points,' and those who are properly attuned to these other layers experience not only the physical but the paraphysical aspects of the sites. You can call this the 'glory' of the site; that is, the energy and the altered consciousness that permeates, surrounds the site, just like the glory around the people we talked about." We paused to rest on a ledge, where the crevice itself was only yards wide and our trail becoming dangerously narrow. *El Viejo* pulled out and stuffed, then lit, his ever-present pipe.

By now the scent of lavender tobacco was a familiar and welcome odor. I realized that I already knew, somewhere deep inside, the things he was telling me, but I listened intently. Having lived in the past, experienced a large portion of humanity's history, didn't make you all-knowing. Some stories had to take priority, and each individual shaman, initiate, acolyte would bring his own perspective to the knowledge of *The All*. I smiled at this realization: *Each individual is important, even in the great game of the gods and* The All. *Each of us truly matters.*

El Viejo continued his discourse, nodding as my revelations about myself showed on my face. "What happens is much the same, on a lesser scale, when a religious person visits a cathedral with his non-believing friend. The friend may appreciate the beauty of stained glass windows, the Gothic architecture, the history and ambience of the physical matter, and can come to truly love the place. But the religious person, while absorbing such external detail, knows that the true meaning of the center of worship, its 'glory', far exceeds any physical manifestation. The untouchable to him is much more meaningful than the touchable; the sense of 'glory' that makes this difference cannot be measured by instruments, but it is there.

"And so it is with this Valley, and other power places around the world, and even beyond it. In these locations, the many dimensions, the many worlds, the Other Places, they converge, overlap, are accessible to certain minds and souls. The sensitives of every culture realize this, either inherently or intellectually, and act accordingly. Witness the Catholic churches built over every pre-Columbian holy place in Mexico and further south. The same happened all over the Mediterranean, even in Jerusalem, where Moslems built over Jewish ruins, and those over others. This has happened all over the world, during all times, except the present era when holiness has been downgraded and ridiculed.

"The 'glory' is still there – mankind, sometimes foolishly, tries to wall off the site, to limit its access, control its meaning, but that is never successful. The 'glory' leaks out, since its converging dimensions are not bound by the physical strictures of this Universe."

"I want to ask more about the structure of the Universe, old one," I interjected, before he could catch his breath between puffs. "The Universal Me you spoke about–"

El Viejo continued on, as if he had finally made me see, understand, comprehend, what had happened. "*Amigo*, all of those other images are you, as I said. Displaced in those other dimensions, displaced in time, displaced in the Other Places." He shook his head in frustration. "Well, just displaced in a manner that you felt, but in a way that can't be described in any human language.

"You have to understand now how this affects all of us, always had, always will – except that when you are Enlightened enough, advanced enough, you will enjoy the effects, recognize them, utilize them for your own benefit.

"Those other sounds, those other colors, those other emanations that you experienced in the Other Places – you can't recall them now because you are back in your own mind, and your memory in this mind cannot reproduce them, except to make you aware you are missing something important." I nodded; the pain of absence, of separation, from that wonderful Being, was receding but could never go away completely. "But for those brief times, you were displaced into one of the other versions of you – versions that had different processing systems in the brain, to be aware of new sounds and colors and those other vibrations you experienced.

"A basic rule is this, something you need to know. Just as you experienced shifts in TimeSpace during your visits to the curtained tunnels, we all of us occasionally shift back and forth to the closest dimensions nearby, up and down and forward and back, in and out, along the Paths of Greatest Invitation. These displacements occur because of natural laws, most of them. But sometimes by the design of greater Beings elsewhere.

"That is how you experienced that service station on the road here from Bernalillo."

Lights were dawning so quickly in my mind that I thought my head would explode. "You mean, when I first drove by, I was in my original dimension, but when I returned, I was in another one?" His smile answered my question.

"But how do we ever know which one is ours, the original? What does it do to us to go back and forth among the infinity of parallel universes?"

He smiled. "*There is no original Universe*, my friend. All of us who are unsatisfied, who are creative, who are inquisitive, we have all switched among so many Universes that it is impossible to tell where we began or where we may end. I cannot tell whether the propensity for changing Universes is what makes us nonconformists, or whether the creativity itself spurs in us the abilities to move among worlds. But I do know that many people, particularly those satisfied with their lot in life, sometimes they stay in one place a long, long time." Grinning widely, he said, "I think I pity them. But I believe that most people do shift around a little bit, and never know it."

Needing something to calm my nerves, I reverted to an old, bad habit: I sat down and gestured for a pipe from him. I needed to whack myself up side the head, do something to give me a sense of belonging, an anchor. *El Viejo* complied, pulling out a pipe from his mysterious bag of tricks, lighting my tobacco himself. I pulled in a hot draught of smoke, exhaled it, feeling the lavender permeate my body. Was I becoming like the old one now? In more ways than one?

"How many times," he asked, "have you met people who swore that one thing happened, when everyone else said otherwise? The source of urban legends is not just a quirk of primitive minds; many times things did happen in one Place and not in the adjacent Place, and those who cross over among the dimensions can argue in all sincerity about their differing experiences, and they are all correct.

"As I have said, getting in touch with yourself in one of these other nearby Places is the easiest to happen – your occasional glimpses of the future come from a future you, of the past from a past version of You. Of alternate realities from yourself in one of those realities; the psychic powers from yourself in different times, different places. This is the true source of all of these powers." I nodded; with my recent experiences guiding me, this all made a lot of sense. He went on.

"Ghosts are those who have slipped the bounds of their other place, but not entirely; appearing in our space as dim playbacks of past or future events, people and events from other places. In your world travels and imaginative writings, you have encountered stories of great battles seen replayed in the sky? Witnessed by hundreds or thousands of people?"

I nodded. English history was full of those. Even in the U.S., some Civil War battles occasionally replayed themselves to the fears of suburbanites living nearby.

"Time slips of the same kind."

"Hey old man," I said, choking on the strong taste of the pipe. "So if we are all just orphans of TimeSpace, careening throughout the infinite universes, how does that help our understanding of things? How does it help me?"

"As I have said – now you don't have to be concerned over the small things: the seemingly false memories, seeing something in your long-time neighborhood as for the first time, smoothing over your frustration at your family and friends and mankind in general, for all their follies. You have a reason, now, to understand why others see their worlds differently than you."

"So why can't we just go out and tell everyone all of this? Save them the trouble? Let them know what reality really is?"

The old man shook his head. "You do realize that we would have to prove it first, and that can only be done by doing for them what you did in the cavern there, with the *atiín*. Do you think we can bring eight billion people to the Valley, and give each one of them all of the experiential training such as you have had?

"Remember my guitar analogy?"

I exploded in frustration, waving the pipe around. "So what is all of this about, if we can't help every other unenlightened person out there in the world? Why just some of us, why not everyone?"

"I have no answer," he said softly, pipesmoke curling around his face now like a Medusa. "When The Valley calls, we answer. We come. We help. Just like you did."

I was calming down now, remembering the "glory" I had felt among the Beings in the Good Place. I wanted so desperately to experience that feeling again, but it was evanescent, slipping away. I couldn't feel the true power of it anymore, but I could feel the memory of the feeling, and that in itself was still nearly all-consuming.

"I am grateful, *Viejo*," I apologized, abashed at my outburst. "Nothing like this has ever happened to me, and in my joy I just want to share it with as many people as I can."

"Maybe you will," he replied gently. "The Valley chose you for some reason. Maybe you will tell about it in your writings, from your memories, even though your electronic recording devices may have failed you. The mind is a wonderful recorder and analyzer."

ALONG THE WAY, *EL VIEJO* THREW OUT THESE CRUMBS OF WISDOM concerning the two criminals who I hoped were hiking northward and eastward to Santa Fe by now. "Some climb the steep walls of the canyon, some live life by the flow of the stream. Each in his own way. No matter where they originate, eventually every canyon opens to the same great lands beyond, and each running stream, regardless of which molten snow field gives it birth, flows at last into the same welcoming river.

"Why are there different paths for different people? Well, first it would be a very boring world if all lives were the same, and we know *The All* wants to experience every conceivable possibility. Like the Continental Divide not far from here, some lives go first one way and some another, traveling a whole world apart, but they still meet in the great vast sea.

"Just as life is easiest in The Valley, and most choose to appreciate the abundance thereof, so others are driven to scale the steeps, to seek other Valleys. Some canyons will be too steep to descend into, others will have no rivers for life. But these visionaries, they must seek and find others. And, if they are to live again, must needs go down into The Valley and there, surrounded by the bounty of the river, take root and live."

How these observations related to my recent little adventure here in The Valley, I didn't have a clue. Sometimes I think he was planting seeds in my mind and my soul, seeds that would eventually blossom and ripen, if only yielding food for thought.

ALONG THE WAY, I ASKED AGAIN, "I STILL DON'T UNDERSTAND, WHY did The Valley ever let *Coyote* and his Tall Friend ever get here in the first place? And find the *atiín*, and cut it out, and bring it to Santa Fe?"

"Think about what you just said, friend. Think about each step."

"I don't get it."

"Maybe, think of those two as tools, a way to get you to come to New Mexico, to search for this Valley, to undergo the physical and the psychic changes you have encountered?"

I started to say something but the import of his words sank in. "For me? A way to get *me* here? What a roundabout way, that mysterious e-mail and all. Why didn't you just send me a marked map? I might've come anyway."

El Viejo shook his head. "You misunderstand. I didn't send that email message to you. The person who did, they knew it would be the one and only way to get you here."

"Who might that be, *Viejo*?"

He pointed at me. "You did, friend. You sent the message to yourself because you knew what it would take to get you going, to make you find The Valley and go through the metaphysical growth you have experienced."

Me? How —?

"Language doesn't cover what you now know. Maybe as you go back to where you began, your electronic equipment will work once more, and you will send that message to yourself."

"How will it get backwards in time, and –?" .

El Viejo's palms came upright and he smiled again. "Now you know one of the utilities of the Infinite You. It will come to you, and you will do it. You are beginning to realize that what you have been taught about the nature of causality is somewhat at odds with what the greater reality happens to be."

WE APPROACHED THE TOP END OF THE UPWARDS TRAIL JUST AT sunset, and I walked ahead, emerging from the crevice, looking around nervously. Nobody was in sight. I sighed with relief. The crack in the mesa ended here, too, and there was just flatland in all directions. I looked into the dark depths of that fissure; strange to think of all the weirdness it led to. As I watched, *El Viejo* lumbered out of the crevice, looking as if he were one of the ancient gods, just emerging to Earth from the underworld. Knowing him as I thought I did, I wouldn't have been surprised if he truly were!

I knew time was short and before long I would be trudging southward alone again. This was one of the new senses I had acquired, that of an aura enfolding upon itself, prior to apporting. I felt the imminent separation of our merged fields of perception. "Before you go, my old friend *Viejo*, tell me the most important thing I should remember from my days here in The Valley."

He squinted at the setting sun. "Isn't that beautiful? And all of this Valley?" He sighed. "You are right to ask, *amigo*. And I shall tell you before I must go."

This is what he said: "*The All* is in the process of experiencing itself. It wants to experience, to integrate, the life experiences of every possible being. A rock, though part of Creation, can only experience a small range of sensations: movement, heat, melting, wind, rain. It does not move except in a geological sense, and can never know pain, pleasure, emotion.

"The smallest living creatures are likewise limited in their range of experiences. Eventually, *The All* creates or directs the creation of thinking beings, humans here on Earth, other species on other worlds and in the parallel worlds of which you experienced just a few with such traumatic effects.

"Inside an educated, appreciative mind, however, *The All* experiences things it never experienced before: not only emotions, but imagination, poetry, stories, music, drama, art, culture, scientific arrangement of data, information, knowledge, wisdom, leading to transcendence.

"That is one definition of Evil, then: a conscious action that deliberately limits *The All* from these experiences. That is why a dictatorship is evil, as Plato even pointed out – one man's personality, one warped mind, makes a population or a nation take one direction – his own. Thus that society is limited by the flaws of that one man. Such a dictatorship hates dissent, and therefore limits *The All* again. Killing innocents, indeed all killing except in self-defense, is an affront to *The All*. Censorship, too. Likewise, ignoring disease and poverty and the desolation of souls – limitations, all. Slavery and mastership, both.

"Good, then is the opposite of Evil – education, stimulation, imagination, exploration, creation, accumulation and dispersal of knowledge, search and research, enjoying and appreciating the Universe and each other. Those nations that limited the range of inquiry of their populations – all died, or are dying. I don't need to name them for you, but they kill themselves. Look around the world today.

"Do you not think the rapid spread of free minds and free markets in the last part of the last millennium were an expression of *The All* becoming recognized by the human race? Only through the free interchange of goods and ideas, of experiences and emotions, of knowledge and wisdom, can every human cross-fertilize with every other, and groups with groups, until great truths emerge, great artists develop, great thoughts be thought, great music and art blossom.

"I realize that geniuses in the past have risen above their conditions of poverty, disease, war and ignorance, but these were in spite of the conditions, not because of them! Just think of how many great ones have died without realizing their potential, just because of those factors. As the poet said, 'Many a flower blooms and dies unseen on the desert floor.' *The All* is expressing Its will that all people should develop."

"Viejo," I wondered aloud, "is this why humans are so important? Environmentalists I've talked to tell me that fungus on the floor of the forest is every bit as important as a human being. Not that I believe it."

He chortled. "See, this new world society of great democracies and great education has produced many alternative views; unfortunately many of these are at odds with the reality you have come to know here in The Valley. Consider this: few insect eggs survive, out of billions laid; few young animals live to maturity, for Nature is harsh with her children. Humans, though, offer *The All* an opportunity to allay the violence, to put an end to the bloody tooth and claw, because we can sense that Nature can change, be changed. Our overlaid cortex, atop the mammalian brain, atop the reptilian stem, represents a higher way, and I have explained to you how *The All* wants to know Itself through us.

"So yes, the other species on this world are important, but they are not human beings, the highest manifestation of *The All* on this world today. You yourself know for a certainty that in the Other Places, there are Beings far beyond us in both good and evil. And these other super-organisms, other ways of thinking, of meditation, of contemplation, even of instinct and revelation, have arisen and these unique manifestations of *The All* also can contribute."

"So friend," I asked, "was there ever a time when mankind was more spiritually advanced than today? Has *The All* ever taken some backward steps in its march toward self-realization?" Technologically, I knew, there had been many backward steps over millions of years. I had seen some of those in the terrible visions at the *atiín* site. I had also experienced the lives of those who had believed they were more spiritual, but I had no true way of determining if they actually were.

El Viejo shook his head. "The myths of perfection in the past derive from what most of humanity has seen until now – things grow old, die, decay; hardly ever did mankind's lot improve, so what was there to look forward to in a future except aging and death, perhaps by disease, most likely by war and destruction?

"If tomorrow is always worse than today, then by the extension of a backwards logic, at some time in the past things should have been better, probably even perfect, in the long enough ago. In the limited vision of the medieval peasant, for example, a full meal, a soft bed without lice and bugs, and comfort from cold and heat, were paradise enough.

"We can't find, in this Valley, or anywhere else, that past perfection. What we have found here, even I as you, is a progression of humanity, a procession of ideas, and a few surprises, insights into how we humans have grown in unexpected ways. And, yes, unrecorded histories, forgotten civilizations, all human, some with a touch of divinity, even an occasional visitor from Beyond, as you saw in those Other Places. And ways to go to those Other Places, where some have gone before, entire nations and tribes, leaving this world behind, disappearing into myth and legend.

"The sum of it all is this: you are human, as am I. But most of us do not know fully what it is to be human. We have not yet awakened the many other senses that we all possess – precognition, clairvoyance, psychometry, telepathy, apportation, clairempathy, and other talents for which there are yet no names. In the millions of years of mankind's existence, countless numbers of wise and foolish have lived and died, each contributing in some way to the unconscious racial memories that can be tapped here in The Valley, through the *atiín*.

"We might call this The Valley of Mankind, for representatives of all races, of many cultures, of every time, have passed this way before, and others will come later. Each leaves a part of himself here, in the very dust under your feet, in the waters that flow through this crack in the world here, on the sheer walls of rock, in the shrubs that line the pathways, in the trees that shade the river.

"Why were *you* asked to come? As you have learned, you yourself will send the message, after you learned to feel the viscosity, the ebb and flow of TimeSpace. But others than I inspired your vision. Perhaps you are to reveal to the world what you have seen here, perhaps you may tell only one friend.

"In the end, you will know what to do. It will be revealed to you.

"By you, yourself. It has to come from within you."

And then *El Viejo* told me what I had seen myself: The Valley is extremely ancient, as old as Man; and mankind in all his varied forms, with all his primal urges, his manifold desires, his deepest secrets, his most precious knowledge, has always found The Valley when it was needed. "Lately," *El Viejo* murmured, "it's been busier than most times." He looked at me through dark deep eyes, as if his soul were reaching out to caress my soul – a caring, yet a sternness of being, a discipline learned in the harsh deserts to the south, and perhaps in many of the Other Places, other worlds. "Maybe something wonderful is about to happen?"

"Transcendence? Judd's theory? Maybe even prophecies of the end of the world?"

El Viejo only shrugged.

I KNEW THEN WHAT THE OLD MAN WAS TELLING ME: FOR ALL OF THE fantastic worlds I visited, the panoply of human history I experienced, the finding of myself, the most important thing I learned in The Valley was this: *The All is beginning to know Itself – and each of us has a role to play in that great Becoming.*

That Great Truth has manifested itself best in divine prophets that different people chose to follow for different reasons. But also it appears in greats of literature, music, science, even in physical feats such as athletics, any time and any place where the pure essence of the human soul is totally focused on excellence, achieving its transcendental states of euphoria. Does this mean that an Olympic athlete is equivalent to a Prophet of God? Of course not; but each person is a small manifestation of *The All*. Some are much, much more – and these are the ones we see as Transcended Ones, with their auras and wisdom – but we each carry a unique piece. We each of us belong, and we each of us are needed. This is the true meaning of Love.

In medicine, in technology, in science, *The All* is making itself known, and none can ignore it. Some will be inspired through dreams, some will make the connection in a song, a dance, a photo, a concert. Even a book or a stunning new view of nature, a photograph of the heart of the Galaxy, a mundane task accomplished superbly. Those fortunate enough to witness these Transcended Ones exercising their missions, have reported the energy, the vitality, the holiness that they emanate.

Yet in lesser ways, the rest of us have occasionally experienced the epiphany of contact with *The All*. The riff in a rock song, the meter of a poem, the lilt of a voice, the melodic cacophony of jazz; sometimes it's just the small voice of a child, or the understanding smile of a spouse forgiving a small sin. These are the moments when you know you have touched *The All*.

There are other smaller, but recognizable, communications from *The All* that have nothing to do with your own achievements or aspirations. These are important as well, for they bring information that you cannot access any other way.

You will know when these moments happen – they occur to us all, almost every day. Be still and listen.

What forms do these moments take? Think. Have you ever looked – everywhere – for lost car keys, glasses, a wallet or a purse? And when you go back, you find them in the very place you've looked at many times before? That's *The All* calling your attention – to the fact that attention is being paid and is being asked.

You drive back and forth to work for years, day after week after month. Then one day, one strange day, for some reason, you see a house on your route that you hadn't noticed before. Again – *The All* is asking you to pay attention: "Here's new information; pay heed."

Other days, you will hear a word or a phrase repeated many times, and other times you will simultaneously hear a word and read it. Pay attention to these words; they are messages, distinct and clear.

And in all these small ways – ways familiar but important – *The All* calls. If you are to become a conscious part of *The All*, you must answer these calls. Otherwise you will spend a lifetime in lesser achievement, and wonder where the years went, and why.

In this generation, above all others, the Will of *The All* is bubbling forth. The meaning of these times is that we may well witness Transcendence in our own lifetimes. Through understanding of the ways the Multiverse works, and yes, even though high technologies that enable us to examine our own minds and bodies and to communicate in a global web, we will be assisting in our very Transcendence, making way for the worlds to come.

With all that has happened, with what is occurring now, with all the potential for fantastic improvements, is it not possible that *The All* must be preparing us for an Age of Transcendence? An age when the entire human race will virtually boot itself up into the equivalent of a planetary computer, a super-consciousness? Become like one of those wonderful Beings I saw in the Other Place? I believe that we will all know together, when it happens.

EL VIEJO REMAINED WITH ME LONGER THAN I HAD EXPECTED, staying as I made camp among some *piñon* trees half a mile from the trailhead. Later that night, I heard noises in the distance. Peeking up around the sagebrush-stabilized sand dune, I saw *Coyote* and Tall Guy come back to the trailhead with flashlights, the lights gesticulating with accompanying shouts of displeasure, finally disappearing back down into the crevice, back down the trail into The Valley.

"Maybe this time they will learn the lessons of The Valley, you think?" my old friend asked rhetorically.

I groaned, "Surely not to steal the *atíin* again, *Viejo*? I don't want to go through that anymore." A part of me passionately wanted to go down and protect that holy place from these intruders, but I knew it wouldn't be.

"No, not this time. I think they may find your cavern soon, and who knows what they may learn there?"

"But they are going the opposite way down The Valley, *Viejo*," I protested. "How can they learn the lessons in reverse?" He looked at me quizzically. "I mean, I found Judd first, then Algona, then you in the *kiva*, then the cavern, then –"

I stopped as he grinned. "Many canyons empty into The Valley. They all run down toward the river. Every path achieves the same destination. But their lessons are not yours."

THE LAST THING EL VIEJO EVER SAID TO ME, AS WE DEPARTED IN

different directions the next morning, was this: "There are other lessons to be learned, my friend, other places to find. Go to these places. Learn of the power of the ancient ways, ways that still resonate with all human beings. Experience the lives of those who came before – learn from their successes, avoid their failures. There is a Flow in *The All* – learn to move with it, in the Paths of Greatest Invitation, by using your abilities. Manifest those abilities by meditating on the meaning of *The All*. Leave this place, go and tell others." He smiled that ancient smile, twinkles and textures that had recorded more of History than anybody I'd ever known, perhaps all of them put together.

"Every person has a Place," he said, shaking my hand for the last time.

"This Valley is the Place for many," he spoke quietly as he began walking northward, toward places unknown. "There are other Places."

"Search with your heart and your mind and your spirit," whispered the desert winds as the Old One vanished into the heat-wrinkled horizon, "and you will always find that Place."

LATER THAT DAY, AS I TRUDGED ALONE, HOT AND HUNGRY, southward toward the SUV and my return to civilization, the tablet computer beeped, signaling that its wireless features were functioning again. I sat down under the shade of a nearby salt cedar and flipped open the flat screen, hoping to e-mail what I had already written during my ten days – or was it *two*? – in another world – other *worlds*! – lest memory and imagination blend and squeeze reality out. As if I would ever be certain of reality ever again! In electronic synchronicity, the smartphone also beeped, telling me of its return to life, its willingness to work again in the wondrous world wide web of microelectronic miracles.

After the ubiquitous flag logo faded on the tablet screen, I punched in the keystrokes to bring up the e-mail program. But the date on the screen was the day I had received the original message! Sighing, I wondered briefly if the weirdness of the worlds had zapped my trusty electronic companion, forever losing many of the files I hadn't backed up. But checking my e-mail "Inbox," I saw that none were any later than the morning I had received the mysterious message. It was definitely true: somehow, the system had reverted backwards, back to the morning when the message came in that began this whole fantastic quest. But both the smartphone clock and my digital watch showed that ten days had passed. Which were correct? Maybe both? *Oh well*, I thought, *I've experienced a lot stranger things in this Valley.*

Once started, the Muse settled on me in usual fashion, blocking out the outside world: in the comfort of the shade and cool breezes, a thousand feet above the floor of The Valley but worlds away from it, I pounded out what I had seen, what I had felt, what I speculated must have happened. Time itself seemed to stop. Often I just downloaded the voice recorder into the computer when I was too tired to continue or too much in awe of my memories. Before I realized it, lengthening shadows told me several hours had passed, though strangely the date and hour on the computer screen had not changed.

Another timeslip in *El Viejo*'s *TimeSpace*? He'd said many times that the flow of Time in The Valley conformed to different laws than in the outside world. And had I ever experienced *that*! So it was possible that down there in The Valley I was living in alternate time streams, on alternate worlds, switching somewhere between time flows, like the switchback trails that went first one direction, then another, but always rising or falling. Was I still in the world I had been in when starting the hike up The Valley wall? Would I see myself going down into The Valley? Could I warn myself? *That way lies madness, old man*, I reminded myself. Regardless of my conjectures, the computer clock showed no sign of changing, and another check of my e-mail, using the wireless connection, showed no new mail.

Here I am with my computer living in the past, with some kind of wireless tablet timeloop that lets me connect to the world wide web a week and a half ago? A sudden realization dawned, an awareness that in times past I would have ignored. Too bad I hadn't been able to look at some stock prices in the last ten days! But now I laughed out loud, dialing up my home office number. I left a deliberately garbled message about "Check your e-mail," and hung up. Then I quickly typed out a message, trusting that my wireless uplink would continue to work in the past. How could it *not*? It already *had*!

You are a searcher for the Truth, I wrote from memory, sending the e-mail message to my own address. *A thirst that only Myth may sate,* the message concluded, *There is a Valley.*

EPILOGUE

I have long since returned from The Valley, finding myself in eventual synchronization with the rest of our apparent Time-Space coordinates. I found Algona as well, but that is another story.

I like to think I found myself, too, during that stay in The Valley.

The Valley changed me forever. I hope that it even changed *Coyote* and Tall Guy, too. If they'd had to endure The Valley's lessons more than once, I felt pity for them, but then some people have to be slapped pretty hard by the Multiverse to get into shape. I know that from personal experience.

Should you try to find The Valley or your own Other Place, these are my words of advice for you: Just as you would not dare to climb a mountain without preparation, for fear of disaster; why then would you not properly ready yourself for the most dangerous, and yet most rewarding journey possible – your own soul's trajectory through time and space?

What is this preparation?

At the very least, meditate. Then, eat properly and exercise moderately – exercise the body through physical routines. Condition the mind through intellectual workouts. And for the soul, the spiritual body, you must achieve its proper balance through research, knowledge, meditation, contemplation, reflection.

Look into the Universe – there are wonders beyond imagination;
Look into your Soul – there is depth beyond understanding.
There is an ending.
But *you* must be the beginning.
There is always hope.
But *you* must be ready.
You will be led.
But *you* must be prepared.
There, is a Valley.

ABOUT THE AUTHOR

Hugo-nominated author Dr. Arlan Andrews, Sr., is the founder of SIGMA, the Science Fiction Think Tank, which works with the US government and non-profit organizations to provide the unique futurism of science fiction writers for those who need it most. See the SIGMA website at SigmaForum(dot)org for more details, and for a membership list of the outstanding authors who participate. Arlan began his technical career working as a missile tracking telescope operator at White Sands Missile Range, where he also honed a lifelong interest in unusual phenomena by exploring the enchantment and mysteries of New Mexico while attending college. He worked for AT&T Bell Laboratories on the antiballistic missile program, spent time in China, was appointed as a Fellow in the White House Science Office, and co-founded both a Virtual Reality software company and a biotech equipment company. All of these groundbreaking activities originated in his fascination with the future and the unknown. He expresses that wonderment by writing both fact and fiction, science and speculation. During his career as engineer, entrepreneur and author, Arlan has published nearly 500 stories, articles, columns and other features in 100 venues worldwide, primarily in science fiction, the paranormal, futurism and the fringe areas of science and folklore. These have appeared in anthologies and in such publications as ANALOG, ASIMOV'S, SCIENCE FICTION AGE, SCIENCE FICTION REVIEW, PULPHOUSE, FATE, STRANGE, ATLANTIS RISING, NEW SCIENTIST, PURSUIT, ALT HISTORY.COM, IDEOMANCER, MENSA BULLETIN, INTEGRA, and a former column in UFO MAGAZINE. His ANALOG novella, "Flow", was on the Hugo Award ballot in 2015, winning the Jovian Award for Best Novella that year. Many of Arlan's stories and articles -- plus new stories and several new novels -- are now available in e-versions and paperback. In addition to appearances at conventions and conferences, Arlan appeared on the History Channel cable presentation of "Ancient Aliens: Ancient Constructions", in September 2011. Recent publications available on Amazon.com include SILICON BLOOD (novel) and FUTURE FLASH (a short story collection), both in e-books and paperback versions.